THE HAMLET

A Tale of Life, Dreams and Epiphanies

GAITHER STEWART

Cyberwit.net
HIG 45 Kaushambi Kunj, Kalindipuram
Allahabad - 211011 (U.P.) India
http://www.cyberwit.net
Tel: +(91) 9415091004
E-mail: info@cyberwit.net

"I therefore conclude that the meaning of life
is the most urgent of questions."

Albert Camus, The Myth of Sisyphus

Other works by Gaither Stewart:

Novels
San Marino Blues
The Fifth Sun
The Trojan Spy
Lily Pad Roll
Time of Exile
Asheville

Short Stories
Signs of the Times
Once In Berlin
To Be A Stranger
Icy Currents, Compulsive Course
Voices From Pisalocca

Essays
Trails of Memory
Babylon Falling.
Recollection of Things Learned,
    Remembering
    Socialism

PREFACE

By Petar Penda

In his seminal book of socio-political essays entitled *Babylon Falling* (Punto Press, 2017), Gaither Stewart, to a certain extent, explains his poetics. In two of his notable essays, "Compromise and Commitment" and in "Transformation" that opens the book, he sees the creative individual's chief goals to be to change and transform the world, to be committed, and to "reject social conformity and political correctness". He further explicates the necessity of writers' engagement by stating that "moral conflicts of the day have a political background and that nearly every aspect of our lives is related to politics. An understanding of politics is fundamental in order to understand what the writer must oppose and what he can defend." Not only has Stewart such a viewpoint in his essays, but also shows it in his novels through the themes he deals with and by the action of his characters. This emphasizes his point of view that the private life of an individual is inseparable from the political, which is hugely visible in his novel *The Hamlet*.

Namely, when Stuart in the little Italian village of San Nicola, learns that something suspicious is happening in his neighborhood, he feels a moral urgency to act and oppose much stronger forces and, in Hamlet's words, "take[s] action against the sea of arms". This action conveys the idea of the moral imperative of every human being to act against any injustice in the world and leave their comfort zone despite possible consequences. Gaither Stewart points out the necessity of taking action against evil by establishing the connection between the characters in the novel who haven't met before. All of them are united by the wish to stop what happens behind the walls of their hamlet, that is, in the research institute which produces deadly botox used in the war between Ukraine and Russia. This idea of connectedness is reinforced by citing John Donne's *No Man Is an Island*, which suggests the close connection of all people around the world because, "Any man's death diminishes me,/Because I am involved in mankind."

Thinking in this fashion, when faced with the decision to do something about the situation, the protagonist named Stuart Stuart thinks like this:

He too was an individual emerging from a retreat in the hamlet, suddenly snapping awake to the realization that he must do something about the state of things in his world. He would perform an act of love.

He sees the act of doing something as a supreme act of love for humankind, for young men poisoned in Zaporozhe, and for his fellow citizens in San Nicola. Stuart feels *involved in mankind* and this involvement makes his action necessary. Even more so, because he loses two dear friends who opposed and, with the help of others, ended one of many biological warfare laboratories in the world.

The greatness of the theme of *The Hamlet* lies in the fact that it deals with the current political situation in the world and our indifference to it. The description of the citizens of Rome who are lulled into sleep by their conformity and are unable to see what happens around them reflects the state of mind of most people in the world. The eternal city is the reflection of all cities and the rise of fascism in Italy reflects such a state in almost all countries throughout the world. This state of sleepy minds of modern-day men and women is emphasized by their implicit comparison to Giordano Bruno, who sacrificed his life for the truth by opposing the Church. Giordano Bruno is seen as a *spiritus movens* who lives through all ages and inspires rebellion and the fight for justice, but, unfortunately, only in rare men and women.

The Hamlet also delves into the dream world and its connection to reality, showing how Stuart's dreams are inseparable from reality. No matter how dreams distort his daily life, they stand for his fears, hopes and the feeling of belonging to the community. The dreams reinforce his principles and they continue in the daily world thus making him a revolutionary. This makes his dream world, and dreams on the whole, inseparable from the real world as they flow one into another, making a never-ending circle. This idea is pointed out by E. A. Poe's poem, which is taken as an introduction to the novel, in particular by the following lines: *All that we see or seem/ Is but a dream within a dream.* It is also confirmed in Stewart's "Dream Song", also serving as an introduction to the novel: *"There is a magical moment when I begin to wake that my dream continues on its own volition, no longer dependent on my sleep for sustenance."*

The dream world, that is, in one part Stuart's imagination, also helps him distinguish appearance from reality, that is, what is given to people as reality by governments versus the real situation in the world. Facing reality is painful and most of us prefer to believe in appearance and avoid seeing the truth. On the other hand, the reality is rewarding as it gives us self-knowledge and knowledge of the world, epiphanies which help both our personal growth and the development of a better world. This means to see things from the inside and not the way they are presented. This is the reason why the main character feels the inner compulsion to go to Zaporozhe and talk to the dying soldiers, feel their pain as his own and tell the world the painful truth. Multiperspectivism aids him to see things more clearly and to appreciate his own life and be able to differentiate illusions from the verity.

One of the chief aspects of *The Hamlet* is intertextuality, which enriches the narrative and strengthens the criticism of the world system and countries in power. There are references to quite a number of works of art, novels, poems, and, in particular, to ancient Greek myths. Myths serve the purpose to remind us that we haven't learned much from the past and that humankind often repeats mistakes, being all the time in a vicious circle. Power corrupts not only those in power but also those who are disempowered. They fight for their liberty, often crossing the line and losing their humanity in the process. Even when they realize their past mistakes and wrong obsession with power, it is too late. So happens to Ermanno, who realizes his mistake in founding a bio lab which produces lethal poison in the hamlet, and he later helps shut it down. But his repentance comes too late and modern-day gods, the Intelligence services of several countries, are after him and they kill him. Similarly, professor Logreco's obsession with Tiresias, the mythic figure of a blind seer who was both man and woman, alludes to his bisexuality. Likewise, he was once a secret agent, and years after he had withdrawn, they found and killed him.

As the story develops, all the characters undergo significant changes. They gain knowledge of themselves and others, are able to distinguish difference between infatuation and love, and the importance of loyalty to their principles and their friends and partners. This personal growth is placed within the political circumstances, which points out the idea of the man as _homo politicus_. This idea is stressed by Stuart's need to do more and to see the poisoned soldiers in Zaporozhe. Seeing two young men in their early twenties dying of botox poisoning, he understands the utter horror of wars and political injustice in the world. The young men wanted to see the world but they faced death in their prime. No matter how painful the revelation of the ugliness of politics, Stuart looks forward to his life. However, he is uncertain about his Donetsk translator and taxi driver's optimism that "life is truly good".

The plot and the narration of _The Hamlet_ are dynamic, they absorb the reader, and make the novel a page-turner. Rhythmical sentences and occasional Italian words contribute to depicting the setting of the hamlet of San Nicola, of La Storta, and Rome. In a similar vein, Russian words add to the description of Donetsk and

Zaporozhe. In addition to descriptions, points of view, and internal and external conflicts, each character is distinguished by their language peculiarities, which proves Gaither Stewart's mastery and deep care for details.

Overlapping of the personal and the political, the commitment to revealing the truth about the current political situation in the world, the universality of the storyline and the characters' internal and external struggles, along with the remarkable and original style of writing, make *The Hamlet* one of the finest pieces of contemporary literature. The telling story of love, betrayal, and the meaning and value of life, given uniquely and imaginatively, will certainly be recognized and appreciated equally by a wide readership and scholars in search of fresh literary voices.

Dr. Petar Penda
Professor of English and American Literature
University of Banja Luka, Bosnia and Herzegovina

A Dream Within A Dream

Yet if hope has flown away
In a night, or in a day
In a vision, or in none,
Is it therefore the less gone?
All that we see or seem
Is but a dream within a dream.
Edgar Allan Poe

Dream Song

There is a magical moment when I begin to wake that my dream continues on its own volition, no longer dependent on my sleep for sustenance. That precise moment was the entrance point into the Dreamings of the Aboriginals, the Dreamtime, as we in the West call it. Those ancient peoples believed the Dreamings—the singular of the idea of time before time existed—was a continuum of past, present and future. And it was during the Dreamings that the land, mountains, hills, rivers, plants, life forms of both animals and humans, and the sky above were formed by the actions of mysterious and supernatural spirits. Since Aboriginal Australians from before time existed had no word for time, they referred to the world creation as the Dreamings. I am also drawn to a shaman's words that I am only a dream image, an insignificant part of a dream within a dream. In my Dreamtime, I am aware that I am awake but that I am also still in the dream. It is so alluring there, in my own Dreamings where time does not exist. Perhaps that is real life, too. Such words ring esoteric— as fantasy and wild imagination, but my words are true. It is bewitching, Dreamtime. When it occurs, I not only participate in the dream, I direct its continuation in a mystical state of consciousness. In that moment, I am conscious that I am an integral part of my dreamscape—the landscape within the dream. I, the sleeper-dreamer-creator-director, hold it together: I hold onto the remaining fragments of sleep; at the same time I live the unfolding dream. We merge—my dream self and my wake self—and become one. I am in the existential no-time, as the Maya believed. The Dreamings—as it always was and always will be, on and on and on. Ancient peoples believed that everything that comes into the world—a song, a story, an idea —is created in the Dreamings; everything derives from the Dreamings. Individual lives are creations of the Dreamings and will return there when the body dies. In all people there must be an eternal part born through the mother in time from the originals of the Dreamings.—of the time before time existed. And Mesoamerican peoples for tens of thousands of years dream of return to old places that existed only for their eternal, indestructible souls.

THE HAMLET

"But if the vision was true and mighty, as I know, it is true and mighty yet; for such things are of the spirit, and it is in the darkness of their eyes that men get lost."

Black Elk

1.

It was the fortieth consecutive day of the rains. Stuart drove cautiously across the South Elevated over a nightmarish labyrinth of trash, junk and garbage. He lowered the window for an instant, gasped, and held his breath at the gaseous stench rising from below. Yesterday's downpour had momentarily relented and become a drizzle but the heat had returned unimpeded. From the sea of garbage below him blackish vapor trails rose skywards. Poetically still referred to as the *rotonda,* the former roundabout marking the entrance to the hamlet had become an open graveyard for rotting dead and half-eaten probably domestic animals, an illegal but public garbage dump, and a gigantic junk yard. The entire area was overrun by fearsome rats, feral cats, vicious dogs and, nights, frequented by whole families of wild boar. Fearful foxes rummaged for leftovers from the growing amount of wet garbage expanding both horizontally and vertically from the roundabout underneath. The Blade Runner whole was now a wild animal paradise where humans seldom ventured; it was observable only from the Elevateds or from the summits of the two colorful art deco style towers just inside the Great Wall. Stuart disliked and feared the towers because of the incubus of the dump they displayed so absolutely, as if it were representative of human life. From its former borders at about one hundred meters distance from the Great Wall, the nauseous neo-roundabout, growing exponentially toward the city, toward La Storta and Olgiata and surrounding townships, displayed stripped automobiles, disemboweled couches and easy chairs, yellowing bathroom furnishings, outdated computers, fifty-year old stereo sets, rusted motorcycles without wheels, saddles or handlebars, blackened lawnmowers sans motors, automobile carcasses denuded of tags, motors, wheels, doors, and seats and now inhabited promiscuously by a variety of animals. There was also an orange school bus without tires or windows where the most fearless homeless of surrounding townships were rumored to overnight. Two steel elevated roadways –one from the south, the other from the north—provided access from the highway that once passed through the roundabout to a labyrinthine roadway leading to a padded, steel-spiked guarded gate in the Great Wall, recently painted a glazed dark brown. A paved road wound and twisted purposefully in successive one-hundred eighty degree turns back and forth for precisely five-hundred and forty-five meters to cover about sixty meters distance—Stuart called it the Ho Chi Minh Trail—as if it were still undecided whether to permit access to the narrow gate in the Great Wall. A high steel fence—on which a cynic had hung upside down a framed painting of a Christ smiling evilly straight at the roundabout chaos and ignoring the carnivorous liana eating its way toward the Savior —stood in a straight line between the neo-*rotonda* chaos and the labyrinth roadway which ultimately ended its mad trajectory at the majestic gate in the Great Wall leading into the hamlet.

His mind returning to recent messages from his Tsalagi friend and dream guide on a reservation in North Carolina and imagining his Cherokee snicker at the upside down Christ, he tried to ignore the armed guards dressed in hamlet-issued black and silver uniforms now checking his car and credentials on their Smartphones. One of two German-speaking guards muttered "Ok", and pointed inside with his thumb.

"*Copacetic*," Stuart answered trenchantly, at which the guard's colleague first frowned, then shrugged. Stuart disliked both of them as much as he did the towers; the guards were as heedless, as indifferent to him as to everybody and to the roundabout mass itself.

"Tower visit", Stuart said maliciously, handing over his shiny golden pass of a landowner resident. On the spur of the moment, he'd decided to visit the left tower chiefly to irritate the two surly guards, one of whom was required to accompany him because of hamlet administrative fears of a blocked elevator or a heart attack on the tightly winding stairs. The guards remembered that he was afraid of the tiny elevator and would walk it.

He drove through the gate, parked in a reserved zone, and ducked under the low tower door. The guard followed. By the time he reached the top, the hard rain had returned. From about forty meters altitude he could see clearly the meeting of the hard rain and the vapors rising from the gray watery mass, its heart throbbing and pulsating as if it had a life of its own—maybe even a soul, Stuart imagined, its heart beating like a living being against the Great Wall— the defensive barricade of the five-hundred inhabitants of the hamlet against the dark mass of the former roundabout now extending toward La Storta and Olgiata. At unpredictable moments it seemed to surge and then just as quickly deflate, like a living organism inhaling and exhaling to a rhythm of its own—not only mysterious, but seen from above, terrifying. Stuart understood that when the rains stopped the vapors would still rise heavenwards from the mass below that since the beginning of the rains had already crept hundreds of meters in the direction of La Storta. He wondered how long the Great Wall could resist the silent uncontrolled invasion of the whole hamlet.

His shaman friend, John Rainwater, would have seen it all otherwise; the Tsalagi had said that Stuart would never see what he sees anywhere. Rainwater said Stuart only imagined he was in an unreal dream. He said that since his Iroquois ancestors had dreamed the world into being during the dreamings, he himself was part of the original creation and that there was one thing Stuart must never forget: the difference between reality and fantasy is a very fine line. From day to day, Rainwater's words were becoming clearer; Stuart sometimes feared his life was only illusion.

Memories and regrets, reveries and hopes are the limitations of reality and Dreamscape is the setting for all creation, Rainwater would say.

He shifted around the tower summit, observing from all points the hamlet, much of which was hidden from view by the patches of woods of normally deep green pines now darkened by the unrelenting water spotting the landscape. He'd never understood the reasons for the Great Wall or the attack of the roundabout dump: to hold the five hundred inhabitants in, or to hold others out? You would have thought that the Great Wall and the impediments to enter or exit would have generated a strong sense of fraternity among its people; but that was not the case. Instead, the sensation of an unhealthy individualism had only intensified daily—individualism, isolation and suspicion one of the other, the real reasons for which remained the only mystery—Stuart had concluded that the hamlet must contain secrets to be defended. So no, the Great Wall was not to hold them in or others out; it was to preserve and defend the secret. Otherwise, why guards? Foreign guards at that. German-speaking guards. Pensively, he descended from the tower, conscious of the pressure of the guard's presence on his heels.

Once again outside, he peered at the inside of a nearby section of the Great Wall and despite its powerful brown color, he thought how flimsy it appeared as compared to the power of the gray mass of the roundabout observed from above. Walls, he recalled, have never worked anyway. Nor could the hamlet's Great Wall work in the long run. A contemporary of the wars of Hannibal when he and his elephants were crossing the Alps southwards, Shih Huang Ti, King of Ch'in, conquered the Six Kingdoms and eliminated the feudal system; he built the Great Wall of China around the kingdom because walls were defenses. Building fortifications is common task to emperors; the only thing singular about Shih history beginning with him, Huang Ti, was the scale on which he operated. Such facts are something more than exaggeration or hyperbole of trivial inclinations. To enclose an orchard or a garden or a hamlet or as in old times, a whole city, is normal—but not an empire. However, this reveals little about the reasons for the wall. Shih Huang Ti—according to millennia of historians—searching for the elixir of immortality, forbade all mention of the word death. The wall for Shih Huang I was a magical barrier intended to halt the advance of death. Baruch Spinoza said that the Emperor and his sages believed that immortality was intrinsic and that its corruption could not penetrate a closed sphere. Perhaps the Emperor hoped to recreate the beginning of time; after all he called himself the First, in order to be truly the First. And he named himself Huang Ti the First in order to be the legendary emperor, the founder of an immortal empire. He ordered that his heirs should be named Second Emperor, Third Emperor, Fourth Emperor, and so on to infinity. Perhaps the wall was a metaphor. Perhaps the wall was a challenge. And Shih Huang Ti thought: "Men love the past and I can do nothing against this love—nor can my executioners—but some day there will come a man who feels as I do, and he will destroy my wall and will erase my memory and will be my shadow and my mirror and will not be aware of it. Perhaps Shih Huang Ti walled in the empire because he knew it was fragile.

2.

Driving in a zigzag pattern, dodging the enormous potholes the rains had created in the road lined by the famous San Nicola pines leading toward his house about two kilometers down the hamlet's main road and thinking aloud about the mad dreams of Shih Huang Ti the First, Stuart abruptly repeated that dreamscape is a realm taking place in a dream … the background in your own or in another's dreamtime.

In dreamtime, skilled dreamers can shape and change their dreamscape and what takes place there—as Shih Huang Ti must have done—the dreamer can fill in the blank canvas on which dreams are painted. A painting however not yet painted. Not yet conceived. A conceptual work in one of the tunnels of a synapse of the brain—a contact between neurons and cells and a possible container of dreams—it too yet to be born, like the place where cartilage eventually breaks down in an arthritic joint. In his dreamscape, he knew, anything can happen.

That same night he followed the mental rules for the creation of a dreamscape and forbade Sophie to interfere with her bedtime games.

"I DID IT!" he related to her the next day after he had let himself return fully to wake time reality.

"I willed it. I dreamt, woke a little but stayed in the dream. I began manipulating it, executing various extensions of the dream. At a certain point I *chose* to stay in my dreaming; I edited it and extended it more, while still remaining in the dream, still there, reluctant to leave it, and for instants only, barely outside of it, all the time working along the fine line separating dream and awake, like the line between fantasy and reality.

"In the dream, I was in Buenos Aires, with or maybe without you. My hosts lived in a huge apartment and led a rich life, but my best friend who accompanied me had no money at all. Our wealthy hosts took us to a special place —we should not consider costs. We seemed to be in a sort of restaurant-club, but I didn't know what it was. In my dream state, I considered this disturbing issue and I couldn't decide what I would make it. Maybe a bordel. 'Beautiful wood,' I said. The place was a series of small roofless rooms, with no doors, no corridors, just walls. No connection, no idea of how we were to get inside … or out again. The problem of connections again. No matter. My friend was Adolfo who'd moved there from Rome. He and the woman I created to be with him said not to worry—Adolfo would do some acrobatics for us if we liked, that he was once a stunt man for Fellini. But I said I would proceed on to Palermo which was located about the distance Rio is from Buenos Aires."

In wake time, Stuart looked at his clock: 8:20 am, time to get up. However, he knew he could stay in his dreaming if he desired and learn what the strange room was all about. But he wanted to be in Palermo. In his dream, Palermo drew him in an inexplicable way. Dream Palermo was not like Sicily. Nor was it like the exclusive quarter of Buenos Aires named Palermo. It was still more beautiful. It had retained its scars of centuries of domination which everyone said made it more beautiful. But no matter. He could make a dreamscape into whatever he pleased. He did not have to leave dreamtime; it was under his control. Still, he decided to exit that conceptual dream world but he was sorry he did for he didn't see Palermo's scars.

Now, hours later, he still feels the effects of his own dreamings that he could have continued, maybe forever. Is that death? he wondered. He feared it might be waiting for him there in dreamtime so he let himself leave and maybe never return. Or perhaps wait until he was very old to try again; they say the older you get, the less you fear death. That's the opinion of philosophers who don't fear death. Take it or leave it! He didn't know, but he was old in the dream and he still feared death. Dreamtime is a most dangerous place; you can enter and never find your way out again even if you hold Ariadne's ball of red thread. Time may hold you forever.

Mayans called their dreamings the "Time of No Time." From that non-time on—like in all visions of the beginning of time—we are on Earth time. They believed that Mother Earth then shakes to her core driving men mad. That is a time of disconnection and hyper-individualism while new energies are coming into the world and people grow new skins. In the Mayan vision we in the West will find safe harbor only if we can journey past a wall of mirrors. Mirrors which will surely drive men mad—unless we have a strong heart. Some mirrors delude us with an infinity of reflections of our vanity and its shadows. Others paralyze us with our terror and rage, feeding an empire that transforms our fear into resignation. But the empire has no roots and is falling to pieces around us. Everyone is called to take a stand. To get beyond the wall of mirrors, the final challenge is to pass through a tiny door which requires us to make ourselves very small. To be very humble. Dostoevsky wrote that "humility is the strongest of all things and there is nothing else like it." To know we know nothing. To be courageous. And then we must burrow down into the earth where consciousness lives. On the other side of the mirrors, there is a clear pond. There, for the first time, we'll be able to see our true reflection.

In the Fifth Century BCE something significant occurred in Greece when the philosopher Heraclitus suggested that a person's dream world was something created within his or her own mind. This was antithetical to other philosophers who until then thought that dreams were the result of *outside* forces, such as the gods. The argument raged, "messages from the gods, or messages from within ourselves?" Aristotle brought the feud to an end by first studying dreams in a rational way; he then concluded in his book, *De divinatione per somnum*, "the most skillful interpreter of dreams is he who has the faculty of *absorbing resemblances*. I mean to say that dream presentations are analogous to the forms reflected in water."

Even though northerners may think this city is nearly tropical, it happens that it snows here in the spring. Here at fifty-two meters above sea level, at 41°53'30" latitude, it sometimes snows in late March or in early April.

The forty days of rain ended four days ago, but the sky had remained of a strange gray-blue-black coloring, something dreamlike about it, Stuart thought, still in his dream mood. A puffy, bloated sky filled with watery remains. A sky, wintry dark, a stone hard sky. Then during the night, a freeze struck and a snowfall made its late appearance concealed within its secretive but snappy military step—presumptuously marching—marching in total command ... like an enlightened dreamer. Its cold white flakes hung suspended in the icy-cold spring air, infectious as a sticky spider snake bite, the kind of snowfall that can drive you crazy. He shook his head to clear his thoughts of return to his dream world and told himself to stay far away from such temptations.

"Look, look, Stuart, not only did the rain transform into fucking snow," Sophie said, "but it's already sticking on the daises and the dandelions that had nearly covered the garden."

They stood at the picture window and watched its silent descent, snow-white, growing, sticking, thickening, spreading faster than the liana on the steel fence at the Great Wall. The tall hamlet pines lining the road and fading in the distance appeared in three distinct colors from top to bottom, white, green and garish-black.

For the last three days they had again lunched on the terrace, taken siestas in the sunshine hammock, surrounded by glorious exploding nature intent on blasting away the winter, dandelions and daises had returned and plants had emitted their perfumed aroma and the huge red roses along the sides of the main house which Sophie pampered were wide open and inviting. Red and black ants were working, bees and wasps buzzing, an occasional butterfly fluttering among the flowers, colorful birds chirping their individual melodies, two small green rose-ringed parakeets rhnnt, rhnnt, rhnnting in their language and the mean crows caw cawing from one tree to the other, signaling, warning, admonishing their brothers. In the gardens, the yellows and purples of the flowers, along the road, the green tops of the San Nicola pines. And on the horizon lambs' clouds hovered over the dark rolling forms of the mountains.

After the long rains, the scene had such a calming effect that Stuart and Sophie again perceived what she called "nature's certitude" so that the two pagans felt empowered to speak of a God. However, that evening at the window framed in the antique damask drapes that Sophie adored, she and Stuart reluctantly recognized the return of low temperatures. Then, later, a bizarre thunderstorm struck and during the night, not just a cold snap but a dramatic freeze brought nature to a standstill, followed in the early morning by an icy rain, quickly transforming, whitening and solidifying.

"Happens like this some years, Sophie," her husband said sadly.

'Still, it's spring and electrical storms give me the fucking creeps anyway,' she said, standing with a dancer's grace at his side, pelvic twisting and swaying, her hands wandering over him as if searching for the security she felt abandoning her. "I don't know. It's like you shouldn't even sleep at night. You've got to be ever alert. Attentive. You have to check things out. You can't let your guard down even during the night—especially not during the night, soul time."

"What do you mean, Sweetheart? What's on your mind?"

The abrupt weather changes. First the weeks of rain, then the freeze, and the spring snow now covering the hammock hanging on the terrace made them both think unpredictable thoughts. Yet his Sophie just couldn't help giving every move she made an unconscious sensuality. Though he too had felt something different in the air, in this seemingly critical moment he was reluctant to support Sophie's mystical tendencies or her dangerous preference for physicality.

Now Sophie Berardenga was petite, brown hair swirling around a beautiful face with huge green eyes, shapely, with beautiful full legs and the narrow Italian ankles that Stuart never tired of caressing. Nor of kissing the dark mole-beauty mark on her left cheek back near her perfect ear.

Standing at the window watching the spring flakes fall, Stuart Stuart towered over her from his basketball height, slim and athletic-looking with long dark hair and full beard and, to Sophie's distress, dressed in the same shirt, pants, and shoes he'd worn the whole year. A third-generation Scot, whom his eccentric father, Domenico Stuart, had given the same name as their surname, he'd said just to make doubly sure the Scotch-Italian Stuarts never became extinct, even though causing Stuart countless bureaucratic conundrums: bureaucrats, who were doubtful in the first place that the Stuarts were real Italians even though one Stuart has a huge tomb inside St. Peter's Cathedral, refused to believe his first and last names were the same. But such things in Rome would go on and on and on, forever.

Sophie and Stuart were both thirty-five.

"Apocalyptic!" Sophie muttered, her nose against the cold windowpane. "A melancholy feeling of times ending comes over me in times like this. You know, lights out in the world. Like it must be in wartime ... when bombs fall and darkness descends like a veil and troubled sensations overcome you. You know what I mean? Like being in a distant foreign country where you don't know a word of the language. Yet there are the omens, the presentiments. The past is vague and the future doesn't exist; only the present counts and it's all strange and incomprehensible. Swirling ceiling fans. Bicycle-crowded streets. Romantic sad cafés, where mysterious people huddle in the corners, scheming, conspiring. Chimes tinkling. Drumbeats rolling steadily in an indeterminate distance. Ghosts roaming among falling shadows becoming darkness. I can't describe the feeling. It's in my head but also in my stomach. Maybe in my soul. Oh, Stuart, the fucking darkness is coming."

"Is that from a new story you're writing ... the musical stage as you call it? You're always true to yourself, *Tesoro*, forever super aware of the present. And your eternal musical language."

"I'll read it to you someday—when all this is over. You'll understand me and our times together better that way."

"When all what is over, Sophie? All this what?"

Sophie pursed her lips and pulled at her long thick hair, sighed and turned back to the picture window giving on to the front yard, at the same time stroking the heavy ancestral damask drapes like those framing each of the room's four big windows and thinking 'if he only knew, he would kill himself.' She said: "Oh, Sweetheart, I don't know what I mean or what I'm saying. It's just … it's just the wretchedness of it all. This crazy weather and the stuff going on in our capital—and up north too. Simply wretched. Now, this end time snow has to fall on us like a punishment."

"All of what going on, Sophie? For God's sake, what's on your mind anyway?"

"Money and land taxes. The brouhaha of the times. Threats from East and West. How are we to survive, snowbound like this? I can't open the shop tomorrow and even if I did nobody would come in and if anyone looked in they wouldn't buy anything. Who needs necklaces in a blizzard? And nobody buys my stories either."

"Oh, Sophie, you know this happens nearly every year. We can wait it out. And by the way, this house doesn't make you bourgeois again. Where are your principles, girl?"

"Ok, Master, our treasury has exactly six euros and I think forty cents in it and our bank deposits are at zero. Practical thoughts. Besides, we'll soon be snowed in, and grocery stores too likely closed … even if they would give us credit. Stu Stuart, things were going so well. Now this … this threat. Oh, for the good old days when things were normal. Stuart, what is to become of us?"

Wringing her hands, Sophie wandered into the adjoining second living room. He watched his wife do what she compulsively did several times a day: unthinkingly she adjusted the wide sash holding apart the yellowish damask drapes within which was woven—Sophie claimed—

the outline of a lamb. Stuart called them blackout drapes and the lambs unicorns. Sophie's *unicorn drapes.*

"Perfect balance," he pronounced in approval. He teased her lovingly about the seventeenth-century drapes and this huge manor house Sophie had inherited, as had her father from his parents—the only things of her mysterious former life that remained in her after ten years with him. Anyway, he had learned to accept the hold tradition seemed to have on her. Like her beloved green velvet couch, the huge heavy armoires in every room, the portraits hanging on the walls of her ancestors none of whom either of them even registered in their consciousness, the tall floor lamps in darkened corners, potted plants, and tall Japanese vases, ancient carpets from Isfahan, the crossed swords on the walls of the rear study. After all, it had simply passed down to her through the many generations since its construction by Sophie's Berardenga Tuscan ancestors, accumulating, accumulating and maturing in its own way out here where time seems to stagnate and life creeps past, while, in reality, Stuart knew it was flying at the speed of light, maturing in its own way. Everything, every single thing, he thought, was far removed from him and his dreams.

"Perfect?" she repeated. "What would you know about traditional Tuscan taste? Stuart Stuart, Scotch-Italian Communist? What could you know about them? You know, when I enter a room for the first time my eyes invariably linger on the drapes. Drapes say a lot about who you are! So there."

"Actually, *Tesoro*, I think many people spend too much time deciding on their drapes, as if drapes guaranteed happiness. Costly fabrics, in any case. Just too much of a life-changing decision. All that wasted thought, discussion and deliberation about drapes. As if deciding what bourgeois political party will best protect your class interests in these times of a stirring working class. When oh when will we rise up? They're just waiting, the elite up there at the top, sneakily, observing us, just waiting to finally yoke us all. And we're down here thinking about drapes. Someday you'll see I'm right."

"There you go again! Your usual diatribe every time I adjust the drapes. Sometimes I wish the designs were really of unicorns! What drapes we would have! Art drapes. To compete with the unicorn tapestries in the museum near the Pantheon ... and how you loved them too, those huge tapestries of a lady and the unicorn. Middle age art. And so our drapes. And lover, these drapes are so old they are again modern."

"Ok, ok. Right. So what do you say about a little run … before the snow gets so high we'd have to wear snowshoes again."

"Snowshoes? Again? You mean we still have them?"

"Four years ago it snowed the first day of May. That time we did some trekking. And from the looks of things we're going to need them every year in this southern spring that never comes anymore. Things get worse every year. Every month. Maybe every day. And so nature, so society."

"Pessimist! And that must have been another woman with you four years ago! I don't recall that snowfall at all." That was his Sophie, doubtful about love.

3.

The snow was dry and inviting, barely covering the soles of their running shoes. In the sudden cold it stuck quickly to the earth of the near sea-level lands. They trotted along the snowy road leading away from other villas and headed into the wildest and most unpeopled and untrammeled part of the hamlet that people here called the Casale ... a white world today. They ran in the direction of the city—not away from it as people in the hamlet were inclined to do.

The old farmstead of the original hamlet is invisible from the road, hidden behind woods of mature trees. In the seventeenth century, what became the hamlet consisted of a congeries of distinct edifices. There was a chapel attached to the north-western end of the northernmost block which would be in the direction of today's Vatican Radio antenna masts. The country estate of the *Tenuta di San Nicola* was bought by Cardinal Ottavio Acquaviva the Elder in 1608, and a small villa or *Casino* was built. This part survives as the *Casale di Acquaviva* at the end of the Via del Casale di Acquaviva, a dead-end country lane paralleling the Via San Nicola. Presumably the Acquaviva family remodeled the old *Casale* in the eighteenth century. The locality of *San Nicola* is still rural, although infiltrated by messy suburbia towards the north-east where it abuts La Storta and Olgiata.

"It's pretty intense, the snowfall," Stuart said as they accelerated their pace to a slow run, still side by side. "But it seems safe enough," he added to reassure claustrophobic Sophie, who, he knew, felt hemmed in by nature's bizarre games. She called the area they lived in behind the Great Wall *the lands of abandoned space*s, even though the spaces she meant had actually never been occupied ... not by anyone but them. His old friend, Patrick Rainwater would have loved their occupied-abandoned spaces where their strides on the snow echoed through the foliage.

Two kilometers from home the snow was still falling copiously, each flake huge and visibly measurable to the naked eye. The level of the now ice cold snow had climbed to more than eight centimeters. And ice had formed on the shallow ponds along each side of the road and ice cycles were lengthening from the pines. The snowfall, the ice, the dark pines with their whitening tops, the limited vision combined to create a new reality of half earth, half heaven. Stuart felt it could be life or it could be the other world beyond, a world in which each object was separate and alone: each tree, the ice, each individual snowflake.

"The whitest snow that ever fell to earth." Sophie noted, short of breath from keeping up with Stuart's long strides.

"And already over my shoes," he said, breathing smoothly through his nose.

For some reason, the more clearly he recalled the scenery from the tower, the faster his pace, as if he were obligated to reach some specific objective far from the tower in the shortest time possible

The road narrowed. Spontaneous, unidentifiable trees pressed on either side, in some places hanging over them like a net, letting in only stray drifting white flakes. Stuart found its beauty excessive and ugly. It was also perilous because its natural enclosure—some still brown dying trees, bushes and underbrush surrounding a clearing under a canopy of green of a network of overhanging trees and the filtering white of the snowfall from the heavens –was a threatening spot for claustrophobic Sophie.

In the same moment they entered the most spectacular of the wildness of nature's own botanical garden, Sophie stopped, peering to the right where the foliage had collapsed under the weight of the snow. A summery green glade had appeared to their right side, small but with the quality of open land. Still and quiet but emitting a certain anguish, there was something horrible and secret about it. Though the treetops were laden in white, the earth of the clearing under the net was black and green.

"Stuart, look over there. Look! Look! The birds. Dozens of

them," she yelled, running into the glade. "I just knew this was all wrong! Just wretched. Dozens of them," she repeated pointing left and right at dead birds lying unmoving on a square of green moss and scattered among low weeds. Crows, black and gray crows, one identical to the other. The scene made Stuart feel somehow in a place beyond himself, a place or a time in which you long to escape to, some faraway land where trees would always be green, snow would remain white, ice colorless and mountains dark blue.

"Dreamscape!" he exclaimed spontaneously.

Sophie stooped and reached toward a bird at her feet.

"No, Sophie, no. Sophie, don't touch them. Don't touch them."

"Just wanted to see if it was warm."

But she didn't touch the bird she hated so much in life. Instead, she looked at Stuart thoughtfully, then back at the bird at her feet, wondering what it meant.

They counted fifteen dead birds.

"Mediterranean crows," Stuart pronounced. "Gray and black. A hooded crow! They look so much smaller dead like that. A whole family I'd bet—you know they live in families—maybe even in tribes. A whole family decimated. They must have lived in that tree, caw cawing one to the other early mornings."

"Well, they're lost to others, just like them. And dead from what? The cold?"

"Who knows? But birds don't die of cold; they fly south. Some rare bird disease, I guess. Maybe even transmittable. We've got to get out of here. Wait, I'll report it to 118. First, I'll photograph some of the birds and the place so they can check it out. This might be dangerous, you know. Remember all the stories from Wuhan about bats and covid-19. In any case, this looks to me like a disease—or poisoning. The health people can examine them, maybe pinpoint the disease."

"Poisoned!" Sophie repeated. "Most people hate this bird, the *cornacchia*. It's so mean to other birds. The fascist in the bird world. Yet, I once heard that some people eat them—disgusting to think of. Hard to believe. Most likely someone discovered this family and poisoned them … and now they've gone missing from their tribe."

"Right! Oh, they're mean all right. Terrorizing other birds with their throaty *caw caw caw*. And their size and power. Why, they're not afraid of anything. An exceptional bird to be sure. At least they act that way. Still, I wonder if they're not afraid sometimes that other birds might gang up against them. I was walking in our rear garden the other day, walked right past a crow and it paid no attention to me whatsoever. Fearless! At the moment a crazy thought struck me. You know, I've long suspected that the city feels menaced by our invading country-side and its wild nature. Kill'em all, they think down there in civilization, birds and sometimes even people. It's puzzling. Sophie, you know. Maybe the city placed the crows out here to kill the other birds in the first place. They've only been here a few years. A crow conspiracy! A false flag of some kind. You know how our people are. I think many of them hate nature—the way they cut down trees without a second thought and pour cement everywhere. And now birds poisoned by humans in this isolated area so far from everyone. I'm not convinced. Still, we might have discovered an—an agent."

"An agent? Now, what the fuck does that mean?"

'Ah, well, uh, uh, well, just an agent. But there's something else. You know my feelings about coincidences. This—this scene, the snow, the woods, the dead birds and you leaning over them, the dreamscape—all this happened before—somewhere—or maybe in a dream. You know, the eternal recurrence of all things ... everything connected."

"Oh, for heaven's fucking sakes, Stuart! But you know, I keep having the feeling that things in general have suddenly changed. Nothing seems to matter anymore. Don't you feel that too?"

Back at home they stood at the window, snow-watching. Wind and snow swirled wildly across the terraces and penetrated the tiniest of apertures or cracks and crevices around the window frame so that from time to time the damask drapes quivered from a particularly strong blast of nature. There was thunder. Streaks of lightning cut zigzag patterns across the darkening sky. You could hardly believe that there had just been spring days of siesta in the hammock and lunch on the sun terrace.

"What things did you mean have changed," Stuart asked. "How have things changed?"

"Oh, I don't know, it's hard to be specific. But like I said before our run and the snowfall—just look at it now. Must be a meter high. The rose bushes and the daisies and bright yellow dandelions frozen under the white. And the sounds! Sounds of a new kind of silence, the end times atmosphere, and now the dead crow family and all those abandoned spaces out there. Things like that. Nothing seems the same. Don't you feel it?"

"Well, Sophie, of course, I … wait, what's that sound. Quick, up to the roof," Stuart yelled, running to the stairs. "Sounds like lorries. It's their snow chains clanging. Like you say, something strange is going on out there."

"Maybe it's nothing," Sophie said.

"Then you mean to say it's everything."

"What the fuck does that mean?" she said, crowding him at the choice vantage point. "You keep speaking in riddles today."

"Some philosophers say nothing is enormous—the total of everything that is nonexistent."

"What? Well, that may be. Anyway, this time it's something. Just look at those army trucks."

"Still, somehow the concept of nothing makes me think of your abandoned spaces. And Sophie, those vehicles are called lorries."

From their protected roof garden they had a good view of their surroundings. Up on the road a column of military trucks and buses ploughed through mounting banks of snow.

"Military vehicles," Stuart said pensively. "Four of them. Maybe a whole brigade of men. For Christ sakes, this is an invasion—of your abandoned spaces. Not the way I expected them to be filled one day. Sophie, like I've told you, things that happen to us is modern capitalism in action! As if power and snow and dying birds and occupied abandoned spaces go together. You know what I mean—nature and space are a measure of the world condition."

"You and your capitalism hang-up! But no, there's no joy in this shit, Stuart. The bliss we've always felt here in the manor house and the wild around us. Now there's no joy here. Not after the snow and the dead birds and now this. Maybe never again. No, no joy at all."

The day was beginning to end when they heard the motors and clanging of chains again. They ran back up to the roof. Darkness was coming down prematurely. The sky and the surrounding hills were mixed in a whorl of cold, wind, snow and ice. Two armored trucks and a bus were fighting their way back toward the Great Wall exit.

"Strange," Stuart said as they watched the vehicles struggle against a meter and a half of fresh snow, 'like German Tiger tanks at the battle at the gates of Moscow in World War Two', he thought. He said: "There were four lorries and I think three buses when they arrived." Where are the others? he wondered. Would they make it out of the snowbound hamlet? Or was nature more powerful than steel?

"I'm going back to check out the birds. Maybe the other vehicles are still there. *Tesoro*, where're my snowshoes anyway? Or are they too among the lost things we're always talking about? Lost things and abandoned spaces have a way of marching hand in hand in this magic hamlet."

Sophie had wanted to return to the glade with Stuart but she knew she couldn't face the enclosure. So she thought and reminisced.

Why, she asked herself for the thousandth time? Yes, that was the real question, WHY? Why am I the way I am? Why my fears? I have him. But I'm a separate being from him. I write my stories to show it. To prove it. My ideas come from my own head—even if that's often the problem. I'm me and always will be only me and will never be able to erase my past. I can't be him … and he, me. Not like the song suggests. With him, things are different. His presence is the difference. He is the difference. He can turn the stars in the skies to purple if he wants to. He's magic. And he thinks he married a lady. So why my manias of fear of closed places like the glade? Me, undaunted, unafraid if anything—others think! The one place I never want to leave is his embrace. But there is this thing of being on top. This needs explaining. Not for erotic reasons but so I can breathe freely. To escape the suffocation. To be in control. We hit the bed and by instinct I immediately flip over on top of him. How can I explain when he asks? He likes it but wonders why. I've always been that way—before I met Stuart. The others—male or female—inevitably asked why I had to be on top. Father had told me to suppress it when I, the eleven year old introvert, complained that uncle smothered me—doing his thing lying on top of me. That's why I began speaking like them: fuck this, fuck that. How was I to escape from the family seclusion. The family incest. They surrounded me, my parents, relatives, the other uncles. Until at sixteen, crazed and inexplicable, I escaped and walked all the way to the capital, the city of closed elevators, closed metro doors, closed palazzo doors, closed police doors, sealed tomb stones over graves in the boundless cemeteries.

But the Berardenga were rich, they have always been rich, they gave her an allowance, however insufficient, which she supplemented with increments from other non-family uncles until in her mid-twenties she met Stuart and to make certain she maintained silence about the uncles at home they willed her the manor hidden away in a place called Casale di San Nicola on the distant outskirts. No metro tunnels, no sealed buses, no triple locks and chains on doors for her, no restrictions to her being on top. No more thoughts of underground that had haunted her since she was eleven. At twenty-five, Stuart took control of her. She would die for him.

Trudging slowly over a meter and a half of snow, Stuart thought of the lorries and buses trying to get back home. Vain idea! Yet everybody needs their place. Then, there was the glade again. The gap in the growing wall of snow. But how strange it seemed now! Not a flake of snow in nature's botanical garden inside the tent-like glade. Everything dark there now. No lorries or buses. What little snow had penetrated the canopy covering it and reached the glade had been cleared. Not a flake remained. Not one single bird body was to be seen either. Carried away by the military? And what kind of military is it whose duty includes clearing away dead birds? Nature provided no answers. Who had won? The State had shown itself in apparent useless earnestness. From the superficial evidence of the missing lorries, the absence of the dead birds and the silence of nature, the secret state seemed to have won the battle. But the snow was still there. Surprisingly then, now getting used to the snowshoes, his trek back home was a cake walk. Sophie's worries were less serious than earlier. The evening cold had hardened the snow and the bare ground of the road. There was no moon, no lights anywhere. And the thoughts churning through his head were dark thoughts. Negative and skeptical thoughts.

Sophie was standing again at the window stroking sensually the damask drapes. It was a relief to see her in her familiar position. For a long moment, she didn't acknowledge his return. Then: "Stuart, I just can't come out of this melancholy," she said, examining pretentiously the damask sash. "After all this time … after all our love … when our lives seemed so perfect. And then, these end times! Times of the birds and the spring snowfall." Again she stroked and adjusted lovingly the yellowish drapes.

4.

Three days later the spring sunshine returned. The snow vanished. The hammock was again in use, as if the great snowfall, the fifteen dead crows and the anomalous passage of the military lorries with their snow chains clanging were all part of a bad dream, a scene that stayed alive in Stuart's mind. Sophie reopened her jewelry shop in La Storta. He should have begun his monthly column for the Scottish magazine he wrote for, but instead his curiosity carried him back to the glade, tentatively, uncertain, unwilling to get still more emotionally involved. Yet, step by step he penetrated ever deeper into the woods that proved to be thicker and more impenetrable than it had seemed earlier. On the fourth day, he pushed through a jungle-like thicket and suddenly stood face to face with what at first seemed a log wall, like the side of a perfectly laid log cabin, indented in the center; it seemed like an invitation to enter this foreign space, a truly abandoned space. Sophie must see this! He stepped forward exactly as it happened in his dream: I'm walking in the woods. I see a wide pile of expensive logs, all similar in size and length. As I approach I notice they form a semi-circle. Now awake but still in the dream, I decide to continue the dream to see what happens. Or what CAN happen if I desire. I maintain limited control. I can do anything I like. For I'm in dreamtime. I walk toward the deepest part of the indentation that becomes a grotto, I touch the smooth walls; it is close and tight. I think "womb". If I like I can enter the womb. I become aware of the significance of my wake thought. Re-enter the womb. Does it mean to prolong life or does it mean my death and the rebirth of a new person? Curious choice. I decide not to risk and let the dream end as it wished.

The real wall moved. With a shoulder, he pushed slightly on the right side of the log wall. It swung open like a door. And practically at his feet—only a meter's distance away—on a perfectly cleared earth lay embedded a steel trapdoor. It was painted green and had large silver handles. Disconcerted, he stared at what seemed the kind of inexplicable and perhaps meaningless vision you encounter in a dream, until out of the corner of an eye he saw at the edge of the clearing about five meters away a partially covered black object and he immediately knew what it was: a dead crow. Forgotten. It was all black. An American crow. Because of the negative superstitions regarding crows—they bring bad luck, they mean death is around the corner, crops will fail. In some countries, murdering crows is a popular "sport". Was this dead American black crow abandoned? Left behind? So far from home? Or simply forgotten by a distracted God? Or perhaps the crow left behind was an immigrant crow, part of another family altogether. He wrapped its frozen body in paper and put it in his sack

He then stooped and lifted one of the trapdoor handles. Locked. Underneath the handle were two key holes side by side like in a safe deposit box. Again he peered around him when he heard one of nature's inexplicable noises. Was he alone here? He hesitated. To the left, he pushed at a funny-looking thicket. Maybe it was false nature. He pushed again. It swung open as had the log wall and revealed a crude roadway leading away from the trapdoor clearing. The road was marked by tire tracks. Chain tracks. Not a scrap of any other object. He closed the artificial thicket behind him and followed the tire tracks about a half-kilometer's distance. To his right, the sun reflected the brilliant brown of the circular Great Wall sending off flecks of golden sparks. Surprised that the Great Wall extended this far from the former roundabout, he noted the faint tracks leading from the trapdoor to what must be another exit from the hamlet, this one pointed directly west in the direction of the maze of perfect stone walls—more formidable and powerful-looking but much lower than the Great Wall of the Hamlet—surrounding the forests of masts and towers supporting the antenna of the Vatican Radio transmitters about four kilometers away and whose signals reach the most distant corners of the earth. Wondering about the significance of the nature of the two walls and if there was a connection, he thought that most definitely there was a connection. He continued on the roadway southwards that opened onto a pasture from which tracks led off in various directions. He held to the main path to the left until—to his surprise—he stepped back onto the main road of the hamlet, Via San Nicola. He'd wandered in a triangle: main road, the mysterious thicket, another road leading back to the main. Stuart knew that the things he had just seen—the trapdoor, the fake thickets, the Vatican transmission masts—were to remain in his mind as a metaphor. The unanswered question was: a metaphor of what? A metaphor, a snapshot of what had happened to them on the day of the snowfall, or of what was happening in the world from Europe to China today, or of what was yet to happen in their world? In any case, he perceived a strong premonition of untold events in arrival.

Once back at home, he wrapped the dead bird in more paper and put it in an empty freezer in the cellar. Details of the snowfall, the dead crows, the military vehicles, the artificial bushes, the log cabin wall, the trapdoor with the silver handles, the safety deposit box-like keyholes, radio masts, the second roadway with tire tracks leading back to the hamlet's main road churned in his mind. The following day, he barely glanced at the first clearing where they'd found the dead crows on the day of the snowfall and continued another half kilometer along the Via San Nicola where the road he'd discovered leading from the trapdoor exited into the main roadway so discreetly that it was nearly invisible. Lorry and bus tire tracks indicated that the vehicles that used that road did not return to the Great Wall and the Elevated over the roundabout. After a slight rise, the unpaved road dropped sharply into a long slanting descent for about another kilometer where the hamlet abruptly ends. What was before a normal steel gate had become a veritable barricade and a number of no trespassing signs were fastened to its joints: "Property of the Maritime Services", "Trespassers will be prosecuted by law," "Beware of dogs," all written in Italian, English and German. Just under the dog warning a small yellow plaque with the word in small letters in brackets: (Forschungsinstitut). Research Institute.

Higher up the hill beyond the barricade, two huge black dogs stood motionless and observed him observing them though high-powered binoculars. A man in uniform stood behind them. The Mastiffs, the canine terror of his nightmares: their black eyes were fixed on him, their terrifying square brown heads, their short muzzle and muscular build were live warnings . Hard to train, it was widely said, unpredictably murderous. Then he turned his sights on the man and he started; it was the same German guard at the hamlet's Great Wall who had accompanied him to the top of the tower.

Trying to shake off his rehashing of a recurrent incubus of a village in a barren valley menaced by invading hordes of Mastiffs pouring down from the mountains, Stuart turned back toward the dead crow glade, his mind repeating over and over: German guards, dead crows, a secret trapdoor, all in the hamlet he called home. Dreamscape again? He pulled on a pair of rubber gloves before touching anything and carefully wiped with a cloth the silver handles and the keyholes of the trapdoor, the only things he recalled touching the day before. Carefully he photographed the key holes before rushing back home.

Somewhere in their manor house he'd seen a drawer containing a collection of keys handed down through decades and maybe centuries; surely two of them would fit the trapdoor. He found the keys in the storage room near the freezer and was surprised at the number: maybe a hundred big and little, round and square keys, a few apparently a couple of centuries old.

The next morning he was back at the trapdoor with a bag of keys the tips of whose blades resembled the keyholes of his photographs. Around him, quiet reigned. No dead crows. No new tracks. No specific signs of human activity whatsoever. Yet he sensed that people had been here. Therefore, he felt growing trepidation as to what he would find underneath the trapdoor—if his keys fit, which he almost hoped was not the case. To his surprise, two of the first fit perfectly. Two turns of the keys and the steel door was unlocked. Open sesamé!

With ever mounting trepidation he lifted the two doors, stood up, stepped back, and leaned over the opening and warily peered into the gaping hole. Blackness! Looking intently into total darkness, the darkness that you only know is there before you has something of the invisible to the human eye. Looking into darkness where light no longer exists is a soul-chilling experience, after which you can no longer be the same person you were before. Yet what else did he expect to see anyway? People in white coats? Mastiffs? No, it was a darkness that sunlight struggled to penetrate as it rose from the pit. Stuart perceived the presence of shadows, something evil and foreboding. Then he noted just under the ledge the first rungs of a vertical ladder leading down into the pit of darkness. He tried to ignore it. "Tartarus!" he exclaimed, remembering the professor's words. His only friend in the hamlet who lived in the villa near theirs, the "Professor", who lectured on Greek mythology at a nearby university branch, had related to him legends of Tartarus, the infernal regions of ancient Greek mythology, the name originally used for the deepest region of the world, the lower of the two parts of the underworld, the professor stipulated, where the gods locked up their enemies … the prison of the damned which gradually came to mean the entire underworld. As such, Tartarus was the opposite of Elysium where happy souls lived after death. In some accounts, Tartarus was one of the personified elements of the world, the primordial *god* of the stormy *pit of Tartarus* that lies beneath the foundations of the earth. Tartarus was the body of the *pit* itself. As a place, *Tartarus* was described simply as the *pit*. So when he flashed his powerful 250000 Lumen Xhp90 into the pit, Tartarus was fixed in his mind. The bottomless pit, he thought, as his torch searched in vain for the bottom. Well, after all, if it was an extension of Tartarus, he was searching beneath the bottom of the earth which means the original blackness. The nothing. The *nada*. The everything of which Sophie had been skeptical.

As his eyes and the LumenXhp90 adjusted to the darkest darkness existent outside of Tartarus, he saw that the smooth walls were so solid looking that his initial Welsh coal miner's concern about security eased while he counted the rungs as he climbed downwards: ten, fifteen, twenty rungs … about two meters.

Down, down, down, one hundred fifty rungs, when at maybe thirty meters depth he stopped at a recess in the wall several meters deep where lay a pile of some fifty sections of rails and various excavation equipment. So there was a miner's tram somewhere, he thought, still deeper beneath him, which again reminded him of the novel, the *Valley of Tears,* about coal mining in Wales in the era of King Coal, when the dangers of the pit were rampant and mother earth devoured its own children: the darkness and the cold and the gases to the clanging of trams, lungs ruined for life by coal dust 'way down in the dark lonely deep'. Men and small boys condemned to Tartarus like enemies of the gods.

And sure enough, the first thing his eyes and his Lumen registered when he landed on the bottom of what was coming to seem more than a mere pit—but truly that which lay in the infinity under the bottom part of the world—was a multiple car tram standing just inside a tunnel pointing east, parallel to the main hamlet road, Via San Nicola, in the direction of the roundabout. Scanning a bit at a time, he spotted an electrical power box hooked onto the pit wall. He pushed "on", and the entire vertical pit, the ladder and the tunnel as far as he could see into it lit up in a pleasant yellowish light. After a hesitation, he jumped into the last car, located a button "go", and carefully pressed it as if placing all his chips on "even" at the roulette table. The tram departed and moved over the rails as smoothly and quietly as the Number One metro line running down the Champs Elysée, while he wondered if he would ever get back to the same exit ladder. Yet if there was a tram, it transported something or other and that meant there were other exits. Moving at around fifteen kph, he passed main branches, left and right, tunnels apparently with their own tunnels, all together forming a huge network and, he believed, dedicated to some less than legitimate activity. Occasionally he heard echoes of a terrifying screeching like the sounds you might hear outside a zoo. He would investigate those sub-tunnels later.

Some minutes later, he arrived at the end of the tram line. After an initial sensation of travelling gradually downhill during the first part of tunnel, he had felt the tram tunnel was rising rapidly toward the end of the line—and though he was convinced there were other exits from this subterranean world, he was glad to see a wooden staircase at the top of which lay a trapdoor. He ran up the stairs in delight and pushed; it was locked from above, as he could have imagined. But he believed he knew where he was: his sense of place and direction told him he was at the main gate near the roundabout and that above that locked wooden trapdoor was the tower on the right side of the entrance through the Great Wall. He smiled to himself. Dreamtime, but pleasant and non-threatening

He pushed "go" and sent the tram back without him. Hurriedly then, he walked along the illuminated tunnel, sketching the network as seen from the tramway, but becoming more and more fearful that he'd overstayed his time. His sensation of a gradual descent from where he'd entered and then the rise at the end of the line proved to be right. The rather narrow side tunnels were marked by white lines and symbols and small cages hanging on the walls. A thought: Were the dead crows once encaged in them? At what seemed the deepest point of the underground he heard through a branch tunnel to the west the sound of the rustling of water.

5.

Exploration in the tunnels seemed useless until he had an idea of what he was searching for; moreover, each minute spent nosing around and idling needlessly in the subterranean complex was dangerous: those two guards and the Mastiffs linked to both the Hamlet Commission and the Forchungsinstitut were warning enough. Before the rains, he mused, before the transformation of the roundabout, and before the corvucide, the hamlet was a peaceful place—truly an Eden. And people of the hamlet had no interest in what was happening on the other hill. Sophie was right: things had changed in recent years and, in a way, nothing in the world seemed to matter anymore. Now, what he had observed, the complex of buildings and private homes on that other hill, surrounded by their own stone wall, an area that until recently was a sort of official Naval Station from where bugle calls marked military ceremonies that echoed over loudspeakers down from the hill and across the hamlet as far as the roundabout and arousing little curiosity, had changed its nature. Normal security measures had been upgraded: no more bugle calls resounded from the hill; only silence. And Stuart had seen the one German guard and two Mastiffs up there observing him. He suspected there was more going on up there than meets the eye, which, in his mind, created a new reality that unlike a naval station, somehow corresponded to Sophie's pessimistic world view. And his attraction to the world of dreams and his belief in coincidence and the role of chance did not impede his acceptance of that reality, some of which he had personally observed.

The next day, he drove off in his twenty-year old Fiat Panda that he loved with a passion but that others either derided or ignored. Sophie too laughed at his little, fragile looking dream car that he pampered, changing the oil often and cleaning the windshield and headlights assiduously; but the car itself had not been washed in years and the heating system had never worked. The surly German guard

42

sneered and waved him through the gate of the Great Wall without even a glance at his exit pass. He weaved back and forth through the labyrinth, took the Elevated South, then minutes later exited west onto Via della Storta that passed in front of the main entrance to the ex-military station and now, Stuart believed, converted into something sinister and nefarious, and most likely criminal: the Research Institute. After a series of sharp curves recalling the maze in front of the Great Wall, a straight stretch, another ninety degree curve and there was the stop light, the bus stop and, set back somewhat from the street, the tall front gate to the institute. He didn't recall having ever seen the gate open, even when a lone car may have just exited: the light was always green for exiting cars or persons.

On the spur of the moment, he slowed, turned sharp right and stopped to the right of the gate. He jumped out of the car and opened the hood and fiddled with the radiator, all the while taking in the scene inside the gate: off to the right, neither hidden nor exposed, two orange buses like those that arrived in the hamlet with the military vehicles on the day of the snowfall, but which had not left via the Great Wall entrance with the others.

Immediately, two guards came out of the guard house inside the gate to the left and rushed toward him, one restraining a snarling Mastiff on a leash. The geography and the link to the hamlet was clear: the institute's internal road from this gate led downhill in a straight line directly to the gate with the warning signs inside the hamlet, about one kilometer distance from where he was standing.

He slammed down the hood unnecessarily loud and called out to the guards, "No problem ... just age," he said, sliding back into the Panda and yelling, "The car's twenty-five years old."

While the guards laughed and calmed the Mastiff with a friendly pat, Stuart read the plaque on an inside wall: *Research Institute*. He imagined a troop of guards like these with their mean Mastiffs and technicians in white jackets gathering the dead crows, checking the trapdoor and re-boarding those buses and returning here via the rear exit from the hamlet. The connection between the research institute and the hamlet was now clear. But why? Not many years earlier, the *Forschungsinstitut* had been that inconsequential military installation: flag raising and lowering, uniforms and saluting, taps and military music, with barracks for the men, houses for officers and families. Back in those days, there was no Great Wall around the hamlet either, no towers, no German guards. What the hell was going on here?

6.

He rang Gianluigi's bell and with an ear close to the intercom waited for the rush to the gate of the professor's three Maremmano sheep dogs barking furiously until they caught Stuart's familiar scent. As usual, the Prof, as he and Sophie called him, answered he would come for him so that his vicious watch dogs didn't tear him limb from limb. The dogs, their tails now wagging furiously, wanted to greet him. From the gate he gazed at the valley and the village on the horizon to the east. From here it looked like a quaint Tuscan hill town; instead La Storta was a traffic-choked, smog-ridden thoroughfare cut in half by Europe's busiest road, Via Cassia, reaching northwards as far as Florence and Fiesole. Strange, the thought suddenly occurred to him, how his eyes had begun seeing everything differently since the death of the fifteen crows.

"Kalimera, Stuart. Do come in, *parakalo, parakalo."* Gianligi said, nearly exhausting his vocabulary of Modern Greek language, to which he often added a reluctant "as the Greeks of today say, ignoring the language of the gods".

The professor's villa sprawled along a slope among hills running in all directions. It was painted the same blood red color of the country houses spread between the city and the sea. Covered terraces wrapped around the somehow forbidding three-story structure topped by multiple chimneys emerging from a rising and falling red tile roof. Gianluigi was wary of the green mass of the swampy area below, surrounded by spontaneous oaks and poplars submerged under nameless bushes and wildly climbing vines all of which seemed to gradually advance toward the villa. Silver tinted olive trees leaned uphill to escape the mortal clutches of the advancing wild. Water in the pool shimmered in the rays of the late afternoon sun. The mysterious quality of the villa had attracted Stuart from the start. Except for the dogs and the former occasionally amplified martial music from the secret military establishment on the hill, silence had reigned here since the beginning of time. The silence of the grape arbor and the poolside palms, the silence of the swamp, the silence of the hills and the olive trees and yellow grain fields and red farmhouses, the silence of the distant sea. It had never been clear why and how he managed to live in this huge house, alone.

They settled in the breakfast room. Gianluigi opened the kitchen door and called, "Bruno, *vieni dentro*." A huge white Maremmano trudged in. "The others will be jealous, Bruno, but they can't all come in." He poured almost warm vermouth into mismatched cups and admitted sadly that a gin tonic would indeed hit the spot, but that his gin had disappeared due to circumstances beyond his control. Professor Gianluigi Logreco had a drinking problem, the ramifications of which he routinely rehashed with Stuart each time he came.

"So sorry about the drink situation today in general, but since the Great Wall and that obnoxious roundabout, I hate going out of the hamlet at all. Our Commission could relent a bit on the ban of commercial activity inside the hamlet and allow a small beverages shop."

"But Gianluigi, I thought you were accepting the offer to sit on that committee."

"Me! With that bunch of Nazis. Not on your life! What gave you that idea?"

"You did. You said the offer was enticing and you would most likely become a hamlet guide. Guide, that's the word you used for administrator."

"Hrumph! I must have been slightly inebriated."

"Yes, you were sloshed."

"Stuart Stuart, I'm surprised at your lack of insight. San Nicola is not a concentration camp after all and besides half of that so-called administrative committee is not even from here. They come from that, er, ahem, that adjoining research institute on the other hill. Not even Italians! From some East Germanic tribe. Prussians probably. Anyway, what I need most of all in this moment is a crate of gin and, well, of course, vermouth, and some cognac and a full wine cellar. Why, I can't even bear going down there now … and facing all those empty shelves. Like going down into Tartarus! Oh, Stuart, you don't know how I hate the summer looming from behind the hills beyond La Storta," he complained. "No longer do we get the pleasant breezes like those that blow over the Peloponnesian islands, from Corfu to Crete. Oh, how I hate the end of winter. Summer has become absolutely destetable! People suddenly become so confident. You know, Stuart, there's nothing more depressing than optimism, that joyful summery mood sweeping the country—for no reason. And in bad taste besides. Like acquaintances who suddenly become friends and come to use the swimming pool. Summer means mosquitoes and sprays and lotions and air-conditioning and cold, cold sweat. Oh, Zeus, how I need a real drink in this moment. I almost feel sympathy for Erysichthon."

"Erysichthon?"

"You might not remember him. Now his story is not exactly mine but….well, his desire was not the same as my thirst for gin, but Erysichthon was a rich and greedy man back in real Greece. According to the story, one day he cut down a sacred grove of trees in order to build another feast hall, as the rich in all times are wont to do. The goddess Demeter was slighted by this, and decided to punish him. She gave him an appetite so strong that he ate everything he could get his hands on. He ate all the food he had, then all the food he could buy, until he had completely exhausted his wealth. He even tried to sell his own beautiful daughter for food! He was reduced to such poverty that he lost all standing, his home, everything he possessed. When he had nothing else left, he turned on himself and died eating his own flesh off his body."

The professor frowned in disgust and turned toward a wall mirror and, again adjusting his tie, said, "I cancelled my lecture for this morning and gave it online. Most students prefer that anyway but still, my frequent physical absences look bad and sully my reputation. After all, I do have my standards … as flexible as they are. But I must maintain the image of Professor Gianluigi Logreco in the corridors of academia, especially in view of the AI threat, you know, artificial intelligence, that is, robots. Can you even imagine: a robot teaching Greek mythology?"

He leaned toward the mirror and suddenly recited: "I'll set you up a glass where you may see the innermost part of you. Uh, Stuart, I always forget, is that Hamlet or Lear?"

"Lear," Stuart said, making a wild guess.

"I doubt it," Gianluigi said, as if Stuart's guess were a polemical attack on him by a rival professor. "No matter!" Then, rummaging in his mind for some expression in his weak Greek language and examining himself in the mirror, he added: "Ah, the good old days, Stuart. When there was at least a beer in the morning to start the day right. 'With no problem,' goes the song so popular these days, by the way, an idea and words plagiarized from the Greek story of Tiresias. You likely think a beer at nine a.m. a bit early. Yet a beer early morning is something like, well, like Paul Bowles wrote: 'A pipe of kif before breakfast gives a man the strength of a hundred camels in the courtyard.' But now all that's behind me. My reckless days are over. From now on it's a *marcia trionfale,* or maybe a marche *funebre.*" Languages humming and translating themselves in his mind, he said: "Here's to you, Bruno, and to your brothers and sisters out there. Still, the vermouth was, what can you say? It was better than nothing at all. Or not?" Peering once more into the refrigerator and frowning, he said: "Well, nothing of interest here."

"Okay, Gianluigi, I need to talk, so let's sit in some quiet place far from the kitchen and the frige, but first what is that story about Tiresias?"

"He was a blind oracle famous for having been transformed

into a woman for seven years and then back to man. In an argument between Hera and her husband Zeus about who got more pleasure in sex, the man or the woman, they asked the opinion of Tiresias since he'd been both. He answered: 'the woman, ten times more,' on which Hera struck him blind but gave him the quality of clairvoyance as compensation. Well, that's mythology for you!"

"Great story though!" Stuart replied as they settled into the professor's study, sprawled on the two couches, which, together with a TV set and a cardboard box for Bruno or one of the dogs were the only pieces of furniture in the professor's study filled with books and small sculptures. *Carmina Burana* was blasting from the CD on top of the TV as it was the last time he was here. "You need here a picture of the curious figure of that Tiresias. I've often wondered about that same subject as did the Greek gods."

"Hmm. I wrote my doctoral dissertation on that."

"A dissertation about Zeus, or about who had the most orgasms?"

"Stuart! Please. No! About the role of Greek gods in Attic culture. My idea was that … anyway, listen to this, written by an academic colleague at Banya Luka University, Petar Penda:

Once my eyes were sea-blue and seeing
And my breasts were round and full of milk.
I breastfed Thebe with my wisdom,
I lived and loved as a man, then as a woman,
And again as a man, and saw
All sides of the world, and the underworld.
My wrinkled breasts stayed with me
To remind me of life and the world,
Of gods' flaws, spite and envy,
And how blindness helped me see
Beyond the gaze of mortal eyes.

I saw my past and felt every hand on my naked body,
Lust and love entwined, reason blurred by lechery,
I recalled each sigh caused by the touch of
Soft and rough fingers, lips and tongues
And how happy my life was
Before I became the seer.
Then I learned that life's secret was in the readiness
To embrace whatever was inevitable.

"Okay, Okay, I get it and it is fascinating." Then, without further circumlocutions, Stuart recounted the high points of his adventures since the day of the snowfall: the fifteen dead crows, the military vehicles, the trapdoor and the underground, the tram ride, the research institute and the orange buses. "Now you confirm a certain amalgamation of our hamlet and the so-called research people on the hill. The question I ask you, Gianluigi, is why? Why the chaos at the roundabout? Why the Great Wall and the towers? Above all, what are the research people doing here? Does the hamlet belong to some foreign power? Or to some evil institution? And what do they want here?"

"Well, Stuart, I must say that I had a false impression of you. Not to say that you seemed one of the herd. Not at all. But I misjudged you anyway ... I suppose, erroneously based on what you don't say or do. That you followed up on the discovery of fifteen dead crows changes everything—a new story has begun. As you likely know birds were omens for the ancient Greeks: the dove symbolized love and was associated with Aphrodite. The crow or raven was the messenger of the gods, and it symbolized bad fortune. Funny thing, allegedly the raven was originally white. But when the god Apollo sent it to spy on a lover, and the bird returned with the news the lover was cheating on him, Apollo flew into a rage and scorched the raven black all over. That's what the gods or early onrnithologists claimed."

"Like the one I have in the freezer ... I thought I saw a certain lightening of its color. Professor, that's a kind of proof that the old Greeks were right."

"Now you're spoofing me again."

"Not really, not crazier than the fish that's born male and becomes female."

"Well, yes, most fish change gender. Many change sex .In the course of life they transform into the opposite, influencing gender change. This phenomenon called sequential hermaphroditism occurs in the bream, a fish from the Mediterranean that remains a male until the age of three, and then becomes a female. Anyway, seeing those dead birds in that protected spot seems to have done for you what my one attendance at a Hamlet Commission gathering did for me. It showed me that our hamlet is not the place it used to be. Not the place we thought it was. Stuart, there are two worlds here in these spaces. Their world of corruption and evil, and the dream world in which the rest of us are living."

"Sophie calls the area down the road beyond our two houses—the woods where we found the birds—*abandoned spaces*. However, I think she has in mind more than that specific area but in general all those unknown and apparently unused or rather misused parts of our whole planet."

"Your wife is a wise woman, Stuart."

"Yes, she is—even if she's hooked on drapes-—but Gianluigi, anyway, why didn't you accept a seat on the hamlet committee where you could influence the issues we face today? Why?"

"Stuart, listen, I'll tell you some things I shouldn't … now that I know who you are. But promise me what I tell you will remain between us!"

"Of course, of course. That's why I'm here now: for information. And I confess that I've long thought that you're not only the absent-minded professor of Greek mythology."

"I have a friend—a very close friend from my native Puglia—

who heads an important division in AISI, Italian Internal Intelligence Agency —like the FBI in the USA. But it competes with AISE, our foreign intelligence agency. Both answer to the Intelligence and Security Department directly under the Prime Ministry. Now, according to my friend there exists a *certain* situation in the hamlet of San Nicola. The so-called research institute on the opposite hill is run by AISE, I believe, though he didn't say that expressly. But for some reason, my friend who has a lot influence says that he himself really runs that 'project'. Now you will be interested in what he calls that 'research institute'. He refers to it as a Biowarfare Lab."

"Good God! What am I hearing? Scary to think that I walked around down in Tarantus like a tourist. And I didn't even know what I was looking for. If I'd known, I doubt I would've crawled down that ladder and taken an underground train ride. What the fuck could they be making down there? Or up on the hill? The two places must be one and the same. Whatever they make killed those crows quite easily."

"My friend might be curious about your underground explorations. Right in the heart of the monster, so to speak. A project also of his rivals in the AISE, remember. May I tell him?"

"Well, I don't want to abandon my own investigation now that I'm in it, so if I can help by speaking with him, why not? Do you think it presents dangers to Sophie and me? Just the idea of biological warfare is a terrifying. Remember the horror stories of mustard gas in World War One? Now we have secret biowarfare labs to develop chemical weapons all over the world. Remember Wuhan and Covid? And they chose San Nicola! To think that if it hadn't snowed that day we might never have known what they're doing here in their underground tunnels. You know, you've got a swamp, but down in Tarantus, I heard water running. Don't know if that's significant. By the way, Gianluigi, do you think this secret biolab pandemic is linked to NATO and the CIA?"

"Why not? Remember Gladio? A super terror agency created right here in our capital that conditions or controls our intelligence agencies. Why not?"

"Gladio? I have seen the name. But what is it?"

"You're a little young for this, but, well, it was founded by the CIA in Rome back in 1956 and officially dissolved in 1990, but actually it's still alive, God knows under what name … and it belongs heart and soul to the USA/NATO/CIA. Founded as a stay-behind army to fight the putative Soviet invasion of Europe—that never happened—it became an all-NATO terrorist organization. Killing people has always been high on its agenda. Sweden's Prime Minister Olaf Palme was assassinated on the streets of Stockholm because of his good relations with the Communist Bloc of Nations. Our prime Minister, Aldo Moro, was assassinated for wanting to bring Italian Communists into the government. U.S.-supported laboratories are developing chemical weapons all over the world, so why not one on home territory, so to speak. The One World Order without limits has long been burgeoning in the minds of secret powers in the West and Gladio is one of its weapons."

"Gianluigi, you speak with the expertise of a person far from academia. You're more than an absent-minded professor of Greek mythology. Not to the extent of Tiresias perhaps, but as if you'd lived another life."

"Hmm. Apparently I've revealed more than I intended. But you're under a pledge to me! Not your fault anyway. You weren't digging into my background but into an underground world I do know something about. The friend I mentioned is real; I got to know him when I was quite young, just out of the university when we both entered AISI. I'd studied Greek, of course, but also Serbian and related languages so I was of interest to them. But I lasted there only about three years before I chose academia and changed my life."

"Why don't we meet your friend somewhere? Maybe outside

the hamlet. He might not want to be seen here and besides it's just too fucking hard getting in and out."

"Oh, Stuart, don't be so gullible like San Nicolians who believe the Commission's story that the Great Wall and the towers and the guards are for their own protection against a strange and still unidentified form of liana like that eating and eroding the steel fencing just at the entrance. A metaphor, of course! You sound like the people of Athens who believed the dictator's ruse to re-conquer power. The story is that when Pisistratus returned from political exile to Athens in a golden chariot he was accompanied by an extremely tall woman dressed in full battle armor. He presented to citizens the imposing figure as the Goddess Athena herself, come to restore order and well-being to the strife-ridden city of Athens. People along the streets knelt down to the goddess and gave thanks for their salvation from the tumult surrounding them. Roberto Calasso narrates in *The Marriage of Cadmo and Harmony* how Pisistratus taught the beautiful country girl, Phye, to act like a goddess. Dressed in armor and mounted in the chariot at his side, she must have looked majestic. Proceeded by heralds announcing to the Athenians that the goddess herself was conducting him back to the Acropolis. Pisistratus returned to power because Athenians believed that the divinity had come to earth to install him. This old story of public gullibility rings contemporary: God was on the side of the dictator. God was stepping in to save Athens, its children, its faith, and its 'way of life'. Aristotle later wrote that the political deception described in the story of the Athenian dictator 'was by far the most ingenuous since the sophisticated Hellenic people had diverged from their barbarian forebears.' So goes the incredible ruse used no less crudely in those times than hundreds of false-flag deceptions in our so-called modern era.

"Anyway, Stuart, my friend is powerful and can get in everywhere. Even San Nicola. Still, a good idea, an outside meet … maybe in La Storta. Wait, I'll call him now."

7.

"*Minchia*, Gianni, you look exactly like an updated Zeus," Ermanno Riccardi exclaimed when they approached his table in the vine covered veranda of the *Fico d'India* restaurant in La Storta. As the two embraced, laughed, punched at each other playfully and spoke of their past, Gianluigi abandoned his professorial mask and Ermanno Riccardi seemed anything but a top secret intelligence agent. Stuart was struck by the mutual admiration they showed one for the other and wished he still had a friend like that. While Gianluigi and his friend reminisced about the "old times", the crazy things they did, what became of one or the other of the people they once knew, those who had mysteriously vanished, one who died in an inexplicable accident in the mountains, another in prison, memories illustrated with a lot of laughing or sad expressions, Stuart's thoughts strayed back to his own complex life of before Sophie. He'd truly loved Stefano, his friend from his school and university years in the capital, the companion with whom he'd shared apartment, girlfriends and a carefree life until a rapid version of leukemia struck down twenty-three year old Stefano, killing him in a period of three weeks. A violent death. So violent, so near, that Stuart found it difficult to recall any high points of his life of those years. He saw no place for optimism in the melee in which he'd lived. Just in time, it came to seem, Sophie appeared to transform his world: from the cramped and loud apartment in the city, to the quiet of the manor house in the hamlet and beautiful Sophie adjusting her damask unicorn drapes. From the brouhaha of an empty party life in a partying time to damask drapes. A revolution, an overturn of everything he once was. He found the changes healthy. Nothing stays the same. Nothing lasts forever. Neither love not hate remains forever. The spirit of the times was exactly that—the quintessence of that age, then the nevermore, as Poe's raven answered. Other times had spawned other spirits in his life. Even the form and outcome of revolution itself change.

France 1789 changed quickly; 1839 was a different spirit. The Russian Revolution had its time. And people and time itself changed.

"Stuart Stuart—what a brilliant idea to have the same given and surname—Stuart, my friend Gianluigi tells me you've made some strange discoveries in that village you live in."

For a moment, Stuart stared, momentarily surprised by the sound of his double name pronounced by a stranger. Who does he mean? Yet when thinking of himself by name—a rare occurrence—he too thought double.

"They say it's less than a village, a mere hamlet. Actually, an estate once upon a time. But it doesn't seem to be either to me. My wife says it consists chiefly of lands of abandoned spaces … and lost objects that suddenly resurface. Now it really is isolated—ever since the Hamlet Commission built the so-called Great Wall and converted the roundabout to a garbage dump. Anyway, crazy things have been happening in the hamlet of San Nicola since the day of the snowfall." And again Stuart related the story of the dead birds, the military clean-up squad, the trapdoor, the underground complex, the hamlet relationship with the ex-naval station on the opposite hill, the German guards, the Mastiffs.

"I suspect links but I don't understand the connections and what it all means, but I hope you—or someone—will look into this."

Riccardi reddened , looked at Gianluigi for a moment, coughed and cleared his throat.

"Well, let's see. How to explain? As you now know, I work where your friend the professor once worked, and suffice it to say there are some bad people there. It's always been that way … and I fear always will be. Lord Corruption plays a big role in my agency and I could disappear too if certain people heard me say these things. People have long spoken of an agency within the agency … a rogue agency, so to speak. I tend to believe there are actually three agencies in one: one real, one rogue, and one anti-rogue. I belong to the last. Stuart Stuart, listen to this! Though I just met you, I trust you more than I do people in my same department, even my own secretary-assistant. Incredible, eh? Now you can imagine what I'm thinking! In any case, if you are what I think you are, then you can help me more than I, you. And Gianluigi here is my cover ... I think he realizes that, eh, Professor?"

"Well, yes," Professor Logreco muttered hesitantly.

"Now, Gianni, no shilly-shallying here! No Greek stuff. We need you and not stories of Greek gods."

Despite Ermanno's playfulness in recalling the old times with Gianluigi, Stuart perceived the subtle hardening of the tone of his voice and recognized immediately his cultivated but well-controlled movements, his long fine hands, his erect posture, not as tall as Stuart but whose height seemed to lend him an air of authority. Riccardi was a man in command, above all of himself and accustomed to commanding others in his well-modulated speech the volume of which he never raised. His sparkling eyes spoke the same language of power and authority: he had those cobalt eyes that could be eager, smiling and all-seeing while at the same time withholding sight into them. His authority was not abstract, hierarchical or bureaucratic, but real. Not a handsome man, he nonetheless exuded magnetism and attraction, Stuart was certain to women as well as men.

"Okay, okay," Gianluigi said," but I'm thinking of both academia and that damned Hamlet Commission. True, I was wrong to reject membership in it earlier but you know my history of denial of my own past ... as if it never happened. Sitting in my thinking room, alone with my gin on my best days, my body disintegrating and falling in pieces around me, I, reduced to a mere brain, I sit there over my gin and wonder what to say to a classroom full of young people only because the course I teach is considered an easy three academic points for a degree. Maybe now I can redeem myself in some way."

"I can help in that. I do know one key person on the committee who might re-sponsor you. After all, it's my job to know things and people."

"Well!" Gianluigi assented, looking at the agent ambivalently.

"You're not really enthusiastic about this project, Gianni. I see that. So what's wrong with committee membership? You'll be our man on the inside who can tell us what's happening."

"That's what bothers me. In ancient Greece too, the spy on the inside pays the heaviest price …"

"There you go again, Gianni, you've got it in your blood. You should've been born as a Greek god … that is, if they were even born."

"Stories of infiltrators and secret operations reach back three millennia to the origins of Western literature," Logreco continued. "That is indisputable, my friends. Remember the adventures of Odysseus, a key figure in the *Iliad*—Homer's epic poem on forty days' fighting in the Trojan War—and the hero of Homer's *Odyssey*, which chronicles his adventurous post-war journey home. Odysseus was not primarily concerned with secret missions and intelligence operations—no more than are you. No, he was a warrior in search of glory and revenge. He enjoyed what might be called recreational violence as he might have called our situation. But he had an exceptional talent for deception. That's why they called him Odysseus the Cunning. The goddess Athena once told Odysseus: 'We're both experts in trickery—you among men, I among the gods.'"

"Hmm! Now, Gianni, that is complicated."

"Complicated but true. Both gods and men have always been tricky. In both the *Iliad* and the *Odyssey*, Odysseus' trickery leads him too into espionage. So during the Trojan War, he volunteered to go with the young warrior- king Diomedes on a secret mission to spy on the enemy camp. Early in their mission they met a captured Trojan spy, Dolon, coming in the opposite direction to spy on the Greeks. By deceiving Dolon into believing that his life would be spared if he cooperated, Odysseus persuaded him to reveal important intelligence about the strength of Trojan forces. As soon as Dolon had spilled the beans, mighty Diomedes killed him. The ancients, especially the gods were always killing the messengers. I can't help but foresee a similar situation for me—Dolon's, I mean."

"Ok, ok, Gianni, you always come up with a related story from the Greeks, but don't worry, you're not exposed. But I might be. And anyway Stuart, this is what I think is going on … and it's bad stuff. NATO-CIA stuff. So hang on … and above all, no more purely spontaneous moves on your part. You've been lucky so far. Pure chance. But as Einstein claimed the world is not governed by chance. God doesn't roll dice, he said. Realism is what counts. "

"Einstein?" Stuart exclaimed, rather startled by the thought of the physics genius and espionage and at the same time mystified by this man Ermanno Riccardi who quotes him. Could anyone be so perfect? Or under his mask was he not also like one of the three, Odysseus, Dolon or the unseen one, the chief warrior of the Trojan army, Hector?

"Yes. He believed everything is determined by forces over which we have no control—and I've learned in my work that he was right. Humans are not free agents. Like me, I'm an agent, but I'm not free. Nor are you. So you have to be very careful."

"I think I understood right away that this whole story was greater than me. Looking for advice from Gianluigi was an attempt to turn it over to someone else. And to think that I walked around that subterranean world like a madman wondering what I was looking for. I guess I was moved only by curiosity—not even by will. Now when I think back on the ladder leading into the darkness that not even my powerful 250000 Lumen penetrated, the world down there seems surrealistic—and honestly my presence down there seemed like a dream."

"Well, you sure opened Pandora's box. Now, gentlemen, let's be clear that we are talking about chemical terrorism. You must know that there are biolabs all over the world ... making God knows what terrible chemical weapons. A news item that somehow got through NATO censorship caught the attention of people, uh, people like us. Russia's defense Ministry reported that Russian soldiers stationed in a village near Zaporozhye were hospitalized with grave chemical poisoning. Traces of botox, or botulinum toxin type B, were found. So I'm not going to tiptoe around the feelings of our officialdom about my views on the use of lethal botox against Russian soldiers —and I don't mean only the government. —I mean all the agencies like mine, private organizations and the general population .And I want to make clear my opposition to sanctions against Russia and my general opposition to that artificial country called Ukraine. It never was and never will be a country! I believe the Russian Ministry charges that as a result of a series of military defeats of Ukrainian forces, the President in Kiev himself authorized terrorist attacks using chemical weapons against Russian soldiers and civilians. And as a result Russia sent the laboratory tests to OPCW, the Organization For the Prohibition of Chemical Weapons …"

"But what the hell is going on down there in the hamlet underground? Was I lucky to get out that underworld alive?"

"Maybe," Riccardi said. He took some papers from his briefcase and read from notes: "Botox is a drug made from a toxin produced by the bacterium Clostridium botulinum. The same toxin that causes a life-threatening type of food poisoning called botulism. Many doctors use it in small doses to treat health problems. For a long period, botox was produced for some reason only in Westport, Mayo, Ireland. Although a toxin, botox has both medical and cosmetic benefits when used in the correct dosage. Yet, just a single gram of the crystalline form of this stuff can kill up to a million people, and a few kilograms can literally annihilate humanity as we know it.' So you see that botulinum neurotoxin—or simply botox—poses a major bioweapon threat because of its extreme potency and lethality; its ease of production, transport, and misuse; and the need for prolonged intensive care of affected persons. As a military or terrorist weapon, botulinum toxin can be disseminated via aerosol or by contamination of water or food as perhaps in Ukraine, causing widespread casualties. And to make matters worse such weapons only seem remote; they're apparently widely available. During the early 1980s, German and French newspapers once reported that the police had raided a Baader-Meinhof safe house in Paris and found a makeshift laboratory that contained flasks full of Clostridium botulinum from which the botulinum toxin is made. The reports were later denied and no such lab was ever found there. Still, biolabs are springing up all over the world."

The secret agent seemed more incensed by the mere idea of the use of chemical weapons than he was by the reality that they were perhaps also produced right here, in the hamlet, no more than a couple of kilometers distance from their pleasant table on the vine-covered veranda of the Fico d'India Restaurant. So it was strange, Stuart thought, that the well-intentioned Riccardi didn't seem to give a shit about the brutal reality of those Russian soldiers either, some of whom came from small villages in distant eastern regions of Russia. Men in the prime of their youth felled on the orders of corrupt politicians in Kiev, only a few hundred kilometers away; people who'd never seen a battlefield; people too far from the reality of death in the trenches and for whom a bullet, a rocket or a toxic chemical spray were all the same, and thus the difference was inconsequential: botox spray killed the enemy. While Gianluigi and Riccardi rehashed the same ideas, Stuart's thoughts wandered as to how he would best express his ideas about the insurmountable distance between soldiers in the trenches and politicians in their plush circumstances back in their capital in his monthly column in the Scottish magazine, *Time and Space*. For what seemed an endless time— time flashing past like an instantaneous image in a dream which he knew could occur—in the dream in which he would see into the mind of a young soldier lying among others in a row of beds in a military hospital, a man who knows he is dying but doesn't know why or of what. His fictitious dying soldier only realizes that he hadn't been shot or stunned by an explosion. He only understands that he is a dead man. And there was no one to tell him how or why. And that, Stuart thought, was the very worst: Why? He wondered if during their dying those soldiers near Zaporozhe dreamed. Did they dream of home or of unfulfilled life goals? Or did they perceive of their short lives as only a dream? Or did they dream they were already dead or had never actually lived? And those who did the spraying of poisons to kill their brothers—like those in San Nicola who sprayed the poisons to kill the crows—were they aware of their murderous action? He was thinking that the lives of the dying and the sprayers were truly only a dream and that their dreamscapes were the most strange and mysterious. Mentally he slapped the side of his head and saw Gianluigi and Riccardi staring at him as if waiting for an answer to an unheard question.

"No," he said guessing at their question, "I know no one there."

Ermanno shrugged. "Irrelevant anyway. I do have a friend there who's been in Donetsk from the start … during all those years while the Ukrainians shelled the whole area killing thousands. My friend decided early on to stay and got assigned to a Donetsk infantry unit. By now, he has various citizenships, speaks good Russian, has a woman friend and says he will stay to the end—until they eliminate the last fascist. Mean people, he always says of Ukrainians, unrepentant for burning alive fifty people in the Trade Union building on Kulikovo Square in the port city of Odessa on May 14, 2014. Some people think one reason we are confronted with hate and evil is a test to see how we respond to it. If we return the hate and evil of another with hate and evil, we fail. Our man from the battlefield said 'bullshit' and that they should have seen people jumping out the windows of the burning Trade Unions Building. He once told me that he doubts his own existence and that his whole life since he arrived in Donetsk seems like a dream—everything is so far from any reality he knew before—maybe something like what you felt riding on the tram in our underground world in the hamlet. In that respect, Stuart, my friend is a very passionate type—hates Ukrainians in general. He says they're a nasty people with a natural Nazi bent. The government in Kiev denies it is Nazi and that the Nazi Azov battalions would be absorbed into the Ukrainian military. But our friend in Donetsk says that the Nazi militias have instead absorbed the whole Ukrainian army. Except for normal working people, they're all Nazis. Anyway, he got to know some Russian soldiers around Zaporozhe, Russian kids, he says, twenty-two years old, from Kazakhstan. Two of them are best pals from the same town who joined up together. And it was their seven-man unit that got hit by that botox spray. Two of their unit died on the spot; the others were in a military hospital—between life and death. Here, Stuart, read my friend's letter yourself. A sad piece of literature indeed and written in English for our own censors!

Stuart took the several sheets of the letter from Ermanno's hands gingerly, holding it with forefingers and thumbs. It had been folded three times into a small square, and then rolled as if to fit into a tube. His first thought before he read a word was that the soiled sheets of thin paper, folded and rolled and magically tubed to Ermanno was connected with the dead crows and underground cages. He recalled the cages hanging on the cold walls of the Welsh-like mine shaft. That their doors were hanging wide open on their hinges was, a small detail that had escaped him at the moment. Now he wondered if it meant permanent abandonment; if not why leave them hanging on their hinges?

Dear Papa and best friend,

I hesitate to pen these words in my present mental state. I don't know if the real me is forming these words, or if my dark self predominates as my psychologist wife suggests. She believes that I count on dreaming to crush the evil that surrounds us—that dominates our world. Each time I leave for the shifting front— here today, there tomorrow, she salutes with a farewell ... forever. I can't dream away the reality that another of the young soldiers died of the deadly botox spray last night.

According to my wife the most important archetype of dream symbols is the animus or the shadow. They're part of me, she says. They're present in my dreams in the form of a person or of Kafka's cockroach. All of us in this conflict must unravel what those figures mean to us. Otherwise, Serdtze, the human race is sunk. My unit, I tell her, fights chiefly in forest areas, enigmatic and strange places. Frightening, and it was precisely in a forest that those boys met that fateful botox. The forests, dark and deep, fill my dreams of the morrow. And the forest is where the most evil events of my life take place.

Stuart looks up from the letter and mutters to Ermanno and Gianluigi, "the forest, my wife's abandoned spaces, are also right here in the hamlet—his battlefield!" Who could've imagined? In any case, he thought he now knew what he would write in his column this month."

From the estranged and faraway look in their eyes, he comprehended that he was reading himself into Ermanno's contact's ruminations about his situation: he himself could have written these thoughts by the simple act of transpositioning himself—that stranger Stuart Stuart—to the forests around Zaporozhe.

Margarita says it is frightening how many of us are so out of touch with our own shadow self, that every person can become unconscious instruments through which evil—which lies hidden within the dark side of the human psyche—can act itself out through us into the world. In the pain and suffering of the psychopath—like the persons who order the use of those deadly chemical weapons temporarily feel the pain less because of their excessive narcissism like Oscar Wilde's Dorian Gray. Like Jung, Oscar Wilde, too, could have written that the dream is a spontaneous self-portrayal, in symbolic form, of the actual situation in the unconscious. In a similar fashion, the soldiers who sing victory songs after spraying to death their own brothers—their victims who die in their hospital beds believing that they never lived, that their lives never happened, that their short lives were truly a dream or someone else's dream— die similar deaths. And we—the others, the witnesses who originate in the same manner as the sprayers and their victims —are left to wonder about who first dreamed their lives that were never really lived. The great mystery is the spirit inhabiting the ultimate perpetrator of evil: the evil spirit of total cognitive dissonance. Narcissism and the accompanying justifying sense of putting things in proper order so that pain caused to others seems a reward to the perpetrator for having done (in his mind) the right thing even though for the wrong reason. Mister E. will note that one says that one shouldn't take sides. That evil lies in all men anyway. But Mister E. I have to take sides. Executioners and victims are not the same. The perpetrators of this act have already committed themselves to evil. Were they to change places, the victims—in reality already dead and dying—might have said no to an order to spray lethal botox toward enemy soldiers in the Zaporozhe forest. So yes, there is a world of difference between the sprayers and their victims. A world. How do I know these things? I know them because I was there. I know what every man must know even without penetrating into the dark forest of evil. Men are born with that knowledge.

8.

From the parking spaces just inside the gate in the Great Wall and beyond the soaring left tower, green rolling hills climb toward the south in the general direction of the city as if the area wanted to exclude itself from the hamlet. The anomalous bad weather was only a memory. Spring had exploded in the hills. Yet those alien spaces removed from the main body of the rest of the hamlet seemed another place and time, hills that speak a foreign language and live another life, so out of harmony with the old manor houses deep in the hamlet. In that hilly zone of some four to five square kilometers, powerful interests had intervened and pressured the Hamlet Commission to permit the construction of groups of attached two-story houses so incompatible with what Stuart considered the real hamlet. Out of curiosity, he occasionally drove in his old Panda through those crisscrossing streets of what he and Sophie called the South Zone and observed groups of neighbors—for the most part young and stylish with something foreign about them—chatting over the low walls or hedges separating their gardens or sunbathing on flagstone terraces or joking and laughing in small groups around swimming pools. It was like being abroad.

Still, meeting some of the people who inhabited those urban houses was an unexpected surprise. On the late morning after the day of the lunch with Ermanno at the Fico d'India, the short, hesitant ring of the bell from the manor gate on their private road sounded softly through the house, again making Stuart conscious of the peculiar idea that the quality of a door bell ring—short or long, weak or strong, one ring or several—reveals the type of person you will find on the other side of your gate: the stranger might be stepping into your life forever so it's good to know something about him. The ferocious devil-may-care ring of a Seventh Day Adventist reveals hopelessness and desperation; that of a salesman proclaims his absolute confidence in his success. Other than such molesters, no one except Gianluigi came to their house and today the professor was back at his lectern, which he refers to as a podium, as if it were his second home—chiefly because the word itself is derived from the Greek *Pothi*. And besides, snob that he is, he detests doorbells as symbols of servility—he who rings, waits for permission. Gianluigi usually telephones first which is less degrading,

So because of the hesitant ring, Stuart felt a tingling of trepidation when at the gate he met an attractive young couple who introduced themselves simply as François-Marie and Férnande. They explained that they had seen Sophie's boutique in La Storta and used the excuse to knock on their door just to meet somebody new and escape from their ghetto on the hill and meet some of the real hamletians—the word coined by Férnande. Faced by what seemed a fait accompli, Stuart—pleased by their visit—invited them in for coffee. When they entered the salon, Férnande stopped in her tracks and gasped: "The drapes! And damask! Simply magnificent. Similar to the drapes in my grandmother's house in Provence. *Magnifique*! *Magnifique*!" When her eyes met those of Sophie standing at the window on the far side of the room, they smiled at each other. The damask drapes had sealed a friendship in a few seconds.

They sat on the terrace adjoining the kitchen. Stuart made a big pot of espresso. His double name seemed to intrigue Férnande who they now knew was a psychologist at a big international company in the city and maintained a private practice in La Storta near Sophie's shop. She was tallish, gaunt, with prominent cheek bones that gave her an oriental look, long blond hair that looked as if it had never been combed. She was not a chatterer, but spoke openly and willingly when she had something to say. In sum, Férnande was an attractive and mysterious person.

Her companion, François-Marie, was another cup of tea. He was the personification of mystery who spoke in two-word sentences about himself, but from time to time asked a detailed question about others. A handsome man of average stature, he had a habit of running his left hand through his long dark hair and crossing and uncrossing his legs, an act which seemed staged for effect. When asked about his profession or job, his answer was one word: "Scientist." Then, to prolong his discourse, he added: "That's us, the psychologist and the scientist." At which point he almost smiled … uncertainly.

"Your location here in the hamlet is truly wonderful," Férnande said. "We look out our windows and only see other houses exactly like ours. Here you see trees and rocks and birds and endlessly rolling hills."

"And it lasts most of the year," Sophie said, "through October and into November and sometimes we lunch on the terrace on New Year's."

"The month of October is the best … golden October. My favorite month," Stuart said, on which François-Marie ran his left hand through his fine long hair and crossed one leg over the other for an answer.

"Yes, he loves October in a special way … and not because of the climate," Sophie added off-handedly: "He's a communist."

François-Marie uncrossed his legs and immediately re-crossed them while furiously hand-combing his hair. The word 'communist' either excites him or irritates him, Stuart guessed.

"I'm of Russian descent," Férnande said. "My maiden name is Volkov. My grandfather emigrated from Russia in the 1930s. And one of his sons, my uncle, was a famous writer."

"But your name now is Dolon. Dolon! " François-Marie said hastily. "Not Dolonov."

"Well, everybody is from somewhere," Stuart said. "Are you by any chance of Greek origin?"

"Greek!" François-Marie repeated. "Why Greek?"

"Professor Logreco told us the story of the Trojan spy, Dolon, who fessed up to Odysseus on the promise of clemency but was betrayed and executed by the Greeks."

"Bad story. But what can you expect from an eccentric Greek mythologist. I know him … in a professional capacity," François-Marie said in English. "A silly old man."

Silly old man? In a professional capacity? What could that mean? Stuart wondered. This Frenchman—not snobbish, just sarcastic—who talks around every subject he happens to react to.

Speaking as if her husband weren't there, Férnande asked Sylvie about the birds of the hamlet. She'd seen a Cardinal recently, of the most brilliant red she'd ever seen in France. But that the many crows seem to come and go. "Sylvie, have you noted that the crow tribes seem to have vanished. Strange!"

"Well, frankly, yes. And it's bizarre. Our part of the hamlet is literally crow-dominated territory. Or it was until a short time ago. They terrorize other birds. But now? None. You see those trees down there at the edge of the field? So many crow families lived there that other birds left for safer places. Now the crows have vanished."

Meanwhile, conversation between François-Marie and Stuart had sputtered and dragged in grunts and two-word sentences until they rather seamlessly switched completely to English, the Frenchman's preferred foreign language—it turned out he hardly spoke Italian.

"I'm lucky they sent me to the university in Glasgow," Stuart said. "Since I write in English, my best client is a magazine in Scotland, *Time and Space,* in which I have a monthly column."

"Curious. What do you write about?"

"European socio-political issues for the most part. But since we do live in a rather strange area, I'm writing a series called *The Hamlet.*"

"*Et alors*? About what in particular?"

"I'm working on a long article about birds and …"

"Birds!" François-Marie exclaimed. "Why that? By the way, I'm an ornithologist, actually only a very minor scientist," he said, glancing at his wife.

"It's as Sylvie just told your wife, the crows have disappeared. And they lived in the hundreds in the trees you can see out our windows. Actually, I was hoping to meet someone like you. I need an ornithologist to clear up some technical aspects. And not only why they disappeared but also a certain anomaly: by chance I found one unlike all the others."

"Found one, by chance! What kind? Maybe it wasn't by chance. Wasn't it Einstein—Einstein, the man who personified the scientific method—didn't he insist until the end of his life that the Lord didn't play dice?"

Abruptly, Stuart stood up and said, " François-Marie, please come with me. I have something to show you."

In the cellar, he opened the freezer and extracted the bird wrapped in a cloth that fell away easily. The coal black crow lay peacefully on its side, as if sleeping. The Frenchman's mouth literally fell open and he gasped: *"Il s'est échappé."*

"What? Escaped? Escaped from where? From whom? 'The beautiful soul of a woman's dark eyes fled and left behind this lifeless shell it had inhabited,' he quoted. "Where did you say you found it, exactly?"

"Down the road another couple of kilometers. On the day of the snow storm. Near the clearing where the others were."

"Others? What others do you mean?"

"The dead crows! Fifteen of them."

"So you saw them! They weren't even supposed to be there. Somehow they all got away ... and died for it."

"You mean the botox?"

François-Marie stared at him, wide-eyed and visibly shaken "Yes," he said after some moments. "It was a test that went wrong. Someone made a mistake—maybe like Wuhan. I've come to regret I took this job now. It seemed so simple at first. I was engaged in a study of crows in Paris. In fact I dream of crows. Crows infest my dreamworld. Ask my wife about my dreams. Anyway, corvidae is a cosmopolitan family—the crow family—and includes ravens, which this one is. And this is an American raven! Imported for experiments which I'm not familiar with. It's the most intelligent bird ornithologists have ever studied. Their brain-to-body mass ratio is the same as the great apes and only a bit lower than that of humans."

"Deep into that darkness peering, long I stood there, wondering, fearing, doubting, dreaming dreams no mortal ever dared to dream before. Quoth the Raven, Nevermore," Stuart now quoted. "It's a great piece of literature."

"Maybe. But no longer for me. It's my nightmare. Despite the light of their intelligence, their wings are those of a dark angel … as black as punishment. No more flurries of black feathers for this one. No more talks in the night. Yet it's said that when a raven dies, all hell breaks loose. The conversation between Poe's scholar and the bird is too long. Too gripping. He just lost his lover and to cope with his feelings of loss, he secludes himself in his study where he reads, seeking solace. Then he hears a knocking on his door and window. It's the raven. To each of the scientist's statements, the raven only answers, *Nevermore*. Ambiguous like the narrator. The raven's repetition of the word *nevermore* to every question can drive you crazy. According to my wife, ravens and crows, all black birds, have dark meanings in dreams … especially if repetitive. And mine are constant in these times. Dreams about crows or ravens mean darkness. Such dreams are symbolic of fears of upcoming troubles or pain—or even death."

"Well, I'm a dreamer too and I'm sorry I even saw the fifteen dead crows, especially afterwards when I saw the arrival of the military vehicles and then the disappearance of their bodies. Sorry too that I showed you the raven."

"No matter! Did you also see the, uh, the underground?" François-Marie asked, running his hand back and forth though his hair. "Some outsider discovered it and went down there. They know that."

"Well, uh … I …"

"Look, Stuart, don't worry about my role here. I'm only an ornithologist called in to follow the health of the birds. I have nothing to do with their experiments and I'm barely aware of what botox is. In a way, they blame me that the birds escaped from their cages … and for this mess, which, as you can imagine, may have international repercussions."

"Well, the repercussions to the botox part have already begun," Stuart said and related the report that Russian soldiers in a village in Ukraine were hospitalized with possible botox poisoning. "Russia sent the laboratory tests to the international Organization For the Prohibition of Chemical Weapons."

"That is absolutely horrible. Maybe I should resign my job up there at the Research Institute and go back to France. Now that Férnande has her work here, she's integrated and has learned the language but I'm an alien."

"On the other hand, you can learn a lot of sensitive information there that maybe should be revealed to someone."

"Yes, there's that too. You know they appointed me to the board of the Hamlet Commission. But they don't need me there and I have no voice. The Research Institute's man chairs the Commission and runs top secret sections of the Institute itself. I'm just a vote on the sometimes five-man board … sometimes even seven persons sit on it."

"Why that? Why's the hamlet so important?"

"You should know! You've been there. For chemical reasons they need the lower altitude and the running water."

"The running water I heard! But tell me something, don't you speak with Férnande about these things."

"*Oh, mon dieux, jamais de la vie.* She would want to lock me up in an asylum somewhere. Or she would think it my excuse to go back home because I don't fit in here. No, she knows little about my work—less about where I work."

"But you do need to talk about it with someone."

"Yes, like right now with you."

"Too bad I can't help you or even use your information. But I'll find someone who can. By the way, Professor Logreco says he's going to join the commission after all. He rejected the offer once before but has changed his mind. Why not speak with him? He's not the silly old man you think he is."

"Hmmm. Maybe."

"Listen, François-Marie, who do you think really runs this so-called Research Institute? The government here, the military, secret services, NATO, or who?"

"I wonder about that every day. Someone very high up, to be sure. I would suspect that another commission runs it, a commission composed of all those elements you list. You know, sometimes I think no one really knows what they're doing. Everything up there on the institute's hill is so compartmentalized that you never know who is who."

"That's one thing I've learned since I started writing the magazine column. Compartmentalization marks our grand new society. With the immediate communication of our times, secrecy has only intensified and compartmentalization is the way things work. The government consists of more and more ministries, none of which know what the other ministries are doing. Then every ministry has sub-ministries, each doing its own thing. Every minister has a deputy minister and in turn the deputy minister has his deputies and so on down the hierarchy to infinity. The hierarchy is the axis of modern society. And compartmentalization its modus operandi. A Council of Ministers is a meeting of semi-strangers; and a commission is a gathering of aliens each of whom is determined to reveal nothing and to vote according to secret instructions and none of whom knows who is who of the others. The Hamlet Commission reflects that reality."

"Pessimist … if not cynical!" François-Marie muttered.

"Optimist … with realistic tendencies," Stuart replied.

"Sounds like you expected an outburst of protests about the use of chemical weapons against the Russians?"

"No. Not at all. I don't expect protests against incidents which our Western world doubts even took place … even though the possibility and the probability exist that the use of botox did happen exactly as reported to the Organization For the Prohibition of Chemical Weapons. You know our country is run by fascists, no? You see, François-Marie, Italian fascism didn't entail equality among individuals but a sense of privilege and a hierarchy of values. And the top determined how the bottom thought and acted. *To* paraphrase Hannah Arendt—I read her book *The Origins of Totalitarianism,"* Stuart said, pulling a paper from his back pocket. Here is my note: *'In an incomprehensible world the masses reach the point where they will believe everything and nothing, that everything is possible and that nothing is true. And they're right. Everything is sham. Everything's fake. No one knows what the others are doing. Propagandists discovered that its audience was ready to believe any absurdity and didn't even object to being deceived because it held every statement to be a lie anyhow. The totalitarian mass leaders based their propaganda on the correct psychological assumption that one can make people believe anything.'*

"Wait a minute Stuart! How did our talk about dead crows, the Research Institute, the subterranean lab and the Hamlet Commission lead to compartmentalization and a secret hierarchy? Though an ornithologist, I know how hierarchy works. But I live my life with birds … in the shadow of birds. And I know them well. Birds are an example of your theories although their hierarchy is less diffused than what you describe. Crows command among small birds, but they're no match for hawks or eagles or vultures."

"Still, the whole animal kingdom adheres to a hierarchical system which by its very nature is totalitarian—like that of military ranks and the division between officers and enlisted men. No kind of disobedience, noncompliance, or insubordination, much less rebellion, is permissible there. That's why I think that though it might *seem* that the hierarchical system conforms to nature—in man's nature too—it's nonetheless anti-social. And, well, politically, its primary enemy is class consciousness. And I consider the human nature theory in this context bullshit. And, François-Marie, maybe God does roll dice after all."

"That makes sense … I think. But I still have birds to deal with in general and this dead raven in particular. I can bury it or I can destroy it. Or I can turn it in and say I found it during a walk near the glade. But still, as you explain, someone—only one is enough to do me in—in this hierarchy is likely to know exactly where the bird was left."

"You have another alternative," Stuart said. "You can also leave it in my freezer until all this blows over."

"I'll go for the last. And thanks. Now I'll look forward to meeting Logreco on new terms."

9.

No one in the hamlet believed reports that during that splendid month of May birds were disappearing in all of Europe. In San Nicola, the great speckled woodpeckers, green parrots, an occasional majestic cardinal, hoot owls, pigeons all chimed into the great avian chorus that belied the morbid statistics of their approaching extinction. But because of what had happened, Stuart was cognizant of the precarious life of birds in general. When he stood on the upper terrace and trained his binoculars on the trees downhill near the ravine. Not a leaf moved. Not one crow!

It was mid-week and he was nervous. He ran up and down the stairs to the roof. Again, he checked the time. His appointment with Férnande was in an hour. Perceiving the apprehension that always came over him at the beginning of a new adventure, he drove his old Panda into La Storta and dropped into Sylvie's boutique before going to Férnande's studio at the top of a steep incline just opposite the supermarket where he parked. Though uneasy at the likelihood that today he would have to delve into the deep recesses of his inner self, he was curious at anything new and especially excited to be speaking with their new friend about the subject that he was writing about for his column: the dreamings and dreamtime. Although Férnande was a psychologist, not a psychotherapist, she'd emphasized that she was fascinated by the many threads deriving from dreams. And despite her young age and her limited academic preparation, dream interpretation was her method and the phenomenon of what she also referred to as dreamtime was her passion. For limited periods, Stuart kept a dream diary. Two days earlier he'd recorded his latest experience in dreamtime, which, along with dreamscape, was part of his daily vocabulary. He was so disappointed that down-to-earth Sophie didn't respond to his attempts to discuss what he called his parallel life and his shadow self that he seldom returned to the subject with his wife. Therefore, the appearance in their lives of the sensual Férnande so eager to examine dreams seemed to him a godsend.

The studio consisted of one spacious room with pastel walls, one light tan like the left tower at the Great Wall, one rose like the color on most hamlet balconies, one soft gray like the underbelly of some of the hooded crows, and in disturbing contrast, the wall at the rear was of a coal black that must make many of her patients unduly careful to parry and control every tumultuous emotion. Colorful, non-figurative art, easy chairs here and there, bare floors with scattered Persian carpets completed what he immediately termed a dreamscape. Hence, his momentary perplexity when he looked out the front window and saw the supermarket with its weekend special signs, huge delivery trucks, and files of cars creeping in and out of the sprawling parking. Seen from the paradise of Férnande's, the food center reminded him of Tartarus.

When he chose to sit facing the black wall, she asked him why there? He shrugged and said he liked the color black but that his choice was just chance.

"Do you really think so?" Férnande asked in a therapist manner. She spoke in an exquisite English acquired at Edinburg university and at the Necker Institute in Paris.

"I don't know. Does that say anything about me? I mean my love for the black color, or if I sat here by chance."

"I don't believe that color choice says much … but I don't really know. One says colors are like astrology. They may influence emotions and behavior but they offer no real insight into your personality … or your shadow self either," she added, and laughed softly. "Still, black as a color represents the determined character of persons not afraid to go after what they want—maybe power or prestige, but as a color preference it actually says nothing about your personality. It seems to me there is simply something timeless about the black color."

"I wonder then about the widespread popularity of black in the world of fashion: black cars, black coats and shirts or simply socks. Strange that it has so little meaning. But I see what you mean: fashion is just fashion. Here today, gone tomorrow. If asked, I usually say my favorite color is red."

Férnande laughed and had never appeared so sultry as in this moment, Stuart thought—maybe because of talk of the color black, her dark eyes and her hauntingly gaunt cheeks. She projected an otherworldly something that he imagined more and more frequently. "But that's for ideological reasons, *n'est pas?*" she added.

"Not only. But still, we in the hamlet had our black-hooded crows—until they disappeared."

"All except that black American raven you've got preserved in your freezer."

They both laughed embarrassedly: he because he hadn't told her about his find; she because François-Marie had shared with her the secret.

"Dreams?" Férnande said. "I think we both want to speak of dreamtime."

"Yes, I had a new dream that carried me again into solid dreamtime. Here it is," he said, reading from notes on his phone. I'll tell it:

I'm walking around the streets of Cherokee City, an alien in a white short-sleeved shirt with an irritating stiff collar that I continuously pull at. It's very cold in Cherokee, a village and a quiet town and also a throbbing city of numbered streets intersecting with great avenues with grassy green dividers, tunnels and bridges and yellow street lamps.

I walk around in a daze and have no idea where I'm going. The whole time I'm freezing. Friends invite me to one party or another where they give everybody a sweater. But I can't find one single party and I feel the cold, cold, cold. Gripped by anxiety, emotions churn through my mind as I search for my friend, Patrick Rainwater. I see the cold in my own eyes, my frozen stance, my shoulders hunched in search of warmth, my clenched fists, uncertainty written on my reddening face. And I realize they take me for one of 'those'. One of those who spread fire and devastation.

My hands grope in the darkness for the blanket of my bed in the hamlet manor house and I ask Sophie to turn on the heat.

'But it's May, Stuart. It's late spring '

I'm partially awake. Still cold. I'm aware that I'm entering dreamtime. I keep pulling vigorously at the covers but get only the sheet and the cold is ever more intense.

'But where is the party?' I ask everyone I meet on the street. I look for a friendly policeman to ask where the party is. There are no policemen. No policemen in Cherokee City. Everyone I meet seem like dream-people. They have no relation to me whatsoever. I feel I've entered the beyond, that I'm in a dream. I have the perception that everything and everyone else exist, are real and I am only a consciousness, a dark part of the dreamscape, cold and alone in the unknown. I know theirs is an unsophisticated culture, maybe rude and wild, but true. Their tastes are inartificial. No idea of the planet being ravaged by fire and the sword. I felt it would be folly to offend anyone—especially the children. Still, no one will tell me the half- awake stranger where the party is where everyone gets a sweater. They fear I'll spoil their secret power of authenticity. I perceive my awakeness. I perceive the hamlet manor. I perceive the presence of Cherokee City. And I still feel cheated. Why does everybody but me find the party and get a sweater? While I freeze, the Cherokee people on the streets complain of the heat and speak only Tsalagi to me the foreigner.

I keep looking for Rainwater the shaman, the Didanvwisgi,

I say in Kituwha. Cherokee people just shrug. No one knows him. Rainwater had told me that a man can never truly know himself or the core self of others. I want to discuss that. We can never know.

I listen and like the sound of Tsalagi but I don't understand and suspect they are mocking me because I don't speak properly. I say ha va, *or okay. I'm afraid they will banish me from the town and I will never get a sweater and could never find my way back to the known, were I to want to return.*

And at that point when everything seemed lost, the birds came. No party. no sweater, no shaman, no one named Rainwater. But the crows were on the attack, their long claws in my hair and biting my bare cold arms with their powerful sharp beaks. The birds, the birds, the birds. The very wildness, the savageness of the attack told me I was still the outsider. An exile.

I huddle under the sheet in the hamlet manor, freezing, terrified of the biting and clawing crows, fifteen of them, I tell Sophie, and at the same time I realize I'm safe. I'm in dreamtime. I'm conscious of being in the beyond. I can stay there if I like but I'm afraid and cold and decide to leave. Permanence in dreamtime is a dangerous venture. I emerge from dreamtime back to full wake life and I feel I have returned from the beyond and to wake consciousness.

"*Alors*, Stuart, your dream testimony is truly amazing, with its peculiar mix of the wild—frantic and otherworldly. What is stupefying and at the same time wonderful is that it all comes from the inner you. Stop and think of that! It is all you. Does it say who you are? Maybe, maybe it does. Jung would say it's your shadow self. Your insistence on understanding yourself. But Stuart, you're so deep into dreamtime— as I conceive of it—that I can't possibly follow you."

"But why not? You heard the dream about the cold and exclusion I felt. I needed someone."

"No, I can't follow you there. No one can. You're alone there. That's your private territory."

"That's what's so terrible."

"I, like Jung himself would say, can only listen to what you reveal. And from this first view of your inner self, I can imagine the terror you must have felt in that subterranean world you told François-Marie about."

"Good he told you about it! Actually, Férnande, I felt chiefly anxiety down there. Fear of being discovered."

"Of course. Fear is natural. But you were also displaced. You were in the wrong place. Like Cherokee City. Another time you might tell me what the real Cherokee is like. Anyway, since this is our first, uh, session, let's call it, I would be curious as to your self-analysis. People like you are always analyzing themselves. So what's your conclusion about yourself?"

"My conclusion about me? You must be joking." Stuart laughed half-heartedly, bamboozled as to what she wanted to hear—but aware that resistance was counterproductive to his presence here—and what he wanted to reveal. "Self-analysis, hmm. My conclusion, I think, is fictive, somewhat autobiographical and reportage, all wrapped in self-searching introversion in which I'm trying to reduce the gap I feel between reality and imagination and reliance on remembrance. Now that sounds like a script, I know; I wrote it this morning. But it's true that I'm always thinking about the importance of remembrances. Am I sick because I sometimes dwell on the past? Like Proust, I worry that I don't describe my own life as it actually is, but as I will remember it in the future. Sounds a little like Cherokee thinking. But in fact, like Proust says, you wake up in the morning and before you know it a web begins to fall around your dreams that minutes before were clear as real life. But then, during the day, if you work at it, practice it—this is me speaking, not Proust— remembrance sets in and the web of forgetting begins to unravel and things become clearer—for things past as well as for the dream itself. By the way, don't think I find

Proust boring. That man could write a hundred pages about a carriage ride in the countryside and make it fascinating. The way he considered resemblances and similarities, and that everything that happens in our dream world happens in a similar way—not exactly the same, but similar."

Férnande turned her head and laughed. "Oh, no! But no matter! That is clear enough."

"Before I go I'll tell you the bits that remain of a recurrent dream. I think it just hints at the dream sometimes, then leaves it up to me to fill it in the blanks. Goes like this: *"I know well the fabulous city of my dreams as if it existed in my dimension. A tall gray cathedral, Gothic, stands at one end of the old town. A web of congested streets lead to the cathedral and flow into a wide avenue circling it. The town itself is a labyrinth of twisting streets, filled with noisy traffic. Yet when the traffic arrives at the cathedral it thins and the silence is total as cars glide silently and methodically over the broad circular avenue around the shadowy cathedral. Its spires reach for the sky and fade in the clouds. It dominates the town and is visible from everywhere. I walk through the alleys of the town. I enter a nightclub and wander through rooms filled with sparkling crystal glasses and white tablecloths and laughing women in beautiful gowns. Then I walk out a rear door and find myself again facing the tenebrous cathedral."*

"Do you do it then?"

"Do what? Fill in the blank spaces. Yes, I do, as if it were all a clean slate."

Two days later, he again trudged up the steep gravel access road to Férnande's studio with the delightful view over the supermarket. The May sun bore down on his neck as he made his way up the hill, but he caught a whiff of a still lingering crispness in the air. He had the thought that just another week and the mosquito-spawning heat that Gianluigi so dreaded will have arrived. Sophie was surprised and maybe a bit jealous that he was already going up the hill again: she saw his sessions with *her* friend as a social visit or perhaps in her imagination something more. For she too was intrigued by Férnande, tall and gaunt Férnande with something witchy about her—perhaps it was the darkness lingering in her dark eyes. He told himself that he was climbing the hill also in search of his inner self. And today various ideas were swirling around in his hippocampus so that when Férnande asked what he had in mind for today, he answered without the slightest hesitation: "human nature!"

"Human nature? That's unexpected. So you really want to get down to brass tacks."

"To essentials, I think."

"Why is human nature so pressing when what we both want to talk about are dreams … and dreamtime?"

Stuart paused for a moment, looked Férnande in the eyes and fearing he might disappear into them, dwelled on her words: "what we both want." He perceived a tingling of guilt when he realized he liked those four words spoken by *her*—isolated from the rest of reality.

"Why?" he muttered, as much in response to her question as to why his guilt for admiring a sexy woman. "I don't know precisely what prompted me to think so much about the human nature that we hear people everywhere speak of: 'Oh, it's just human nature,' people say to excuse anything, even the most nefarious acts. So I searched a bit on internet and read some surprising articles on the subject and, well, why not—since it's so basic?"

"Right, Stuart. After all that's why we're here … to talk about what is pressing you."

And again he perceived the same combination of delight and guilt and told himself, smiling internally, that it was only human nature that his wife's friend attracted him sexually. Oh, fuck! If it were just not for that fucking human nature.

Férnande read from her phone: "*Human nature refers to the natural qualities and ways of behavior of most people, the general psychological characteristics, feelings, and behavioral traits of humankind, regarded as shared by all humans.*" She let a few seconds pass before lifting her head and turning her sensual eyes on him, her cheeks sunk to the bone, her facial features dark and fiery at the same time.

"But that's not the way things really are," he protested. "In fact it seems to me that's where the problems begin. As if we humans had some generalized God-given immunity. I don't believe for a minute that humans are blank slates, that we are malleable and pliable and that our actions in life are determined only by social-cultural factors. Fuck that! White humans, Western humans above all, act like we own the earth we live on, while the Aboriginals of Australia and the Native Peoples of the Americas that interest you and me know that we're just passing through … and that the planet Earth just permit us to live here, lending us space to live before our bodies return to it. Human nature! People excuse the humans who cause disasters like wars because they're just behaving as humans! Ugh. Life seems like a duel. I shoot at you, you shoot at me, who survives is the winner and deserves it. It's just our human proclivity to kill each other. We can't help it. Fuck that! Our nature. Our instinct. Therefore, we're not guilty at all. We're just being human, the way God made us. Shit! God is the guilty one, not his poor creatures. Human nature is only an excuse. Gives an airtight immunity! I find it hard not to believe that people simply want to gain from the devastation of others … including the elimination of non-humans who are actually so necessary to make our planet function. Oh God, yes, humans have made a mess of the planet. Humans made the mess and they must clean things up. We should repent and ask forgiveness. But we don't. We just go on savagely doing the same stupid things and blaming it on human nature. That 'it's just human nature' refrain doesn't work. There are literally billions of people on the planet who do not destroy each other and the earth they live on—but the destroyers are another story. They keep on destroying and then claiming they've done their best."

"Yet they know they're doing harm, don't you think? It's not human instinct to destroy and kill," Férnande said. "Such an instinct is pure suicidal. It's *their* psychopathic instinct, not *human* nature. And there we have the answer! François-Marie said you were a pessimist but that you believe you're just realistic."

Stuart waved away her words and saying he had to talk seriously with François-Marie, that he worried about him and that he was walking a tight rope of danger. "His work is not a tea party and he knows it. He should look for a way out … although exit routes are admittedly tight."

Férnande stared at him with such perplexity in her sunken sexy eyes that he regretted having spoken of the danger he knew that her husband faced. "Still, Férnande, we don't have to proclaim all the important things we want to say; we don't even have to share everything with those closest to us. We can hold onto them in memory and use them at the right time. A writer I love, Walter Benjamin, wrote that to speak of the past historically means to seize hold of a memory as it flashes up at a moment of danger."

On his third run up that gravel hill of his dreams, he was conscious of strange things going on in his hippocampus, deep inside the temporal lobe of his brain. There where lay his memory and his ability to imagine and, above all in these days, to dream. He was conscious of the curious replication of the altered reality marking his dreams------a detailed replay of the old or a preview of the new, a combination of disparate objects, actions and perceptions into a detailed hallucinatory experience. He didn't hate his dreams as some people allegedly do; he awaited them in anxiety and anticipation … and in hope. And he felt lucky those times he succeeded in grasping his dreams and making them part of his conscious life. On such days, as he let himself leave dreamtime, he still perceived the presence of his dream in his entrails; and he knew the aftereffects would persist all day. Sometimes, instead of exiting dreamtime, he held onto the dream and onto the Stuart who was in it for a while yet, to relive it, to coddle it—and sometimes to fear it. Then, over the next days, its force gradually diminished and slipped away like a summer breeze.

She was waiting. In her mysterious glory, Férnande was standing at the rear of the room. She was dressed in a light gray skirt and green blouse. Her silhouette stood out against the black wall; her eyes, full of black fire looked ferocious. At the same time she looked subdued even though her eyes still emitted live sparks that reflected off the black wall that he had come to believe she herself had selected. Maybe she had staged it all—but what the fuck!

Wondering if François-Marie knew his wife was a witch, he tried to look away but quickly turned back toward her magnetic eyes. Yes; he had to tell her the dream immediately:

"Last night's dream was both terror and allure, intimate and actually conversant with me. At first, it seemed like any other scary nightmare. As if what happened hadn't really happened at all. It was like a dream within a dream; when you try to evoke the first dream, both dreams slip through cerebral fingers into some inaccessible chamber of your mind. But I don't hate them," he said. "Even though I know I will never be free of them either. Nor do I want to be free of them They're like my warders, but welcome ones. Last night—or rather this morning—I saw myself standing on a wide plain watching the night die. The sun then rose from beyond the Abruzzi mountains. I recognized the Abruzzi where I used to ski. Darkness turned to light. The mountains drew near as they do on days after the *tramontana* winds. Though they were distant, I could see individual pines and oaks. The air was crisp and pure. I shivered as the stillness of night was transmuted into the new day bursting out in colors, bright flowers everywhere, intense lights, blinding, disorienting. I squinted at the new sun until it turned black and I knew I was to die that day. And I was scared. The sun drew nearer. Should I run? Or was it useless? That was the conundrum. My legs were leaden. A killer's knife appeared. It was a thin slice of steel, a star racing across the sky red from the new sun. I saw my pulsating heart, huge and alive, hanging against the sky and dripping red and black. My soul floated free. My body rolled down the steps of Saint Peter's. I was no longer. Still, the crazy thing was that I was aware of my nothingness."

"Such horrid details are hard to remember," Férnande said, "because we want to be free of them as quickly as possible. But actually we're never free of our dreams—they're part of us. And yes, in my experience too, dreams are also our warders. That's the eternal problem, distinguishing between dream and reality. Some dreams seem to contain the seeds of both assurance and doubt. Dreams can also seem to be the enemy, terrifying—not simply *after-dinner* dreams. But the reality is that we reject horror dreams … as if we could choose them! And it's true that sometimes you need courage to face them."

"Afterwards, Férnande, I stared into an old murky mirror in the upstairs bathroom. My face looked like a shadow, deformed, dependent; I had sunken cheeks and eyes. I looked like you. I *was* Férnande."

"I read somewhere that Shakespeare once remarked that a dream is a shadow, the shadow of ourselves."

"My reflection was not Shakespeare's; it was mine. And it was also you, Férnande. Do you understand what I am saying … and not saying?"

"Stuart Stuart, I look into mirrors too. And things do change ... in reflections in a mirror. Everything is changing everywhere. What used to be right is now left. Dreamtime is a curious time, when the new is created. The dreamings, the foundation of Aboriginal religion and culture, sixty-five thousand years ago, is the story of how the universe came to be, how human beings were created and how their Creator intended for humans to function within the world as they knew it. Aboriginal people understood the dreamings as a beginning that never ended," Férnande continued. "During what has become known as the dreamtime to Westerners and many historians, mysterious and supernatural spirits created our world, the earth and its beings. The dreamings told how the mythical creators suddenly disappeared— but only from the sight of mortals; they continued to live in secret places. Some lived in rock crevices, trees and water holes. Others changed into natural forces such as wind, rain, thunder and lightning. Many of the creators are believed to live on the land or in the sky above watching over their creation Those supernatural creators were men and women who had the ability to change shapes, into animals and other creatures such as the Rainbow Serpent in the North Lands."

"They sound like the jinn," Stuart said. "Living in crevices and water holes."

"Probably a related legend."

"Maybe! Anyway, the similarity of the versions of the origins of man and the universe in ancient cultures so distant geographically one from the other is inexplicable," Stuart added. "I recently wrote an article about my experiences among Mexico's indigenous peoples, so the following is fresh and rather heavy but I can relate it anyway … if you will just turn your eyes away!

"The symbol of Mexico's Huichol people's dream of time in pre-Hispanic Mexico was the pilgrimage they make to their sacred site of Viricota, a wild place three thousand meters high in the mountains where they leave the profane behind and undertake a mystical ascension in order to reacquire purity. To escape chaos or to return to it but always in search of original time. For the Huichols, the high place at Viricota is the axis of the world. Where sacred time and sacred space reign. Their trail of ascension was their search for eternal time. And Férnande, I learned that the urge to return to original time and achieve the eternal united all the many millions of Mesoamerican peoples: all the indigenous peoples of ancient Mexico. In a way, they existed only in their own dreams. I try to imagine such a life: each day, each hour, walking the walks of their dreams. Their life is only a dream of life, an interval between birth and death. Where man is forever a stranger but free as in a dream where you can do anything you like, for as long as you like. When you are ageless. Time is free and time flies forwards and backwards. Eternity is vivid and visible, but formless, shapeless and silent.

"For these people the conquest by the Spanish five centuries ago changed little. I learned from the shaman that for them walking this path of dreams is to leave everyday life behind and penetrate the eternal. But what is astounding is that such is the life of whole peoples."

"Well, your account is bewildering and also bewitching, Stuart. You must know that the best psychiatrists agree that dreaming is a product of unconscious forces in the psyche with roots deep in the evolutionary biology of the human species, whether Aboriginals in Australia or Huichols in Mexico. It's a collective unconscious. It belongs to us all. And because they are common to all of us, dreams are valuable allies in healing people suffering from mental illness. Jung and Freud and Trevi worked on that premise. That's why we seek insights into the nature of dreaming in mythology, history, and art in order to understand better the mysteries of how the mind and body interact."

"Férnande, I also spent some study time among the Cherokee in the USA. I learned that dreams are not only an essential part of Native American tribal culture but that the indigenous peoples of all of the Americas consider dreams an extension of reality. A means of experiencing other realms, and of communicating with their ancestors. They teach their children to remember their dreams so that they can use them for spiritual guidance and also for healing. Then their shamans help to heal the soul by inducing altered dream states with their words and actions but also with hallucinatory herbs like peyote and mushrooms. The shaman I met in western Mexico said that a dream is not different from life—they are one and the same and that therefore life is limitless. And we can connect to it—because we are the dream. One thing I know about myself is that though dreams go through me, they always leave something behind. Something of a dream remains and changes the feel, the color, the sound in my life and in my mind. It has happened that a year later, or even years later, some of a dream once dreamt returns to remind me. It happens that way with me. Since I discovered that was happening, I've lived more intensely. More in myself too. And hopefully less superficially."

"You're fortunate. I hope you know that," Férnande said, moving nearer to Stuart, her dark eyes seeming to reflect him.

"Yes, I do. And I've come to think that I'm also afflicted by uncontrollable invasions of my subconscious that account for many such issues … and more."

"In what way?"

"Uh, hmm, well you're my therapist so I can say it. Férnande, Doctor, I keep wanting to fuck women who are not my wife."

"Hmm. Just sounds like an urge for more sex." Férnande murmured, a faint smile at the corners of her mouth and her now bluish eyes.

"Actually, no. It's not that. I have a lovely wife. But that's not what I mean. I should emphasize the other women part. Different sex and different women."

"In other words, you want it all. But do we ever get all we want in life?'

"That's why I said uncontrolled invasions. By the way, that's Jung via Mario Trevi, that Rome analyst. I can't control that desire. It's just there. Tormenting me right now."

"It seems that the sex urge is among the things pressing you most. If it were an invasion of your conscious, it would be controlled. But your subconscious has no control, and lets you desire the other women. And Stuart, since you are my uh, patient, I think I can say that I understand your words perfectly well."

10.

It was like in his dreamtime. Those moments that magnified her sunken cheeks and high cheekbones and the darkness of her deep set eyes that could turn blue. The possibility had never so much as crossed his mind that it could happen to him, but there with him, inside him, was the new reality—that he unsuccessfully tried to relegate to the corners of his mind: it seemed he was losing himself in someone else. He asked himself if he could be falling in love again. For the last ten years he had thought it impossible. Most definitely not. This was not a matter of the heart. It was a cerebral affair. Not romantic love at all. Yet most definitely something was happening in his mind. A kind of hypnosis. A thing becoming but most definitely, he believed, unrelated to love.

Pessimist, Férnande had said of him. Realist—as he'd rebutted—was an honest answer, even though only conversational repartee when he said it. Falling in love with someone else still seemed irrational and improbable. That's the way his life had unfolded until he met Sophie. Before her, he fell for women left and right, forever sort of in love with one or the other. Body and soul, it had seemed then. But those times died in San Nicola. For ten years he had felt sure of himself, secure in his love for Sophie … and of hers for him. But now? Now he thought in broader terms. Maybe of the soul where full feeling resides.

This time, he lumbered up the hill feeling like Prometheus with the past and the unstoppable future weighing on his shoulders, insecure for the first time in ten years, uncertain of what seemed to be happening in his life, haunted by the unknown. Nothing had changed in the rooms of his heart. But what about in his soul? Not only irrational, it was illogical and implausible and hence improbable that it could happen. Yet he felt something new already in place. But what? On the one hand, it seemed impossible to amend the invasion of the chambers of his inner being that had definitely taken place up there on the hill, thus the distinct possibility of a different future than he would have thought possible. But no, that was not the issue. The problem was that the irrational stood in the way. Yet, Stuart told himself, he wasn't about to bring down existential chaos onto all their heads—only to awaken later and realize that part of the story was due to dreams and only partly to the usual sex urge. Férnande seemed to understand that better than he. Stuart Stuart, false Scotsman, false Italian, perceived his uncertainty. His every doubt seemed like betrayal. He pondered the word: soul. Or did he mean really mean sex as Férnande had grasped immediately?

Most likely today they would continue to speak of one thing, while thinking another. Such was this therapy … which was not only therapy but seduction. There! He'd thought it. Finally, he'd admitted what was happening from the start. That is, it was therapeutic, but in ways unexpected to them both. Moral questions always crept into the things they said and apparently what they thought too. Human nature, they'd said. Today, the human instinct seemed more to the point, permitting them to continue to live in what seemed a constant state of emergency—for her, for him. Stuart thought that his consciousness of new emotions was pre-fundamental, which he knew was his real hill to climb. For years, he'd lived in the certainty of Sophie and himself as one. Now there was this hill … and at the summit stood Férnande. Férnande with her deep, unfathomable eyes. The dreamings and the Cherokee Nation and the Huichols and the Aboriginals seemed far away. Moreover, the subject that he'd suggested for this session— social and economic justice and racism—was in these esoteric moments dry theory. Justice was distant from the real thoughts of his therapist, Férnande Dolon Volkov.

"What's on your mind, Stuart?" she asked, he thought, sardonically, as if she didn't know. Her job was to know that and to probe for more. Uncertainly, he answered in a sudden brash tone: "the same thing on your mind."

Quickly, he added: "Moral questions. Everything boils down to the moral question. Like our presence here." Stuart believed she too was cognizant of the power of morality—as per Walter Benjamin— that was sufficient to literally explode also the continuum of their personal histories.

"Specifically?"

He hesitated. The moment was crucial. The wrong word was like a hidden landmine. Férnande wanted details. That was her method. Why, how, when, who? Nonetheless, he knew she was stalling; and she knew he knew.

"People just don't think rationally," he murmured, his chief thoughts still fixed on the situation that he knew was critical, that he firmly believed was two-sided, not just within him. "No vision, no intellect. People just don't bother to think. They just act, irrationally. Things like economic justice and … and universal brotherhood are not only old-fashioned and forgotten; they are ignored. Yet it's an obligation for morally conscientious people to think."

"Think or act?"

"Well, thoughts do come before action. But yes, in the final analysis it is what one does—what we do—that counts, but first of all there are concrete things to think about."

Name some, he thought. Stay away from sex with other women. Stay away from her dark eyes.

"Take for example, our new political prisoners. The West has Julian Assange and Russia has Alex Navalny. People imprisoned because of their political beliefs and their rebellion. Prisoners of conscience and of what has always been."

"Why does that situation exist? Who are they? What have they done wrong."

"They, the others, the other-thinkers. And they've committed no crimes. But anti-terrorism laws have criminalized other-thinkers and opened prison doors for millions. The law permits pursuit of anything power determines are bad thoughts."

"And who are these other-thinkers?" she asked, manipulating not only his emotions, but his thinking too. "These prisoners of conscience?"

"I named two prominent examples; one is a journalist and tells the truth; the other is a criminal and a liar, but also a rebel. But our prisons are full of Muslims, black people, brown people. Also today just traveling abroad can become a criminal offence. And off to prison they go—not jail. Not the same thing. Justice overlooks its own racism and xenophobia. So the jails are full of black and brown people. Férnande, our civilization is fake. A satire of real social life."

"So what is to be done?" she asked, smiling her sardonic smile and holding him hook, line and sinker.

"I don't know but society should defend the weak. It doesn't do it because social inequality gets in the way. At this pace, the most normal of acts by you and me will be criminal in the future—like our talk today. We're potential criminals. The criminals of the future. We're already criminals, Férnande, because we comprehend the truth of what's going on. You and I, we're both criminals because we resist. You'll see! We'll see. Many people will come to understand … but too late. Social inequality alienates the lower classes, the weak classes to which we already belong. What's happening, I believe, is a sort of universal transition from the old dreamworld—as dreamers like us call it—to a new mold of humanity in a world with leaders without the thing called souls. Without hearts. One thing, Férnande, is unclear: are they born that way or do they lose their hearts and their souls along the way? With such people running things—deciding war or peace, deciding who will be rich or poor, who stands at the top and commands and who is the slave at the bottom who just obeys orders, things like that—you have to look closely and think in order to see what's really real. In any case, I see it there, ubiquitous, the fraudulence of our civilization. It's really very, very sad for it seems all hope has vanished, and worst of all, it will likely never return."

Stuart thought it a tragedy that he never had access to all the parts of himself at the same time—he was either this or he was that, husband or adventurer, one thing or the other—and because as a human being he had sought what was pleasant and distanced himself from depressing, scary things, he sought in dreams—and now in Férnande—a way to use what was becoming clear to him in his work. Therefore, he told himself, his altered states, and the ever more frequent entrance into dreamtime each time he wakened gave him some hope. He had long believed that the writer has the latent power to awe readers in a way that takes the breath away. With understandable words, he thought, the writer can show the way better—simple or complex and contorted as the way may be—than the painter does with colors which may only describe whatever he desires, or than the musician who projects emotion and mood. In an essay, he wrote that awe tears away the veil of illusion and lends a profound understanding of how the world actually works instead of how people imagine it. Awe revives our primal childlike selves, and obliterates social teaching designed to conceal our impulses that do not serve conformity, obedience to authority and decorum—to crush anything that kills innate spontaneity and creativity and connection to the natural world.

"Many writers—Férnande, *I* am a writer, even though I write little—many writers use their dreams for ideas and inspiration in their literary creations. Years ago I underwent one year of therapy because of psychological problems resulting from the tragic loss of a loved one—and two things emerged: my own fear of death and my dream life. My German therapist, a Freudian, prompted me to begin recording and making a "conscious" effort to remember parts of my dream life. Doing that I became aware of how difficult it is to recount even the most vivid dream about which I had even made notes during the night. That memory deficiency is well-known to creators of the arts. The gap between the vivid and maybe significant dream and the ragged bits and pieces I succeeded in assembling and reproducing was a veritable morass of memory and language incapacity. The words I managed to save—or liberate, according to Freud—emerged vague, gray and dull, incommensurate with the original. It's the same as the difference between real-life experiences, what you see or do in reality and the pale, inadequate words you find to describe in a literary fashion that experience and what you really felt about the experience at the time. I do better now."

"You just never know," Férnande said.

"No, right, you never know what lurks in our minds."

"And not only there."

"What do you mean?"

"You never know what resides in our hearts or the hearts of others," she said.

"Now you're thinking like me."

"So anyway, Freud or not, how's your journalistic career going?"

"Career? Me? Journalism is hardly a career ... but I should be doing more. Like a weekly column, not monthly There's just too much happening around the world and I do have some ideas."

"Like? Dreams, you mean?"

"And other things ... you know! Oh, yes, also dreams." He wanted to add, 'like of you.' Instead he flipped on his phone." I'll read you some excerpts from my draft article this month ...if you want to hear my thoughts."

"*Vas- y!*"

"*War!*" the article begins. *"It's not true that nobody wins wars. The disastrous proxy conflict between the U.S. and Russia is draining human relationships of all human reason, truth, and honesty. If little else, this war shows clearly who loses: civilians, animals and the environment are the great losers. Morality is a loser. War seems like a chess game where the people playing and the people fighting are essentially disconnected at the roots. The global leaders' mental microscope obsessed with evil and abessed (sic.) with ignorance appears to perceive an irresistible necessity to deprive humanity of a future. This perversion sees people only in numbers and digits, not as human beings with voices of reason for change and human unity. Most of us cannot even imagine the devastation of the first two world wars, but a potential third one would include nuclear and space-based weaponry which would eclipse the disasters of earlier wars. The global leaders compete in number games of an imaginary role of conflict resolution. No sense of time and history, how ignorance and political wickedness are leading to unthinkable calamities and disruption of a natural world order. Advanced weaponry is self-destructive. Leaders are afraid of being replaced by change, but they are intellectually bankrupt. No comprehension of the aspirations of mankind. Most 'peoples' of the world aspire to peace, not wars. Enough of the unthinkable horrors, bloodbaths, and massacres of innocent civilians of the two world wars of our times—still fresh on a human slate of memories. Ignorance prevents them from thinking outside the mindless box.*

"*Mon Dieu!*"

"Férnande, that's only an excerpt. The reality is that our situation is truly crucial—a greater conundrum than that of you and me. But that situation too has to be resolved … right here in La Storta."

"So what do you want, Stuart?" she asked in a husky voice.

"You know what I want! I want you."

"Yes, I know. Now it's been said. And it can never be unsaid."

"I feel …" he began. "I feel as I do many early mornings. I'm in dreamtime. But lately I experience a kind of semi-dreamtime—in and out—and it lasts for days. Like a nearly extinct indigenous people in Mexico I visited, when for three days and nights a whole people lived in permanent dreamtime to celebrate the Day of the Dead. As if their search for the soul of man had induced a suspension of every other unrelated activity. Their contemplative state of mind leads to fantastic states of the souls of the whole people."

Férnande moved closer, looking up into his eyes. Her lips were apart as if to speak. She waited. Stuart leaned forward, She met him, her eyes wide open. The long postponed, long feared kiss. Both confused. Both relieved that it was done. And both momentarily wondering, now what?

It was settled then and there. There was no going back. Both of them knew that. Like their words, like the kiss, it couldn't be unkised, undone, unlived.

11.

As he had from his first work day there, François-Marie Lecash still felt ill at ease in the research institute. Ill at ease, and ill-advised his acceptance of this ill-defined job in Italy. Likewise, his agreement with Férnande to live abroad was foolhardy. In her opinion his field was too limited, too narrow for the man of intellect she thought him to be. Still, she didn't perceive of ornithology as something regarding planetary life as he did; she'd never grasped the implications of animal life for mankind. In general, her mindset differed from his. This morning after she left for the city to her job overseeing the mental health of a crowd of marionettes of some unnamable multinational, he lay in their bed and looked out the window toward the ridiculous Great Wall. Today, he would observe the surroundings and the small things around him more closely than ever before and compare his life here with the future his field had promised him in France. He called in sick at the institute for which he felt no guilt whatsoever; as a matter of fact he did feel ill. But above all, he felt tormented by the idea that he was wasting his life in this institute in a non-descript Rome suburb, no less than in this artificial house. His life was not what he considered real life. It was charade. That thought brought with it a sense of anguish and humiliation that he was a mere puppet in the services of evil. He didn't want to get used to his sense of uselessness. In his high school in Orléans, his shyness had made him feel like a non-participant, with no sense of himself, which today he perceived as the tragedy of his life in which he'd tried to be what others—his parents and siblings and rare friends—expected him to be. He lay in the big bed with the Bill Blass sheets disconsolately, conscious of the fake house they lived in, a large two-story structure exactly like the many others around theirs. With his head half on the pillow, half against the iron bedstead, his half-closed eyes barely discerning the rectangle of the big window, it too exactly like the windows of all the houses on the hills running along the inside of the Great Wall, the thought kept recurring of the enormity of the mistake he'd made in coming here. He grew up in a real house in the real small city south of Paris; he was used to real things in his life. His interest in birds was genuine curiosity and early love for the bird kingdom. How he'd loved the woods around his hometown. He came to know well the ospreys and various woodpeckers and warblers and he admired the cranes on their migrations and had even been attacked once by an eagle when he stood too near its nest: he blamed himself, not the bird. No wonder that for most of his adult life he'd felt more at ease and secure and above all more himself with his birds than with most human beings. Birds, each and every one, he thought, were truly themselves, even though they lived collectively. So Stuart's words echoed in his mind that his knowledge of the hamlet birds could be his chance to do something positive for humanity: he could help expose many secrets of chemical warfare and the presence of a biolab right here in this so-called hamlet. François-Marie Lecash: chief witness. A role in life. He was not a chemist and knew little about botox, but he had experienced firsthand its lethality on *his* birds. After all, he was there to care for them. He felt like a protector of all birds, especially now when they were being used as guinea pigs. Test tube birds. That beautiful coal black raven lay in Stuart's freezer as if waiting for a new life. Yet they were dead. All his birds. Dead like his love, he thought , turning away from the window view of the Great Wall and redirecting his thoughts to Férnande. Admittedly, it had never been a great love affair; in fact today there was precious little love lost between them. He knew that. From the start, five years ago, he'd loved her, even though she repeatedly said that she 'cared' for him. To this day, he still wondered why she even married him. And why he accepted such a demeaning compromise relationship remained a mystery to him. Now, even that minimal 'caring' had transformed into indifference. She had other things on her mind. Others, perhaps. An attractive woman like Férnande, in the city every day, free of him. Férnande in her private studio examining the minds of others and in doing so revealing her own secret thoughts. An exchange of emotions, each new one finding its place among the emotions of others instilled in her—and her own emotions transmitted to others. He was not a jealous person, a display of which in such circumstances would be ridiculous, like throwing the gauntlet to that rapidly expiring remnant of what remained of their relationship. In a way, François-Marie had long suspected that it all came down to the science she had first considered ornithology. Ornithology *was* a science. Still, as meaningful as it was to the very existence of mankind, it was considered at the most a minor science. For him, it was a personal commitment and by chance fell under the category of science. He couldn't care less. For him, ornithology meant his curiosity about and love for birds. He perceived emotions about birds that few people shared. Some still called him birdman. He thought that in order to see birds, it was necessary to become a part of silence. He lived his day-to-day life to the cries of a broken-winged bird that can no longer fly. For François-Marie, birds prove that there exists a finer, a simpler state of being which we should strive to attain. Step by step, marrying Férnande, going abroad, and accepting this job that was suspicious from the start, he had as if abandoned that state of simplicity and to his chagrin willy-nilly ended up engaged in international intrigue and perhaps crime. Thinking such thoughts, the world seemed to spin without rhyme or reason, disconnected from the whole. He remembered that when he was in school, little things unnoticed by his classmates fed his convictions of the perfect connectedness of nature and non-human things in the universe. The belief of human beings that they possessed the earth was the anomaly; they themselves were merely transitory parts of one great whole. And the words of the poem he had learned in school came back to him in all its clarity:

No man is an island entire of itself; every man
is a piece of the continent, a part of the main;
if a clod be washed away by the sea, Europe
is the less, as well as if a promontory were, as
well as any manner of thy friends or of thine
own were; any man's death diminishes me,
because I am involved in mankind.
And therefore never send to know for whom
the bell tolls; it tolls for thee.

As a boy of thirteen he'd found the poem honest because it shows the true position of human beings in the universal order. Today, he still related to the poem in all its humanness; the poet makes clear our physical limitations and the necessity of facing the reality of our mortality. Though it wasn't intended to create false encouragement and optimism, he'd always considered Donne's work a brilliant piece of world literature. And in these days the annual visit of a million starlings that came each year to this great city during their migration to the south seemed to François-Marie a most intimate illustration of the poet's work: their beautiful—for humans inexplicable—avian performance in the southern skies directly overhead—which he viewed, photographed and documented from their house on the hill. The sky was suddenly darkened by the gyrating bird formations when the starlings performed, dark masses, swelling and shrinking, inhaling and exhaling like breathing lungs. As if the purpose of their endless lives was to collectively astound the humans below. Then their scouts rocketed earthwards in search of landing places in the stone city they loved; it was the winter migration of millions of European starlings. Each year they come. And they love the stone of the city itself, the massive embankments along the river. They come for days, maybe weeks. They arrive and stay their stay and when they depart, still collectively, they seem eternal; they never die or leave a victim behind. They leave behind only their white cement-like excrement as a reminder of their existence. Observing the arrival of the starlings, he had the thought that also the life of successful families was marked by regular recurrences and repetition like that of the migratory birds. Birthdays and marriages and the birth of children proceeded according to fixed codes. But he and Férnande had no such core. No markers in their lives. No traditions to hold to. Nothing in common to which to belong. No tangible object to hold onto. He was aware that his apparent estrangement made him a social recluse—Donne's clod that clings— he who more than others perceived the wholeness of life. He perceived that everything was connected by those cords of which none of his associates seemed aware. People just don't care, he now knew. Therefore, his despair, his resignation, which in turn deepened the cleft between Férnande and him. There had never been a more dismal period in his life. Therefore, he would do it. He would live up to his name: Dolon, the Greek spy. He would spy for Logreco. For Ermanno Riccardi. For the third rung of AISI. He would do it for the dead birds. For the black of the raven in Stuart's freezer. He would do it for himself. He was the third man on the side of justice on the Hamlet Commission. But he was the only ornithologist in the NATO Research Institute and the underground Chemical Weapons Laboratory. He realized that he already knew many things. And what he didn't know yet, he would learn. More than once he'd seen the arrival at the institute of the black suv with CD plates, Corps Diplomatique. He knew what that meant: it meant NATO; it meant CIA. He'd seen them piling out of the car: two fashionably dressed men trying to act like gentlemen who kept looking around them, left and right, as if searching for spies. And two action types, marine haircuts, nervous eyes, twitching fingers as if hoping to pull the trigger, who even stopped a guard holding a big dog on a leash and checked his ID. Once he'd answered a wrong number phone call and the English speaker asked if things down below were secure. He knew how things were down there, he had heard the chemists talking among themselves in the lunch room: running water, positive tests, problems of vaporization. Bizarrely, the general atmosphere in what he now knew was a top secret biolab was surprisingly lackadaisical and indifferent to the world outside— as if such dirty work proceeded in a vacuum. All such acts and events prejudiced François-Marie against the laboratory a priori. In fact if he had not called in sick, he would go to the lunch room today and spy. He would sit at some strategic place with his work notes and listen closely, interpreting what he overheard. Today, in the security of his bed, François-Marie retraced events and concluded that the death of the birds was accidental-sacrificial; and he realized that although he was not caged as were his crows, he like them was a potential victim. So now he had to get up and prepare himself for the meeting that he suspected was going to change his life.

12.

Since Gianluigi Logreco refused outright to sit for one second in the now summery veranda-garden of the Fico d'India, he had arrived first and arranged a table for four in a discreet corner of a secondary air-conditioned room of La Storta's best eatery. Ermanno Riccardi gazed around the room with the disguised but unconvinced secret agent look, then hung his jacket on the back of his chair and sat down with his back toward the room. When they arrived together, Stuart mumbled his introduction of "François-Marie" and sat down on the opposite side of the table with a yellow tablecloth and sparkling silverware and two impressive crystal glasses at each place. Stuart noted that table places seemed significant in the dark world of people like Riccardi, who didn't say one word of acknowledgment of the presence of the newcomer, although his eyes were fixed on the Frenchman as if deciding whether or not he was to be trusted. It seemed Riccardi ran his own security check in his mind: he decided himself who was to be trusted. Ah well, Stuart thought: each profession has its quirks.

Gianluigi Logreco broke the silence, leaning forward and saying in a low voice directly to Riccardi that the new man in their circle was an ornithologist.

"A what?"

"Ornitholgist, a specialist in birds. A derivation from the Greek, naturally: *ornis*-bird and *logos*-science."

François-Marie smiled to himself: a science, of course. In reality he had come to hate the word. He hated the word "science" as he hated the word "specialist", the expert. He disliked the person, the specialist with his detailed knowledge of one profession. without any connection with the rest of the world. His ideal was the non-specialized person, the all-round, strongly social, universal person developed on all sides and in many directions, with a clear preference for the aesthetic, while his contempt grew for professional specialization. He loved birds and the life of nature as only one of the many directions that he hoped to undertake; and he was curious about the unlimited fields of knowledge, one of, if not the chief reason he regretted his acceptance of employment at the Institute.

"So we're back to the birds!" Riccardi said. "What about them?"

"In a way, they're my birds," François-Marie said. "I check them and test their reactions. That's why I'm here".

"Test them? Test them for what and how do you do that? Sorry for this, er, this sort of interrogation, but I'm trying to understand what's happening in the field of chemical warfare and, by the way, I heard about the dead crows."

"Murdered crows," François-Marie mumbled indistinctly.

"Well!" Riccardi said.

"Murdered?" Logreco asked, polemically.

Stuart smiled to himself. He knew about François-Marie's estimation of avian intelligence.

"The crows were sort of like my patients. My job was to control their temperature, their movements and also their responses. What I did NOT know was that at the same time lab technicians were injecting into them—or into some of them—mild doses of botulinum toxin type B. In other words, they were killing the crows gradually until someone—and now the chemists act as if they didn't know who—released them from their cages and they flew to the trees that had been sprayed just for them, I suppose with some other form of botox. And that, of course, was the real test: they were freed from their underground cages on purpose—to test the lethality of varying strengths of botox spray. And it killed them all. I believe the botox used on the Russian soldiers near Zaporozhe was exactly the strength they wanted: kill some people, maim others."

"Jesus Christus!" Ermnano Riccardi exclaimed.

"For the love of Zeus," muttered Gianluigi Logreco.

Stuart looked from one to the other of his commensals, as unobtrusively as possible studying each face and wondering what playful dreamer had willed together four so distinct persons at this particular table in the Fico d'India in the suburb named La Storta—named after the bend in the once great north-south highway: Ermanno Riccardi, a twice removed self-declared rogue intelligence agent driven by a desire to catch his ideological enemy off-guard; a Greek professor who hated the summer in arrival as much as he disliked the intelligence world to which he too had once been linked; an ornithologist-minor scientist who loved 'his' birds more than he did his beautiful psychologist wife; and he, himself, who had set the whole affair in motion when he and Sophie found the fifteen dead crows several weeks earlier; he, a curious writer onto the story of his life and obsessed by his lust for the ornithologist's wife.

"So you're convinced the Ukrainians did it, are you?" Riccardo asked.

"Well, the Under-Secretary of State, Victoria Nuland, admits Ukraine has 'biological research facilities'," Stuart interjected. "If she says so, it must be true. That's not something you admit easily—or maybe she was bragging.""And if they have secret biolabs, you can be certain they are working and experimenting also with botox," François-Marie added."Our chemists use my birds in their tests; up there they use Russian soldiers."

"What the fuck is that stuff anyway? I know its composition" Riccardi said. "And I know what it does but I still don't know "*che cazzo é*? What the fuck it really is? Sounds worse than the hydrogen bomb."

"It's bad stuff, that's for sure," their French friend said. "You can't compare these chemical weapons with old-fashioned mustard gas. I hear the chemists at the Institute talk about it every day. In vapor form, this stuff can be absorbed through the eyes, mucous membranes, respiratory tract, and skin. Also, the effects of botulinum toxin are different from those of nerve agents insofar as botulism symptoms develop slowly—over several days—while nerve agent effects are generally rapid. In short, it's a killer and a slow killer at that. Those boys in Zaporozhe still alive still have to suffer its final effects."

"Well, friends, what are we going to do about it?" Riccardi asked in a determined manner, looking from one to the other.

Gianluigi sighed. "We know there are biolabs in the Ukraine where botox has been used. Every western country is making this stuff and only Zeus knows what else. Realistically, I don't see how we can stop it."

"We can at least slow down what our country produces," Riccardi said. "And we have a man on the inside who can provide details," he added, looking hard at François-Marie.

"And we can disclose it to the world and show how they hid it underground in our remote hamlet," Stuart said.

"And save the lives of a few birds here in this avian paradise," François-Marie added. "Anyway, what should I do?"

"Ok, let's collect all details possible,' Riccardi began. "Chemical weapon production: how long has this been going on? Or is this to be the first shipment from here? And if so, how and where and when? At that point, I have some people who'll most likely be glad to disrupt it. But seems to me this is a well-oiled system. Another important question is where else in our country are they produced? Also to keep in mind: botox is certainly not the only chemical weapon. There must be dozens, or hundreds of other such illegal, unethical, lethal chemical weapons that the Bel Paese, the land of art and culture, produces.

"Now gentlemen, I did some research and have some general but pertinent information for your consideration: our country is the eighth exporter in the world of major weapons of war, after the United States, Russia, France, Germany and others. No, *mon ami,* your France is not omitted from this nefarious list. Oto Melara up north in La Spezia sells arms world-wide. It's a subsidiary of our industrial giant, Finmecannica,. And they don't manufacture small stuff like hand grenades or rifles. They sell the Ariete Main Battle Tank, Centauro Tank Destroyer, Wheeled Infantry Fighting Vehicle, Palmaria self-propelled artillery, Otomatic anti-aircraft tank, Pack howitzers, naval guns. So you see when Rome sends arms to Ukraine, they are lethal weapons of war—not playthings—and they make a difference. Stuart, I understand you know that place in La Spezia."

"Sort of. I went up there once. Inhospitable people. They showed me around a bit. Not very much. And the little I saw, they showed me reluctantly. Everyone there was so secretive that you had to really insist to get any information whatsoever. But I wrote an article about it anyway. Created a stir in Scotland when people learned that Italy, the land of art and love and beautiful seaside resorts, sells such killing machines. At the time, Oto Melara was selling tanks to the Saudi for their war against Yemen. You know, the forgotten war! So I think I can safely say that any disclosures that Italy produces chemical weapons will both enlighten and disappoint the millions who come here to see Michelangelo. And just maybe there's a newspaper left in this country that will cooperate in our, er, crusade."

"Well, the name of Oto Melara will get my full attention if I hear it … and I'm sure I will. " François-Marie said. "And now that the birds are gone, I'll have plenty of time to make the rounds of the institute offices—at least those open to me. Morning is my best time at the institute, when everybody heads for the canteen for coffee and cognac. Office doors are open and computers on and desks covered with notes, charts, and, I imagine, addresses. The chemists love blackboards and formulas and equations. So I will be doing a lot of photography of stuff like this that I found in the chemists' conference room written by some psychopath in big letters on the blackboard." And he passed around his phone photos to the others:

Clostridium botulinum neurotoxins are among the most potent toxins. The crystal structures of intact Clostridium botulinum neurotoxin type B are the most potent in nature, one thousand times more toxic than even Cobra venom. It causes paralysis-muscle relaxation. Man's muscles are unable to contract due to the toxin's ability to block the secretion of acetylcolin to the synaptic space. The lethal dose is less than one micro gram in humans.

"A funny thing was a note written in red chalk by some potential dissident-jokester who added just underneath: 'If botox is so small, why not send a sample to their President in a sealed envelope, express and special delivery if you want to be sure he gets it! Hahaha.' So that person—well, among the ten chemists there's a sexy, outspoken redheaded woman who I believe did it and who seems to like me— that person was making a morbid joke, so we have at least one potential ally among them. I'll try to get close to her."

"Hopefully it's her," Stuart muttered, his budding relationship with François-Marie's wife on his mind. Human nature! Stuart mused, recalling the session with Férnande on that subject. Human males in general seem irremediably promiscuous: I want François-Marie's's wife. François-Marie wants the sexy redheaded chemist; Gianluigi the Greek likely wants Sophie—or me—in the same way I want Férnande. Nor do emancipated human females yearn less than males for what they don't have. The nest at home is one thing; sexuality another. We all experience it one way or the other all our lives—even asexuality is sexual—in ourselves or in others. And there's no getting around it: human sexuality is promiscuous—even though in everyday life it's ideally of a romantic nature. And besides, he thought, if life is but a dream, what does it matter? Still. though the human needs pure sex, both males and females need also romantic love to go along with it. Not many, but even some rare animals are loyal to their mates: like the bald eagle or the swan, the wolves in packs in the mountains and beavers building their dams. But every human being I've ever known was at least in thought promiscuous. And my world is not vastly different from others. Life itself seems also like a search for eternal youth. Sex and youth. New sex for a new life. For Chrissakes, since I haven't reached the age to think such thoughts, this sounds like advance pardon for my mental waywardness. But, in my defense, Férnande is the first aberration in ten years. A long or short period for a very human being like me? And in any case, it's not even romantic love I feel for Férnande. The reader will judge. But the thing about human instinct which as a rule differs from that of most animals—whose sexual act is carpe diem—humans can plan devilishly ingenious strategies and play false roles in the process of seduction. In other words, we rely on a mental plan, not instinct—and wrangle and seek the right occasion long in advance to have that one specific human being … not just the first who comes along. Real life is not always—maybe never—only a one-night stand. In real life, most people want love too. Even a street-walker's love, will do. I once wrote that 'hesitation, reason, insecurity, and a sense of surviving but fading loyalty to a loved one stand like disintegrating turrets of a weakened fortress in the sand of the desert of human emotions.'

Ermanno Riccardi looked from one to the other of his growing team and debated with himself the question of the political affinities and possible connections of each. His team was now destined to soon include also an institute chemist—the redhead Frenchy had the hots for. And he had to count on his own instinct about each since official background vetting was excluded considering the extreme compartmentalization of his own organization, not only three separate entities, but also each part inimical to the others. The only problem with his old friend Gianluigi Logreco was disinterest; however, he could be counted on to keep his promises … well, when sober. This guy

Stuart-Stuart was, he believed, the most solid. The fact that he was a self-professed Communist was a kind of guarantee in this project: he'd shown immediately his sympathies for the Russian soldiers infected with botox poisoning.

At this point, François-Marie Lecash was odd man out. But again, Ermanno trusted his own instinct: the Frenchman was really pissed about the dead birds and hated their being used for lethal experiments. Moreover, he became more than an ornithologist when speaking of the sexy redheaded chemist. Get a Frenchman ideologically or amorously committed and he was yours.

"Let's see, friends," he said. "I suggest we meet again here next week. Let's make it on Tuesday and for dinner instead of lunch … at around nine," he added, rising and again looking at each individually in his deeply engrained secret agent manner. "After which we'll have to find a new place."

Gianluigi sighed and nearly ran out the door in his rush home where a full drink cupboard waited. He would entertain himself. François-Marie headed for the Institute in search of Helen the Redhead and Stuart for his three o'clock appointment with Férnande.

13.

Humming and singing under his breath: 'a deal with god … swap places,' Stuart crossed Via Cassia and began his run up the hill. 'Back to Férnande', he thought, seeking the comprehension hidden away in one of the chambers of his hearts to clarify the conundrum he faced: he loved Sophie but he yearned for Férnande— 'most definitely not the same thing.' Certainly not. It could never be the same thing. But in recent times he had admitted to himself the minimum acceptable: he wanted *her*, Férnande his therapist, who, he was convinced, was waiting at the top of the hill with the same thing on her mind.

He found her standing in the middle of the room on the red, brown and yellow Persian carpet with a tense look on her face, no longer the self-confident, assertive and reserved therapist of earlier meetings. She was not aware that the bright expression in her dark eyes and her supple body language were exactly as Stuart had imagined. He closed the door behind him and stood there for a full minute, his eyes fixed in hers.

He believed he knew *how* she was waiting and what she was thinking while she waited. Later, both of them would wonder how he knew. Her story was after all a woman's story; a man would never understand it, she was thinking. But Stuart did know what she was feeling and what she expected and he was no Tiresias.

Today, Férnande felt her complete womanhood, a vivid, powerful sensation accumulated over the years, which she transmitted to him through her dark eyes that in the reflections from the sun sliding toward the west seemed pale blue. No thoughts today of Aboriginals or Huichols. No dreamscapes other than the one in which they each stood waiting. No dead crows or frozen ravens. She was fully cognizant that she was feeling her own libido in a way she hadn't perceived since she was twenty years old. And she felt desired in a way that corresponded to her own desire of back then. To her, such sentiments were still new and unexplored territory. In this moment, sedate panorama turns around la Grande Rue in Paris or on the childish Ferris Wheel with François-Marie back at home held no interest. Nor just barely moving in one of the room-like cabins of the giant *Riesenrad* in Vienna's Prater Park with her parents as a child. Never again would such suffice. Today, she perceived instead the wild sensations of her first ride on a roller coaster at the Amusement Park in Orléans: her spontaneous screams at the hot-cold thrill of the sudden rush of cold air in her ears, the frisson of alarm at the rapid rise and then the sharp precipitous plunge of the precarious cart, her stomach in her throat, up and then down, up and down, her hands reaching out for support from that boy of twenty. Later, she would never reach out for François-Marie in the same way. She never forgot the roller coaster. Now she reached out blindly as if for a similar support for the roller coaster plunge and found Stuart on the thick Mashad carpet where she wanted to stay forever. She thought her sensations now were the same as those that François-Marie had searched for in her from the start, sensations that she thought she would never be capable of sharing with him—long-sought-for sensations that however never occurred. There on the thick Mashad carpet she shared with a friend what she had withheld from the person who loved her. But not as she desired to be loved. First, she thought, must come unlimited desire. Desire and desire, desire without limits, entwined in him, she repeated 'Be me!' *Moi! Moi! Moi!* Over and over, 'Be me, you must be me. I am you. Be me, I'll still feel you. I'll be you. You, me.' They were two different sentiments, she knew—passion and love. Férnande's loveless passion alone was deep and mysterious, especially to her the therapist; it was like time which escaped her, unlimited: she was conscious there was still much more inside her to be unraveled and unveiled. She was cognizant of an unknown something—maybe something demonic in the emotional chamber of her heart. In her heart. More than a feeling, more than an emotion, something much deeper, much more profound than love that she believed was located in another chamber of her heart. Only once had she experienced it, the thing, the something she felt—not love, but total chaotic passion—and then for minutes only. But something had remained, some raging, rogue remnant, a reminder that the sensation existed and had always existed. It lay in waiting, in waiting, something that had to return someday. A mental female 'thing' that neither François-Marie nor Stuart would ever experience. And yet, yet, despite the doubts about herself, she believed instinctively that her passion was natural, spontaneous and generous, the passion that in that moment she believed only women perceive, that she thought she would never perceive again, the ultimate counterpoint to male passion –to merge, to exchange so that one becomes the other.

From the instant they'd *entered* the Mashad, one enlaced in the other, Stuart observed Férnande; he was obsessed by her transformation from the self-assured woman to whom he climbed the hill as often as she granted him access to the stranger now merging into him. He watched her wide-open, unseeing eyes. He couldn't know that she was experiencing once more the unnamable sensation of the twenty-year old girl on the roller coaster. The sensation had remained inside her, accumulating, accumulating, until the pressure became so pent-up that the eventual explosion was inevitable. She'd always known that pressure would have to be released. It had remained inside her all these years— for the most part sedate while she advised others. It had remained intact in her and continued accumulating. All those ten years it had lain there, if not sedate, then subdued by substitutes when it flared up. All the ten years since roller coaster night, Férnande felt as if she were inhabited by another self and that one day that other self would remerge. She herself wondered if it was her demon as she thought of her dark side that since roller coaster night had occupied part of her.

Stuart envied her in her apparent dreamtime. During the unfathomable period on the Mashad carpet, at a depth no less simultaneously thrilling and alarming than Tartarus Pit, his initial ecstasy at her reciprocation to his sexual fantasies had undergone an unexpected metamorphosis of what he had perceived since the day he defined what both recognized as their intent: he had wanted her from the first time he climbed that hill to her—and he knew, he sensed, that she wanted him—yet neither understood *how* they wanted each other. Maybe it was the abrupt incongruous height of the hill on the kilometers long slope pointing away from the city. A hill so high and out of place that the very altitude made his head spin. As malapropos as the false placidity behind her demonic eyes that he had perceived the first moment in her studio. From the outset he had seen a woman on the run, fleeing her own everyday life. But to where? And from what? Was it something beyond human nature? She must wonder about that too.

In any case, Férnande was still in dreamtime when he left her; he, in wake time. The two times, they both knew, were incompatible.

14.

Stuart slipped and slid back down the hill. It was again muddy, its ruts, hollows and ditches filled with water after a summer shower while he was with Férnande—a weak remainder of the forty days of rains. He thought that many no less inexplicable things could have taken place while he was lost in her dream on the Mashad carpet. Mashad? At the bottom of the hill he flipped on his phone and checked on the map: near Turkmenistan and only five hundred miles from Kabul. Curious, he thought, Mashad was near the top of the world … not distant at all. He turned right onto the Via Cassia headed north in the direction of Tuscany, quickly leaving behind the supermarket, the hill and Sophie's *bottega*, and still in a daze with no precise destination in mind—just distance. A long distance adventure. Running or walking on the sidewalk when there was one, all of the places he knew so well seemed different this afternoon, strange and out of place. The big newsstand with a huge clientele on the central corner, the best location in La Storta, was still closed, one said because the owners hated getting up early mornings to receive the daily press. No sense of the news—likely because they knew it was all fake anyhow. Why participate in the dissemination of such trash as media news when you can simply pull down the shutters? Stuart knew and the *edicola* entrepreneurs knew—like any sensible person could know but did not want to know—the real news. But for him, the new times were extraordinary; he had Férnande. Though of course the signs of the times were disastrous, but strangely not for him. Things were falling apart in San Nicola, in Italy, in Europe, in the western world, but he was still flying at dizzying altitudes on the Mashad carpet with emotion-crazed Férnande. Well, he thought, stopping for a moment to contemplate the garage. The mechanic had his shutters at half-mast; he was not certain what was happening in the world either. "Cars are plentiful," the mechanic said. Dressed in white linens with a black silken scarf, he was sitting outside on a deck chair as if he didn't have a care in the world. "And license plates identify most as brand new, new, or nearly new. But they just don't seem to break down anymore. No problems with the brakes. No transmission problems. Cars today are perfect. A mystery to me." Stuart advised him to hire a car breaker and moved on. At a gym, the beautiful hostess was sitting at the door while the shadows of beautiful people inside doing things reflected against inside walls. An optician with a for rent sign hanging in the window of his store witnessed everything, all events, local, national, European, international. Stuart wondered why he wanted to rent. It turned out the eyeglass man was also a businessman; rent five locations, sub-let four of them at a higher price, and work with no overhead in the fifth and then sell his wares at lower prices so that the others dried up and died. He asked people waiting patiently in a long line at a bakery distinguished by the sign—*authentic French Croissants from Le Moulin de la Vierge on Rue Saint-Dominique, Paris, France*— what they were waiting for? "Can't you read? Real Parisian croissants." Stuart hoped their patience would be rewarded. What a patient people we are! Patient or simply gullible: we believe the promises of dictators and their assurance that the bad are the good, and the good, the bad. A fish monger offering fresh north sea sole half-price swore to an old lady asking how they could be half price, that the fishermen still had to catch the fish and they still had to deliver their catch to that fish monger in La Storta—the last curve before the city. Stuart shrugged and read the room price list illuminated in the stairway to the local bordel in an upstairs hotel like an offer from Tartarus. After Férnande, he thought, who needed heaven. He rested at a coffee bar with scattered outside tables frequented chiefly by old men who all seemed the same age, had the same faces like persons out of dreamtime. As one, they examined him quizzically, the man out of place, a mere shadow, alone. They called him, Doctor, and asked if he thought the two women who threw themselves under metro trains almost simultaneously two hours ago knew each other and planned it that way. "Or," the youngest of the old men said, "were they pushed over the edge?", at which the others nodded. Stuart said he believed there was a connection. Noticing that all the tables were bare, he offered coffee for all. "I'd prefer a beer," one said and the others seconded him. Stuart counted seven, went inside and asked them to send out beer for all. So that's what the seven men did all day, every day, wait for an offer and exchange it for a beer. Everybody these days seems to have an angle. Ingenuity, he thought. Then, on and on he tramped, the immediate smell of beer trailing behind him. Commercial strips interrupted by heavily trafficked though nearly invisible side streets leading to more of Sophie's abandoned places, places forgotten in this small city within the huge city, an Irish Bar with green awnings, surrounded by shrubbery and signs, which however he had never seen open. Mafia, he thought, as any thinking Roman would. He stopped outside a shop with a big sign in front: MISTER FIX ANYTHING. He looked in and asked the man sitting in a rickety chair if he could really fix anything. Mister looked back and said: "I remember you. You were sitting in that dinky Panda and asked me for my visiting card. Well, I can fix a Panda, for sure. See that little yellow car over there? A thirty-year old Panda. Cult car now. They built them in Spain then. A trial run. Used wood in the body. Runs like a dream. What's you problem?"

"No problems. It's got a motor like a Ferrari. I really wanted to know if you can revive a frozen bird … you know, thaw it out and make it fly again?"

"I don't know. I've never tried."

Stuart grinned happily at his daring optimism, shrugged and continued along his curious sight-seeing route, feeling like Leopold Bloom even though by no stretch of the imagination could La Storta be compared to Dublin. Places that should be full of people were abandoned; places that looked abandoned were teeming with life.

On the spur of the moment, he entered once elegant Olgiata with its shopping centers, cafés and restaurants, and luxurious villas in one of which a famous gruesome murder of a wealthy divorcee once took place for which her Filipino servant was suspected, arraigned but never convicted; he was probably in solitary today where he would remain for another few years until one day he would suddenly be released a lonely, sick man. Kafkaesque affair, with no explanations. He stopped on a small bridge over a brook that during the rains had overflowed its banks and flooded a nearby pastry shop and a launderette and ran unimpeded across the flagstones of the piazza, ankle deep at the outdoor cafés. Today the stream was a mere trickle, a shadow of its momentary fame, inhabited by swarms of mosquitoes and distinguished by an unidentifiable stench. He passed through the open and uncontrolled gates to take a look at Olgiata's renowned international eighteen- hole golf course where Tiger Woods once played; no one was golfing and swaths of weeds marked the neglected fields where one rich Olgiatian—a Saudi, so it was said—had parked his Cessna 172 Skyhawk near his villa bordering on the eighteenth hole. In disgust at the general deterioration of famed Olgiata, obvious to everyone but the Olgiatians, he decided not to walk to Viterbo—not even to Campagnano. Instead, he sat at a café facing the piazza and considered getting drunk like Stephen Dedalus. He ordered three gins and tonic, telling the waiter that his drinker friend Stephen would be along shortly. He pulled a wad of scraps of paper from a pocket, smoothed them out on the table and read his latest notes, they too abandoned in the depths of his memory, and magically there they were in Petar Penda's *Looking Back,* the poetic images that he'd found so beautiful just before what happened on the Mashad carpet now only short hours ago:

> *The wind stirs the glassy surface*
> *And the even perfection is alive,*

The water heaves and murmurs,
Woken up from its quiet sleep.
It tells you of joyous departures,
Of leaving your old world and
The rapture of meeting the unknown,
Freedom to create your new self,
Face fears and purge the enemies within.
The sea is mighty and inciting,
Calling you to force the moment.
But one more look around and
You freeze, fearing if you ever return,
You'll be alien to your home.

Stunned by the images on the first read and the first gin, he recalled his own conviction that there are places from which you never return. He drank another and read the poem again and once more feeling the sense of the beyond thought he should write congratulations to the poet, but swiftly changed his mind, persuaded that poets were entitled to so much more than a word of felicitation since they existed to save the world. That done, he replaced the poem in his pocket and decided not to wait to drink with Stephen Dedalus, who anyway and wherever he was, had too much of a head start. He drank the third gin and tonic and looked up at the young waiter and asked if he knew Stephen.

"Who?"

"Stephen, Stephen Dedalus."

"What's he look like?"

"About my age. Dark, dark like an Irishman. You know, like a shadow. He's always late."

"Maybe."

"You're not too young to know him. I was a lot older than you are when I met him the first time; he made a big impression then."

The waiter looked at him skeptically for some seconds, then grinned: "Ah ha, you're pulling my leg. I'll bring you more gin—whether this Stephen comes or not."

Stuart grabbed hurriedly at the fourth drink, for fear it would escape him; in doing so he perceived the sudden sensation that these random events meant that his feelings for Sophie had dramatically changed, a sensation which was unsettling to his whole nature. Yet there were no doubts that for Férnande he merely shared the sensation of mingled sentiments and eroticism on a thick Persian carpet from Mashad.

Stuart smiled back at the very sensible kid, drank off the fourth gin and was glad he did; he had exaggerated with all that phony euphemistic bourgeois intellectual talk. When he paid the bill, he left the kid a five euro tip. From a distance he looked back at his table; the kid was standing there watching him and gave him a thumbs up.

He abandoned his walk in the beyond and the people he had met on the way, took the bus back up the Cassia to his Panda parked at the supermarket and headed for the gate to the Great Wall and finally home. Home, home, home in order to declare his everlasting love to Sophie, sleep off the gin, and with luck start his article for *Time and Space*.

15.

Férnande Volkov denied she was beautiful—"I'm sexy," she would say, "not beautiful." Words like 'You've got great legs, you know' sent her eyes to the skies. "My legs are shaped like a drawn Sioux bow ... but I am sexy." Férnande's looks and her intelligence had always created problems for her: she had enough of the former to send the boys in her Orléans lycée into ecstasy; the latter scared them away. So that she herself claimed the distinction of being the most unpopular student ever to frequent local schools. Thus Férnande's unresolved issues with beauty, sex and intelligence prompted her in the direction of psychology, which she undertook at Edinburg University where her father had studied, as did his father as well. Her Russian Communist grandfather had first studied philology under Erich Auerbach at Marburg University in Nazi Germany until the Jewish Auerbach had to flee in 1939, at which time Arkady Volkov moved on to Edinburg, until finally settling in Orléans and marrying Férnande's French grandmother. In Edinburg, Férnande lived alone in a small apartment in the Old City and was naturally first in her department, to the joy of her parents financing her studies abroad. Besides the basic courses for psychology, she studied world literature and the German and Russian languages spoken by both her father and grandfather.

So determined was she to speak the languages of Père and Grand-pére that during the summer vacation period Férnande remained in Edinburg two months longer for intensive courses of Russian and German languages. Though the language spoken at home was rigorously French, she had picked up from her grandfather a smattering of spoken Russian so that she concentrated on the complex grammar in her studies and consequently each year surprised her grandfather with her improving Russian. Orléans was a festive place during her month there. The personal disaster of her lycée years was forgotten, and she was like other twenty-year olds at home on vacation.

Though she still excelled academically, her beauty had matured and deepened, and she perceived that she was different from others.

It seemed of the greatest moment—and far-reaching—that what happened, happened when she was twenty years old: she lost her virginity. A year earlier, she believed, she would have still been too girlishly young; a year later, she would have been too mature and worldly-wise to perceive the reality that would guide the rest of her life. It was the year that she not only lost her virginity but also when she learned that sexual passion and romantic love were two separate matters. But for Férnande the most momentous discovery was the existence of a deeper sensual sensation that most people never experience.

A boy named Luc had been in her class in her last year at the lycée, a studious type, rather shy, who had not been one of those envious of her achievements, and though she was aware that he was attracted to her, he had never said to her more than *bonjour, ça va?* and smiled his timid smile, which concealed, she thought, a certain charm. He too was home for vacation from his medical studies in Paris, had lost his timidity but not his charm. So when they met on the street one day and had a coffee together, he suggested a film, then a few days later a rock concert during which he kissed her and to her surprise she kissed him back. The Saturday afternoon they spent at the amusement park, a thin Atlantic wind was blowing up the Loire Valley and autumnal clouds marked the horizon to the west. Summer was ending and they too felt the *tristesse* that arrives with the end. Hand in hand they strolled through the grounds commenting on the sideshows—the fattest lady in the world, the house of horrors, the cabin of the hermaphrodite with a huge sign hanging on the wall reading: THE THIRD SEX and underneath: *where your dreams come true*. They rode the Ferris Wheel from the top rung of which they searched unsuccessfully for their own homes. "They no longer exist ... not for us," Luc said, she thought the most perceptive words he'd ever uttered

And then they rode the roller coaster, the ride and the aftermath about which Férnande never spoke with anyone but held fast in her memory. Not of Luc, however. No memories of Luc remained, only the memory of a boy who took her virginity that she had so wanted to get behind her and for which she still silently thanked him. His surname forgotten, he vanished. Only she and her perception of the **All** remained. The feeling had come to her on the roller coaster, on the third precipitous plunge straight down and into the sex they had in his own room at his home in the center of Orléans. What she believed then a one-time sensation—a rapture, an extreme euphoria impossible for any other to feel, a euphoria that she would then seek forever, but feared she would never feel again—swept over her. It was not the sex as such, not the long-awaited penetration of her body by another, not her pleasant orgasm that she had easily experienced shortly after her virginity left her forever. The real climax, the climax of her first twenty years, was everything together: the autumnal sensations, the Atlantic breezes drifting up the valley, it was also the hermaphrodite in her little house in the amusement park, all of which for her at twenty years old were encapsulated in the moment of that terrifying-exhilarating plunge of the cart on the *montagnes russes* of Orléans. That one-time sensation, the solitary, potent, inexplicable, perhaps irrepressible rapture that was echoed by the sensation of being one with that foreign body penetrating hers: Would it ever come again?

Her last two years in Edinburg passed as was expected of her; she was first in her class, first in everything she undertook, a favorite of male and female students alike, with whom she had unimportant flings or discreet affairs, none of which interfered one iota with the chosen direction of her life.

So there were no blemishes on her record when she was contacted by the Esplanade Institute For Psychology of Paris and eventually hired despite her lack of advanced academic degrees. In

Paris, Férnande lived in a walk-up apartment in Rue Valadon, around the corner from Place de L'Ecole Militaire and from the most famous market street in Paris, Rue Clair: specialty food stores, pastry shops, butchers, delicatessens, cheese specialists, fishmongers, greengrocers, chocolate shops and cafés. And a meeting point for future lovers. And as fate would have it, she and François-Marie Lecash met there at the fishmongers. He was good-looking, well-spoken, and moreover was a scientist, so what more could she desire? They drank a beer together at the street café and by that same afternoon they were in bed in her apartment from which was visible the Tour Eiffel. By the time darkness descended on Rue Valadon, they had just finished making love for the second time and she was lying on her back and observing the now illuminated Eiffel Tower. Férnande imagined that she was experiencing a preview of a future life together with François-Marie Lecash, scientist, yes, though only a minor scientist, in fact an ornithologist, which was no issue with her whatsoever. Major or minor, who cares? Yet from time to time, she thought that this day, this afternoon, this evening, had nothing to do with the Roller Coaster sensation of two years earlier. None whatsoever. Her deep feelings were what had counted that time in Orléans. Above all, her own feelings weighed. At twenty-two years old she was still a kid for her parents and a child for her grandfather. Life had its own hierarchy and its own plan for everyone, but Férnande felt she was outside of all that; she lived in a world apart, an unshareable world. Oh, she followed the rules; she was not a bohemian and did not even aspire to live an unconventional life. She would not delude the expectations of others, but she would remain Férnande, the outsider, the outrider in search of something only she knew. That search was her secret; only she knew about its existence, even though she herself was incapable of defining what exactly it was. To François-Marie's declarations and avowals of undying love, she responded in endearing terms of her "care" for him, of the gift of their togetherness.

Then, the surprise: Stuart, there in the outskirts of Rome. Not on their first meeting, not even during the first couple of sessions in her studio, but then, inevitably she later thought, the very air changed. The atmosphere in which they met changed . She perceived the air of the epoch of Luc, a lifetime ago, it now seemed. Not Luc the person; he had nothing to do with it. If she'd forgotten his last name years ago, now she could hardly call up the image of him the person. Hers was a deeper remembrance; she remembered herself of that period. Especially her inner self. There on the roller coaster she had felt herself as a separate, individual being, it seemed for the first time. No longer the daughter and granddaughter Volkov, that twenty year old woman who had perhaps cut the umbilical cord on that precipitous plunge on the roller coaster, which came to seem the most significant landmark of her life. And that individual magically merged with another. However, Stuart was not Luc; yet willy-nilly he had quickly become part of her life. Yet making love with him on the carpet of her studio recalled but was still not the same sensation of the roller coaster plunge. There you stand high above and then you plummet down displaying all your built-up power. Still, she considered Stuart, eight years after Orléans, a landmark too. Nonetheless, the idea that love had anything to do with it did not occur to her; Férnande looked into herself much longer, much harder than she did into her patients, into what she believed was her innermost self, her shadow self and admitted that what was generally spoken of as romantic love remained alien to her. She had liked the now ghost-like Luc; she "cared" for François-Marie; she had been exhilarated as never before making love with Stuart on the carpet; she loved to a certain extent mankind; although she loved her own life and being, romantic love for another person was beyond her.

Almost daily she spoke frankly, lovingly with Sophie about the question when they lunched together in a trattoria on Via Cassia just over the hill of La Storta. Sometimes even forgetting that Sophie was Stuart's wife, she plied her friend about the question of love:

"What is it?" she asked.

"When does it happen? Only as part of the sex act?"

"How do you know it's love and not just sex?"

The first time Férnande asked her such questions, Sophie looked her in the eyes for it seemed minutes before answering playfully that she fell in love with Stuart because of his height, hovering over her … and absorbing her. But she then admitted that she didn't know the answer:

"It just happens and you recognize the difference between liking or caring for or desiring another person. Yet though I sometimes consider my sexual drive maniacal—and that still after ten years together—maybe that's a sign of love. You specified 'romantic love', which is what I too have in mind."

"Maybe," Férnande said doubtfully. Thinking, thinking, dwelling on the very genesis, the etiology of the love that everyone around her talked about. Love? What is it? That property absent in her? Or was it still only elusive? That sensation, not only rare, but so minute as to pass you by and vanish forever into the ether if you turn your head in the wrong direction. Only then, during the great plunge on the roller coaster, had the sensation come. Just that one brief time, after which— as François-Marie's raven repeated so poetically—*Nevermore*. Was that one-time showing enough to be able to dichotomize the remainder of her life? No, she again warned herself: no binary thinking for me, no division of the world into either 'this' or 'that', 'good' or 'evil', with nothing in between, creating the conflict that most of my patients expect me to cure.

16.

That same day just up the street at the Fico d'India, Ermanno Riccardi spoke to his group which now included the red-headed chemist whom François-Marie couldn't keep his hands off of, so that Riccardi stopped several times in mid speech and cleared his throat to call the love-struck Frenchman back to their common objective: "By the way," he said, "they were your fucking birds … oh, I beg your pardon, Helen."

Stuart likewise was distracted and deviated from his experiences of dead crows and biological weapons and underground tunnels and trams. His mind kept returning to the Mashad carpet and Férnande's recessed eyes turning pale blue. An already inebriated Gianluigi was drinking nearly straight gin and visibly struggling to follow Riccardi's relation of his recent one-day blitz trip to Kiev and his meeting with the Operations Director of Ukraine's Security Service or UBU, its CIA. According to Ermanno, the UBU was run by Americans. "Those I met ALL spoke perfect English with American accents!"

"What the fuck were you doing there," Stuart exclaimed, shocked back to reality by the presence of one of Italy's high-ranking security men in Kiev.

"And if you'd only kept those crows in their cages where they belong," he said to François-Marie, "I wouldn't have seen them and found that raven and … and."

"And you wouldn't have known what dirty stuff your government was up to right here in your hamlet," Riccardi said as if he were not part of the government. "And Stuart, I was in Kiev to ask about their biolabs. They've got plenty of them and not only for producing botox. In fact they don't even need ours! They want to make Italy co-responsible for their war crimes—just in case a new Nuremberg threatens. So it's all for the best that the birds escaped and died and that you found them and that underground lab and exposed the

Forschungsinstitut on the hill. And listen, you people should see Kiev! I've been there many times but this time in the three hours I was there the air raid sirens sounded several times, all sham, just theater, so they could force visiting foreign dignitaries—a foreign President was there the same hours as I—down into shelters so they'd go back home and publicize the image of poor Ukraine under attack by big Russia and we've got to send more money!"

François-Marie pushed his chair back from the table, crossed and uncrossed his legs and ran his hand though his long silky hair, cleared his throat and said: "So what does all this mean for us in the Institute? Are our jobs in danger?"

"There will be an official government investigation," Riccardi said.

"But work can't continue under such conditions."

"In a way, it can and it will," Riccardi said. "My organization will report it to the control agency and that takes time. Then that agency will do its own study of the situation. Budgetary considerations will take precedence, of course. That takes more time. Hierarchy reigns supreme. Meanwhile the Institute will continue to produce botox. You never know. Ukraine is not the only country in the world that counts" he added enigmatically. "I will write memos and call urgent meetings. But other agencies will quickly forget. Besides, elections are coming up. Elections are always just around the corner … and if not here, then in the USA or to a much lesser degree in France or Germany … but all of which have more importance than what Italians in Puglia or Veneto think. Compartmentalization! Remember? In any case, I would say your jobs are secure for some years yet. Anyway, you surely don't want to make a career in that obscure Research Institute!"

François-Marie uncrossed and re-crossed his legs, cleared his throat and automatically covered Helen's hand with his own and said that was not very reassuring. By that time however everyone at the table knew that job or no job, his chief concern was Helen—somehow keeping her near.

"So why are we hanging around this place then?" Stuart asked, looking around at everyone at the table. "Have we finished?" He knew Gianluigi wanted to get home to his gin and vermouth as quickly as possible. François-Marie and red-headed Helen seemed more interested in a bed than birds or botox. And he himself was ready to leave the birds-botox question to Ermanno Riccardi and get back to dreams, shadow selves and the unfathomable pale blue depths of Férnande's eyes. But since this is a story with political overtones, an unconvinced Stuart mentally corrected himself: we can't dwell forever on the problems of new lovers or on a drinker's preferences or the ambitions of secret agents; by the same token, he couldn't get lost in the changing colors of a woman's eyes either.

He knew he was right on all counts.

"Before we break up today's meet," Ermanno said, "I want to ask Helen—whom I welcome to our project—if next time she would tell us exactly what botox is. We speak easily of nerve agents as if we knew what we're talking about. Meeting our friend Igor in Kiev showed me that when I first heard about the Russian soldiers and botox, I thought simply poison gas or mustard gas like in World War One, or some such. But I didn't really know the significance of what our biolab in San Nicola was producing. Helen as a chemist can clarify these matters."

17.

As they dispersed and while Riccardi spoke with Helen—he too apparently taken by her flaming red hair—François-Marie put a hand on Stuart's arm and asked softly about a nearby hotel. "One deserving of her!" he added, looking back toward Helen with a glow in his eyes. Stuart comprehended that today was the culmination of an intensive courtship and now that the time had arrived, he was making his commitment.

"The Imperial on Via Cassia, about eight kilometers straight south, Church style architecture," Stuart began rather hesitantly. Was he wronging Férnande by abetting her husband's affair? It reminded him of the story of King David an adaptation of which he'd recently used in a short story. David wanted the beautiful wife of his soldier Uriah so he ordered his general to send him to the front to be killed, after which David took his soldier's wife as his own. But God was displeased with King David. *'I have given you palaces and wives and kingdoms,'* God said, *'and now you have murdered Uriah and stolen his wife. Therefore, from now on, murder will be a constant threat in your family.'*

On the other hand, Stuart perceived his sending Férnande's husband off to the place of his assignment as a slight alleviation for his own ... his own, his own what? His betrayal? Yes, his betrayal of his love for Sophie with his clear and certain desire for the wife of another. But as far as the other actors in this play were concerned, betrayal of love was not a consideration: he knew that it was not a question of love between Férnande and François-Marie, nor was it a question of love between himself and Férnande—that he knew nothing about Helen herself was beside the point.

"It's never crowded, so no reservation is necessary," he said in a fake urbane manner. "Ask for a room in the back where the original rooms are bigger and better. I stayed there once."

"Thanks so much, my friend. An emergency, you see … or I wouldn't have asked. Things came to a head unexpectedly."

"Good room service too, if you go in for that sort of thing," Stuart added, cognizant of a hint of sarcasm in his words—"which I somehow doubt."

As Stuart turned to leave, Riccardi called from the table: Would he stay for a moment longer? The government agent and Gianluigi were again ensconced at the table. The Fico d'India was now empty except for them—even the waiters had vanished as if on command.

"There's more to the Kiev story than I said before. After I left my official meeting—arranged by the way by the Aisi-Aise chiefs themselves—I taxied back to the old City Airport where my private plane was waiting for the return flight when a man tapped my arm in passing; 'Ermanno! Remember me?' he said and kept walking. He was carrying a small valise as if departing. I did remember him. Very well, in fact. Igor is our best man in Ukraine. And he shouldn't have been there in that airport, in that corridor. I followed him. He entered an exit tunnel toward the reserved hangar space for secret flights entering and leaving Kiev. He stopped at a bend in the narrow passage where it was shadowy, nearly dark. 'We have ten seconds,' he said. 'I followed your meetings. I know what's happening here. You must know that Americans are running nearly everything here. Especially they are the real chefs of the UBU. Everything. I know of dozens of secret biolabs in this country alone. Here is a list. They are using or are ready to use botox … and much more,' he said, handing me a piece of paper folded into a tiny square. 'And of course they poisoned those Russian soldiers near Zaporozhe—which he pronounced in Russian—the last of them are dying now.'

"Now Igor is a sleeper. Once KGB as a young man when the Ukraine was part of the Soviet Union, he became Ukrainian UBU when the USSR was dissolved. When I asked him to hang on a while yet if he could, that things would get better soon, he answered:

'No, they will not get better. Nothing will ever get better in this land. Things will get worse. Much worse.'

"He was not afraid, not even of that bunch of Nazis or their US-run regime. But it was as if they had emptied him of himself, leaving him a shell. He felt worthless there. A shadow of what he once was. He would gladly remain a shadow but he and I both knew you can do that only so long. The longer I looked him in the eyes, the more I knew we had to save him.

"After his words 'no, things will get worse,' he rushed down to the hangars. I think he meant worse for himself. That's why I advised the AISE to get him out of there; that man is in danger and we owe him security—as much as possible in his line of work. It's not only a question of courage; few people have the nerves to resist.

"Secondly, AISE and its advisers have decided to keep the San Nicola lab open and running until we can see clearly what is happening in the world. I personally still think this Ukrainian thing is going to end soon—in Russia's favor. And Ukrainians are only a liability now—besides the so-called country is in shambles. But nonetheless—and I don't want to believe it—but I suspect that Igor is no longer alive."

18.

As the afternoon passed in the corner rear room that Stuart had recommended at the Imperial, François-Marie, attempting to control the passion that had overcome him, repeated reassuringly to Helen that they fit perfectly one into the other. And he would tighten his embrace as if fearful that now that their initial passion had quieted, she would soon escape, like Férnande always had, like his birds in the underground lab had done. For him, their sexual union seemed like the first time, as if he had lost his virginity. Each time he said that, she smiled contentedly and pressed harder against him in response. Their physical union, the union of the two still near strangers, was truly immediate, of the kind you rarely experience, in which every movement, even the slightest indication of a desire met the corresponding response. He interpreted the significance of their union in the very broadest physical sense, which though he had never experienced it before, he nevertheless considered it the basis of a future spiritual union, a kind of union that was alien to Férnande and truant in their relationship. Helen also understood the relationship between physical and spiritual union—she had divorced her Italian husband because of his lack of the latter.

"When I married Romano, I was too young. I misunderstood him: he had no idea of a relationship beyond the physical, which admittedly held me too—but for a limited time. Then when he started wandering, I said *arrivederci*."

Helen Peterson worked in the San Nicola Research Institute because of her background in chemistry—and only now did she reveal that her father, Roland Peterson, an Austrian from Klagenfurt, was a renowned ornithologist, one of whose books François-Marie had used in his studies of Central European birdlife. While Helen spoke of relations with her family, François-Marie stood up, looking at her and following her words, pulled on his boxer shorts and walked meditatively around the big room, his hands clasped behind his back and for one of rare times in his life he was cognizant of a woman's admiration of him physically—as if checking if he measured up to feminine expectations of the perfect lover. At the corner window, he was nevertheless taken momentarily by the view of the blue mountains rising on the horizon across Via Cassia, and to the West toward the sea, a flatland of fields marked by patches of woods and speckled in the distance by red-roofed houses. He followed the circling flight of several gulls testifying to the proximity of the sea near Ladispoli. Near a farm house, a horse, early afternoon shadows flickering over its strong brown body, nibbled at the rich green grass, occasionally looking around as if marveling that all this abundance was his. For a moment, François-Marie didn't believe that he was himself. Every aspect of what was happening between Helen and him seemed like hallucination. He felt he should struggle against the idea that he was really here in a hotel room with a beautiful sexy woman who was not only not his wife, but a stranger. But then Helen's voice interrupted his meditations to say that her mother was an Italian from Rome where they had lived off and on during her childhood. She herself had studied chemistry in Vienna in an English institution and later somewhere else before she too settled in Rome.

"If I only hadn't come to Rome!" she sighed. "That's where I married my short-time husband."

"But if you hadn't come back to Rome, you wouldn't be here today and I would've never known of your existence!" he said from the back window looking out over the green fields and a woods of tall trees that looked like another world in another time rather than that of the hamlet today and the Great Wall and the twin towers. On that ugly thought, he took off his shorts and returned to Helen's waiting arms. Was this all a dream? he wondered. A dream? Just a dream? If so, whose dream? It couldn't be reality. Yet everything that was happening, the drive out Via Cassia, the hotel, the total lack of secrecy or awkwardness in their behavior one to the other, had happened. It was reality. Only their desire and their bodies counted. There were moments when it seemed endless. Then he would be surprised that it had *already* finished. Too soon. Moments passed. Epochs passed and echoed. And he would remember briefly two thousand year old Tossa de Mar that July with Férnande, night after night in their discoteca singing *Dime cuando tu vendras.* That was another life, another epoch. Férnande who "cared" for me flirted with everyone and everyone wanted to fuck her, male and female. And she vaunted it there. In Tossa de Mar. She vaunted it. So that now, with Helen in his arms, what guilt was he to feel? Why should he feel guilty? And to whom was he responsible anyway? No, guilt was not the problem. Actually, now he knew that guilt was only a small part of it. The question of guilt alone once sufficed to make him feel homeless. More important than guilt had always been the shame. Recently he'd recognized that he'd always felt a sense of shame. Shame? Shame of what? Guilt and shame. He was considered a good-looking man, as he had when he was a boy. And 'promising'. Parents sufficiently well-to-do to send him to a good university. Yet there was the shame he hid in his inner self. His sense of guilt for his real interests. Parents and friends said he would get over his fixation on birds when he got out into the real world. Ornithology? Most people didn't even know what the word meant and besides it was just an expensive and useless hobby for a wandering intellectual, which he was not. It was surprising to François-Marie that ornithology was categorized even as a minor science. For heaven's sake, people thought, working in a cellar or a garage at a table covered with encyclopedias and charts and catalogs and the flocks of stuffed birds hanging on the walls. Something you did in your spare time after your real job earning a living, a collection you could take guests down to the cellar or to the garage to view. As if birds were something to get over. He gave up trying to tell them that birds are living beings after all. And a minor science? Is ornithology something to be treated and cured and take pills for? Gradually birds and studies of birds—he could name and identify thousands of them—came to echo as an accusation against him. Yes, he will get over it with time. Gradually he too came to feel a kind of shame about his ridiculed activity. His profession, his life work, Scientists were chemists and astrologists and psychiatrists. But ornithologists? A science? Even a minor one? Shameful! And François-Marie perceived an accumulated concomitant guilt. That guilt then marked his relationship with Férnande. But not here. Not with Helen. If they could just stay here forever. Why go home on the hill behind the Great Wall to a house exactly like all the others and distinguishable only by a number and to a woman who 'cared for him'? Why? There where his guilt for being a minor scientist, an ornithologist, and his resulting shame loomed. I don't want her care. I want sex and love. Fuck it all! No, Férnande, I reject your kind of care, your care for me. Not only sex, I also want love. And love doesn't come on command. You chose years ago; now I'm choosing too. I say, NO. No! No! I choose the Imperial with Helen and sex and love.

Helen—a real scientist—comprehends the role of ornithology in the Research Institute. And I can feel pride, not guilt; self-esteem, not shame. She's also in Ermanno's small team—a rogue secret service team. Helen will instruct us in the chemistry of botox, Botulinum toxin, she always calls it, respectful of its murderous power, she explained.

19.

In those same days, Stuart finally got to work on his already late column for the Glasgow magazine. He had never learned why the editors had granted him the vast latitude—almost a carte blanche—to write whatever he wanted. Rarely they might inform him that the next issues would pay attention to certain subjects: climate change, the effects of the European Union in the individual member nations, the future of a multipolar world, the changing role of literature. Rarely did his subject coincide, although, as a rule, his articles had a certain wide-ranging generality so that they fit in with the specificity of other articles.

Depravity Becomes Salvation

I will begin at a tricky and chancy time where I think literary people find themselves today. I am presently reading Walter Benjamin's ILLUMINATIONS. Now this project might seem considerably easier than reading complex Hannah Arendt, who edited this book of Benjamin's Essays and Reflections. That is not the case. The thing about Benjamin is that his beguiling style misleads you and you might think reading him is a piece of cake. That, however, is the mistake of taking fischi per fiaschi as Italians say any chance they get, literally "taking whistles for flasks", with the meaning of "barking up the wrong tree." For Benjamin, like a Pied Piper, on one single page can set so many innocent appearing traps and introduce such seductive prods to lure the reader off into dark perturbing labyrinths with its tunnels and sub-tunnels so that your head swims, vertigo arrives in wave after wave, and you spin like a top, undecided whether to close the book and get drunk on a fiasco *of Chianti or to follow him into a darkness so deep that you will need that proverbial red thread to find your way back out. That is Benjamin, whose work I will use as a springboard for this month's column.*

Today I studied his essay, The Storyteller, allegedly about the Russian fabulist, Nikolai Leskov, in which I naively hoped to gather Benjamin's thoughts on literary forms which I intended combining with the ideas of György Lukàcs in his THEORY OF THE NOVEL into a coherent discourse on the art of fiction writing. Instead, I found myself dealing with antinomian ethics, without an understanding of which ploughing ahead with The Storyteller was senseless. So I went to the web to learn that Antinomianism was born among Christian thinkers after the Protestant Reformation. The term Antinomianism was coined by Martin Luther himself to criticize extreme interpretations arising in the Free Grace Controversy: Antinomians believed that only faith, on the one hand, and divine grace, on the other, guaranteed salvation in the hereafter; merit and good works of mercy counted little. Today, as Benjamin helpfully points out, Antinomianism is the theological opposite of legalism and works of righteousness and obedience to Christian law, which, apparently, are never enough. By the same token, that belief may be applied to an individual who rejects a socially established morality: defiance of societal rules; that is, freedom from moral law. It seems then that this old form of Christianity—and unfortunately we're still thrashing around within it—would support both the White Supremacists and/or, at the same time, anti-bourgeois revolutionary morals and goals. Beautiful thought, indeed! You have faith, make a divine revolution and you gain salvation. Delightful conclusion, too. Muslims do it. Too many modern Christians have also converted to Antinomianism—without knowing it. Have your cake and eat it too is their credo. Still, to carry that a step farther, the same mechanism—faith in exchange for salvation—seems to work well for religious terrorists, Christian and surprisingly also Islamic fundamentalists, though I've never heard either of them called Antinomians.

Still, we know that radical Muslims—often, it seems, on some foreign payroll—believe the same. Antinomians all, albeit unbeknownst to themselves. Or, perhaps—and I introduce here the confusing element of the Islamic Bektashi Order who were similar to Antinomians: deviate groups in Turkish Anatolia and among some Sufis and former Ottoman intellectuals, people who abandon mainstream Islam and permit practices like drinking alcohol and not wearing the veil. Yell 'Allah u akhbar' as a sign of your faith, blow yourself up and carry fifty people with you to Paradise.

Seen in that light, revolution seems to have unexpected merits, both on Earth and in Paradise. Oh, the devil take such thoughts and also those of diabolical Benjamin that are running around absolutely wild, like weirdness unleashed. Unfettered. Unbridled. This is where mysterious, arcane and baffling Walter Benjamin—in my opinion, one of the major thinkers of the twentieth century—draws closer and closer to nineteenth century Fyodor Dostoevsky to the point that he writes: "depravity becomes saintliness" and I myself—and hopefully my readers, too—now understand what he meant. Both writers were seers: they foresaw the socio-political terminology and the absurdities of our times. And those two writers of different places and times prepared the way for new ideologies and counter-ideologies.

Ideology Today and Yesterday

You should therefore know that there are two ways to fight: one while abiding by the rules, the other by using force. The first approach is unique to Man; the second is that of beasts. But because in many cases the first method will not suffice, one must be prepared to resort to force. This is why a ruler needs to know how to conduct himself: in the manner of a beast as well as that of man.

Niccolo Machiavelli

Although our new epoch can hardly be defined as ideological, I believe Left and Right are still meaningful terms. Social-political maturity is movement toward Left, not away from it. History shows that when one abandons one faith for another, dogmatism threatens. Exes are a dangerous species. But one fact remains clear in the East and the West, in the North and the South: one must hate Fascism and its manifestations. Romantic dispositions! Rebellious inclinations! You have to be able to say no. Consequently, left ideology—of which Jean-Paul Sartre was a prime exponent—morphed not into philosophy or politics, but into morality. Nevertheless, one was not a moral man without a political ideology, and the only acceptable view was anti-bourgeois, anti-capitalist, anti-imperialist Marxism. Such views and such persuasions subsequently hang on, leaving enormous footprints behind.

The faith—and views—that a large group of leftist writers such as Gide, Wright, Koestler, Orwell, Chiaromonte, Silone, first embraced, then abandoned was a faith of all or nothing. Theirs was the great ideological swerve, the ideological turning point. For several decades earlier if you did not see the truth of Left absolutism like Stalinism, you were reactionary. Stalin and Stalinism has always been a conundrum for the left. At that point, Chiaromonte says, a religion of progress replaced integral atheism and in a sense united with the new universal God of progress. Happiness! Paradise on earth! In this view, the progressive God could be satisfied only by a will to progress pushed to the extreme limit that for some of them ended in totalitarianism. They looked right, rushed past Stalin and just kept going until they reached their goal.

The Grand Inquisitor in Dostoevsky's The Brothers Karamazov tells Christ returned to earth after fifteen centuries that "man only wants to be happy. Man wants earthly bread.

And that is the job of the Church (for Church, think totalitarian state): to guarantee man's happiness on earth. The Church," the inquisitor claims, "loves man more than does the Creator who placed on man's shoulders a burden too heavy to bear: the freedom of choice. Religion (think: State and ideology) must be for the masses. It must comfort all, the ignorant and the weak and the mean and the sick." Instead of the freedom and the uncertainty and suffering that the original Christ offers, the Church-totalitarian State offers happiness. Since the weak and hungry and mean masses are not interested in heavenly bread, the Church-State promises earthly bread. The Grand Inquisitor and his Church-State have chosen for man.In a chapter of twenty-one pages, the Grand Inquisitor articulates his devastating message: God is God and the Church is the Church; the Church does not believe in God and man no longer needs God; the Church promotes His work like a product and uses His name, but it renounces Christ; the Church does God's work for Him; it is a Church without God. The Grand Inquisitor and his Church have chosen for mankind. The Church's work, he says, is to correct Christ's work. The earth is thus the reign of mediocre happiness.

Jean-Paul Sartre

Dirty hands in literature refers to a leader who encounters a conflict of duties with values and must choose between alternatives, none of which are entirely satisfactory. In Jean-Paul Sartre's play Les Mains Sales (Dirty Hands), Communist leader Hoederer explains his view to the bourgeois, Hugo, who has joined the Proletarian Party in the fictive East European country of Illyria at the end of World War Two. Despite his love and admiration for Hoederer and the model he makes, Hugo is steadfast in his refusal to "dirty" his hands:

Hoederer: You hold so tightly to your purity, my lad. How afraid you are of dirtying your hands. Well, then, stay pure. But what good will it do, and why bother coming here among us? Purity is a concept of fakirs and friars. But you, the intellectuals, the bourgeois anarchists, invoke purity as the pretext for doing nothing. Do nothing, don't move, clasp your arms tight around your body, put on gloves. As for me, my hands are dirty. I have plunged my arms up to the elbows in shit and blood. And what then should one do later? Do you imagine it possible to govern innocently?

("Comme tu tiens à ta pureté ... comme tu as peur de te salir les mains. A qui cela servira-t-il et pourquoi viens-tu parmi nous? La pureté c'est une idée de fakir et de moine. Vous autres, les intellectuels, les anarchistes bourgeois, vous en tirez prétexts pour ne rien faire. Ne rien faire, rester immobile, serrer les coudes contre le corps, porter des gants. Moi j'ai les mains sales. Jusqu'aux coudes. Je les ai plongées dans la merde et dans le sang. Et puis après? Est'ce que tu t'imagines qu'on peut gouverner innocemment?")

Hugo is in total admiration of this man. Ecce homo, he apparently thinks. Hugo, the bourgeois convert who hangs onto some of his fundamental bourgeois values, nonetheless approves of the Nietzschian element in his hero Hoederer whom he professes to love more than he has loved anyone else in his life. Hoederer is the philosopher's "a man". He is the full human being. More than a Christ. A man who can say: Hear me!... and above all do not mistake me for someone else. The reality is that Hoederer loves other men with all their faults; Hugo loves the image of men as they could become.

But like Hoederer, Hugo too must distinguish opportunists from those who become infected with the disease of corruption through their sincere efforts to govern well. Hugo recognizes that self-serving opportunists rationalize their dubious measures through self-deceptive references to "the good of the whole" or that "the end justifies the means". So, for him, egocentric opportunism differs conceptually from dirty hands. The question thus remains open: Does corruption in the political realm arise as a result of the very nature of governance and morality? Do rulers simply have more opportunities for temptation and therefore succumb more often than do private citizens? Or does good governance sometimes require the sacrifice of moral standards as Machiavelli suggests and Hoederer believes? We see in nations worldwide that when corrupt governmental leaders are detected, society tends toward leniency in its "punishment" of them. Italy and the United States are both examples. But I don't believe this leniency reflects recognition of the problem of dirty hands in which setting people forgive and forget so easily the crimes of their governments. I think the reason for leniency is fear and awe vis-à-vis power. They don't want to risk punishment for dissent and social scorn for being "different". Yet, yet, Italian political leaders since Machiavelli have recognized that power truly corrupts.

It is an amazing curiosity to me writing this text in the third decade of the twenty-first century in my hamlet in Italy that Nathaniel Hawthorne over one hundred years earlier writing about the American Puritan society of the 1600s in his novel, The Scarlet Letter, approaches a moral theme similar to the modern one illustrated by Sartre in Dirty Hands—however from a different angle. His character, the Reverend Arthur Dimmesdale, in his life of everlasting guilt and penance for a previous violation of the severe moral code of his times in a moment of enlightenment feels driven to commit "some strange, wild, wicked thing or other, with a sense that it would be at once both involuntary and intentional: involuntary in his human rejection of an unfair social-moral code; intentional in that after seven years of suffering the pain of his penitence his most ardent desire is to say NO."

Dimmesdale thinks: "No man, for any considerable period, can wear one face to himself, and another to the multitude, without finally becoming bewildered as to which may be true." Dimmesdale's penance is transformed into an accusation against an entire bigoted, hypocritical and mendacious Puritan society of the New England of the 1600s, which remained branded on subsequent generations of its descendants, including those of the Nineteenth century when his creator Nathaniel Hawthorne wrote, and so on until today as seen in the American reverence toward corrupt power, and one hundred and seventy years since he wrote The Scarlet Letter. In the two books, The Scarlet Letter, set in the seventeenth century and Dirty Hands set in the twentieth, the two self-sacrificing social leaders, Hoederer the Proletarian and Reverend Dimmesdale the Moralist feel they are the chosen, the elect destined to perform the supreme acts for which they are willing to die, acts beyond the reach of common man.

20.

When François-Marie turned on his computer the next morning, the big yellow letters jumped off the opening first page spelling out: "Beyond the Limits". His device was old, but this morning in the Hotel Imperial the words—Beyond the Limits—leapt straight into his brain where it would be lodged all day. His first thought was Férnande. His first limit. Not only did *she* limit *him*; she demeaned him. His minor science! Therefore, she must think him likewise minor. Day after day, the same refrain. Like a line or the melody of an old song you might have heard the evening before that haunts you the next day. The exact words you've forgotten, the melody escapes you, but the essence of the song remains. And the more you tell yourself not to think about it, it keeps coming back. In unthinking moments or while reading a complex document or speaking with another person, the words "beyond the limits" would echo in his mind. What did it really mean? Or was it a symbol, a very general one? You buy a new computer, an *Ordinateur* in his native France, and it tells you to *Go Beyond the Limits With Us.* Were those words the same in all languages? Was the meaning the same? Was there no need to interpret them? Were there hidden meanings? Or did the words suggest to others to do different things? It was as if something or someone were directing him in new directions. He perceived that the words went straight into an old and trusty synapse of his mind. Technology had already taken that step toward the beyond: artificial intelligence, AI, was already flooding the universities. The beyond lay beyond the limits that he should follow. But hang on a moment! The key word here was of course *beyond*. Limits have been established. Down through the epochs, over and over again—limits. Many have been fixed by religion. Others by a generalized human morality. In a way, he thought, it's disguised propaganda. Propaganda at its apogee. Only slightly different from the best of commercial advertising. But nonetheless the *beyond* lay beyond limits after all. He'd seen those same yellow letters looking out at him every morning for years, but he'd never reacted, never even considered the words, never so much as thought about the words there before his eyes while the computer booted. Yellow letters, yellow stars! Beyond the Limits! Go for it! A symbol. A very broad one. Symbolic of itself, he thought. Did it transcend the artistic propagandists who coined it for this computer? The meaning must be: 'You too can have it all' It was saying that most people led such puny lives that they needed reassurance that they are already beyond the limits each time they open this device. 'Going beyond' had likely been lodged in his deepest sub-conscious. Camus would turn over in his grave. He got the Nobel for disagreeing. Live like the Greeks of antiquity, he said poetically. Recognize life's limits. Observe the boundaries of reason. As Camus emphasized, we of today put the impulse of will in the center of reason, which has had deadly results. For the Greeks, values pre-existed all action, of which they set definite limits. Man today places values at the end of action instead of before. Limits in that sense are therefore not something that *is* but that which *is becoming* and we will not know them until the end of history. Well, one thing is sure, François-Marie thought, this time I have gone beyond … and I'm going much farther in this my private affair and I have no need of a late model computer for instructions or for philosophers to define my limits. He hadn't seen the need or value of informing Férnande that he would not be home last night; and now the view of red tousle-headed Helen through the open door to the sitting room confirmed his resolve to go farther, far beyond the limits. Yet he kept in mind Camus' terrible warning that the Greeks never said that the limit could not be overstepped and that whoever dared exceed it was struck down. When Camus wrote that in 1948 he had found nothing in present history that contradicted his reasoning. François-Marie thought the unforeseen was like that: unpredictable. Yet more often than you think, you imagine the future holding as if in reserve something grand for you. Oh yes, most certainly you do have a life plan—well, maybe not a precise plan—let's say a hope for a life—and you think things in your planned life, maybe a normal life, are proceeding accordingly. And you realize that life consists of many, countless little things, repetitive things you may do every day: You get up and do little things in the bathroom, wash the gook from your eyes or shave or whatever; you might return to bed for another moment of love with your wife or lover; you dress and breakfast; you go to work; during the day you deal with little things and return home for dinner and whatever little things are to be tended to. You look at the calendar: two more days before the weekend interruption and you perform different little operations and you think you are happy and that this is life. Little things! Until the day bad fate steps forward to play its hand. Let's say by way of example, until your beloved dog, best friend and companion, vanishes. No explanations. Run over by an eighteen-wheeler truck? Kidnapped? Or just maybe its animal nature prevailed in its dna and it ran away with the pack. Who knows such things? Kafka's Joseph K. doesn't know what he is accused of even when he is condemned … unknown to what. For Kafka, we are all guilty. Guilty because of that indestructibility of our deep inner self. You can be evasive all you want, but you are guilty because of that indestructibility. No, that will not do at all. Power must break you. Meanwhile, Joseph K. just goes on living a normal life of little things until one day two very courteous men take him out and cut his throat. The ultimate attack on human dignity. Why? You don't know. It's all so natural. Normal. And that too is life, they say. Little things or objects, or big things and objects, are different from people; things may remain and be passed down to the next generation. We can hold them and love them but things have a different destiny from people. Interpretation! The meaning may be that which happens to Joseph K. is the representation of Camus's absurdity of the human condition: he lives and is condemned and never knows of what, never knows what is happening or why. Stuart says that the ultimate dreamer who dreamed it all has the answer. But responsibility for what happens is another matter. Still, François-Marie prefers to consider everything just so much *merde*. A mere turd of merde. But his hero Camus says that 'man cannot do without beauty and this is what our era pretends to want to disregard. It steels itself to attain the absolute and authority; it wants to transfigure the world before having exhausted it; to set it to rights before having understood it.' No matter that in his second and third years in his general course at the university in Paris, they had analyzed and debated Existentialism all the way back to Kierkegaard. Then he re-learned that the Greeks had placed boundaries and limits to will—before the happening, not afterwards like in international pacts and accords that few hold to anyway. Disproportion itself. Like Heraclitus's conflagration. Minor science indeed! The words drove him crazy. His dream in his first night in Helen's arms returns to him in shocking clarity: He's walking down a rather narrow road and sees coming toward him a flock of peacocks, beautiful peacocks, all with their trains of tail feathers spread and some are making rattling sounds. The vision of color in movement occupying the entire space before him is frightening. He slows but continues moving forward and as he approaches the ambulatory flock, they make space for his passage and cluck-cluck in approval of him, François-Marie Lecash, the bird scientist. He perceives their approval. Tell the dream to your wife, someone may suggest. She might have an idea—it's her job. Tell it to Férnande? His dream? Not a chance. The peacock is beauty. Beauty of the soul. Beauty surrounds him, applauds him, loves him. On the other hand, he admits that he no longer sees the beauty in Férnande even though he knows it is there; he knows he is unjust and blind.

He sits down beside Helen and as minutes before he'd so desired when he saw her through the open door waiting for him, he runs his hand through her red tousled hair just as he does his own, which somehow reminds him of peacocks feathers and he tells her the dream. When she asks what he thinks it means he tells her about a visit to a peacock farm with his high school class when he was about seventeen .

"Actually it was a normal agricultural farm but the farmer's wife who was Iranian loved her country's nationalistic symbol of the peacock and raised them herself. Our teacher, a fervent communist and opposed to the Shah, apparently didn't know beforehand about the Iranian monarchist wife or he would have chosen another farm to show to the students the corn and potato fields and hogs raised brutally and slaughtered even more brutally. Henceforth, he always started his lessons with the date 1953—that I remember well. The main point of the lessons was the date when the USA organized a coup d'état in Tehran and overthrew the democratically elected moderate socialist leader Mohammad Mossadeq because he nationalized Iran's petroleum—not because he was pro-Soviet as some claimed—and installed its vassal Shah Pahlavi as head of a state that he ruled together with the cruel, U.S.- run SAVAK secret police. In my sketchy, romantic memory of that evening with the peacocks at the farm, night has fallen and lights from the country house illuminated—eerily in my dream-like remembrance—the sprawling yard and its big trees from which the peacocks observed us. But more significantly for my dreamscapes and my subsequent life, their avian brothers on the ground theatrically spread their tail trains, their many colors sparkling in the night under the eyes of rows and rows of peacocks thickening the spreading branches of the peacock trees. You know, Helen, I think it was that almost unearthly scene and the beauty of the peacocks roosting on the illuminated tree branches that night that led me to ornithological studies. I would like to ask your father about the significance of peacocks. I don't regret one minute of my minor science; it took me all over the world for a few years … until I met Férnande. But I still dream of those peacocks."

"François-Marie, have you never thought that maybe you gave up too much for another person, instead of being yourself—as I once did too?" "Oh, yes. Yes, I did. But you know, it didn't seem like a sacrifice at the time. I was still doing what I wanted, just without the world travels. Still, I did go to India … on the trail of the peacock—the paon. To India where it originated. Their national bird. Its feathers in peoples' houses to ward off evil and bring good luck and prosperity. In Iran and in Indian stories, I learned about the origins of the Peacock Throne which each new shah *ascended*. The original throne, built for the Mugdal Emperor of India in the early seventeenth century, is remembered as the most resplendent throne ever made. The throne was ascended via silver steps and stood on golden feet set with jewels and was backed by representations of two open peacocks tails, gilded and enameled and inset with diamonds, rubies and other stones. The Mugdal throne was seized along with other plunder when the Iranian conqueror, Nadir Shah, captured Delhi in 1739. The Shah had a divan made in the same style and took it and the Peacock Throne back to Iran, only to lose both to the Kurds who tore them down and distributed the precious stones. Later Peacock Thrones or divans were made for subsequent *shahs*. The dazzling thrones used by the two Pahlavi shahs at their coronations in 1926 and in 1941 were reproductions of the ancient Peacock Throne.

"I went to the Indian state of Kerala, Communist by the way, on the southern tip of India, which devotes twenty percent of its area to the raising of peacocks, so much so that after a man was hit and killed by a peacock in Kerala, the spotlight fell on the increasing population of peacocks in that state, like the wild boar right here where we live that people even club to death.

"So you see Helen Peterson, as you know from your father, to refer to ornithology as a minor science is not only reductive, it's nonsense: it's unclassifiable. It's animal life, it's climate, it's food, it's security—it's philosophy and the world."

"François-Marie Lecash, my father will love *you*. He's never liked the types I seemed to fall for—especially not playboy Romano. Why, I can hardly remember his last name."

"I can imagine the men hanging around you—all trying to bed you."

"That's what my father says … and he was right. Some did."

"Some did what?"

"Bed me! But being with you is not the same thing. It's different. The reason I said my father will love you is because, well, you're the most sensitive person who ever did bed me. He says only very sensitive people love birds deeply."

"Whoever bedded you? I hope it's more than that."

François-Marie understood from the way Helen just looked back at him that he would soon meet her father. They were no longer kids, but he believed that Roland Peterson too was to be important in his life—in one way or the other.

And strangely, Férnande Volkov was fading, fading, like a falling angel. No ill will, no enmity, not even rancor toward her for the wasted years of his life. She had been honest from the start: while he thought he loved her, she cared for him! She said so. Nor did they ever become real friends. She was still a stranger. *Fini, schluss*. One door closed, ever so softly. Another opened, through which Helen entered.

"Helen, what if we stay here in the hotel in one of their apartments, together, near our work, you far from the city and I far from the Great Wall, the roundabout garbage dump and that crazy hamlet?"

"I'll go for that. But anyway I very much want to see the hamlet and the underground that you know well. They won't let me even get near the that part of the lab."

"Ok. Why not? Anyway, I spoke to the manager and there's a three-room apartment with a kitchen just down the hall and we can move in anytime we want. About the underground lab, maybe Stuart who has keys can sneak us down into the lab that he calls the Tartarus pit … from Greek mythology. We can also visit Professor Logreco while we're there—whom you know as Gianluigi—another of your admirers."

They arrived at the Research Institute compound in separate cars at one of the two times of day when an outside observer could see evidence of activity at the obscure former naval station on Via della Storta about two kilometers from the township: the opening of steel gates at 9:30 a.m. and official closure at 5:30 p.m. Nonplussed and unhurriedly Helen and François-Marie reached their respective offices to begin their guerrilla sabotage of the Institute's chemical warfare: the chemist, Helen, in her war against the criminal usage of botulinum toxin; the ornithologist, François-Marie, in defense of birdlife and in the name of morality.

When at eleven, the other employees retired to the bar downstairs, Helen rushed to a deserted room she had spotted in advance where there was an unused computer and a dusty printer. She put on thin gloves, plugged in her pen drive and printed thirty copies of her manifesto that she had written on a computer in a downtown bar. She left two copies in conspicuous places in each of the eight offices including her own and that of François-Marie, after which she rushed to the bar and soon had a ring of men around her— red-headed, indestructible Helen was very much present in the bar with all those adoring men when the dirty act was perpetrated.

I wrote this manifesto because chemists like myself have created the most terrible chemical weapons capable of devastating civilian populations of the world. In my opinion, unscrupulous chemists also created the worldwide pandemic of Covid-19 and its variants. I have dedicated my scientific background and my acquired knowledge to exposing these criminal and inhuman creations and their use. And I call on chemists of the world to rise up and join me and like-minded chemists in our opposition, and say NO! No to this travesty.

I support the Chemical Weapons Convention, the CWC, which is a multilateral treaty that bans the development, production, acquisition, stockpiling, transfer, and use of chemical weapons and requires all possessor states to destroy their stockpiles safely. The CWC is by no means enough but it is all we have to protect mankind from us. For even the United Nations Security Council voted against probes into U.S. biolabs.

A chemical weapon is any toxic chemical that can cause death, injury, incapacitation, and sensory irritation, deployed via a delivery system, such as an artillery shell, rocket, or ballistic missile or spray guns. Chemical weapons are weapons of mass destruction and their use in armed conflict is a violation of international law.

Chemical weapons include nerve agents, blister agents, choking agents, and blood agents. These agents are categorized based on how they affect the human body.

Nerve agents are the most deadly of the different categories of chemical weapons. In liquid or gas form nerve agents can be inhaled or even absorbed through skin lesions. Nerve agents inhibit the body's respiratory and cardiovascular capability by causing severe damage to the central nervous system, and can result in death. The most common nerve agents include Sarin, Soman, and VX. The last is a human-made chemical warfare nerve agent, the most toxic and rapidly acting of chemical warfare weapons of the present.

Blister agents are transmitted in the forms of gas, aerosol, or liquid. They cause severe burns and blistering of the skin. They can also cause complications to the respiratory system if inhaled and of the digestive tract if ingested. Common forms of blister agents include Sulfur Mustard, Nitrogen Mustard, Lewisite and Phosgene Oximine.

Choking agents are chemical toxins that attack the body's respiratory system when inhaled and cause respiratory failure. Common forms: phosgene, chlorine, and chloropicrin.

Blood agents interfere with the body's ability to use and transfer oxygen through the bloodstream. Blood agents are generally inhaled and then absorbed into the bloodstream. Common forms: Hydrogen Chloride and Cyanogen Chloride.

Certain common industrial chemicals, such as chlorine, are not prohibited under the 1997 Chemicals Weapons Convention, but the treaty prohibits their use as weapons. Similarly, riot control agents, such as tear gas, are considered chemical weapons if used as a method of warfare. According to the convention, states can legitimately possess riot control agents and use them for domestic law enforcement purposes, but states that are members of the Chemical Weapons Convention must declare what type of riot control agents they possess. I oppose riot agents in any form, in any place. My opposition is my mission in life.

That morning, François-Marie, who never went to the bar at the assigned time—an absence which cast immediate suspicion on him even though he was not a chemist. And so opined the technician responsible for the Institute communication network, who shared the office with him even though he was seldom there; François-Marie believed he was also the assistant to the security chief just across the hall from him. The putative security man rushed into the office and found the ornithologist absorbed in some document about birds, he assumed, while from several meters distance away he noted the copy of the now ill-famed manifesto lying to the side of the Frenchman's desk, marked by red underlings and hand-written remarks. He picked up the copy glaring at him suspiciously from the middle of his own desk, glanced over it, shrugged in disgust, threw it into a wastebasket, looked dismissively at the prissy bird-lover and walked out.

When that evening they met Ermanno and the others at an obscure trattoria a kilometer beyond Olgiata, the first subject on the agenda was Helen's reading of her manifesto and what, if any, countermeasures should be undertaken to protect her and François-Marie from discovery. Helen read the first paragraph aloud and passed copies around to the others.

"Friends, it's not by pure chance that I work in the Institute biolab or that I joined this group. I am here because chemists like myself have created the most terrible chemical weapons capable of devastating civilian populations. In my opinion chemists also created the worldwide pandemic of Covid-19 and all its derivatives—no less toxic than the enemy's military forces on the battlefield. I have dedicated my scientific background and acquired knowledge to exposing these criminal and inhuman creations and their use.

"Google, "she continued—"not the most honest of sources—reports some surprising numbers. First of all, that there are fifty-nine biolabs in the world producing the deadliest of pathogens—in reality there are many, many times more considering the official USA-run forty-six biolabs in Ukraine alone! Besides the USA has three hundred and thirty-six mostly secret labs in the homeland. The real numbers most likely run in the thousands. Every year, young chemists just finishing their studies are looking for jobs; many accept whatever they find.

"Therefore I call on chemists of the world to rise up and join me and like-minded chemists in our opposition, and say NO! No, to this travesty and demand that biolabs be tightly controlled so that chemists can perform the jobs they train for: the development of medicines and products that serve man."

Ermanno was puzzled by the enormity of what he so lightheartedly had created. Something that had started with a snow storm, fifteen dead crows and a press item reporting the botox death of an undetermined number of Russian soldiers in a small hospital near Zaporozhe. Now after Helen's words, he suspected he could be witnessing the genesis of an international protest movement opposing biolabs worldwide, and besides in open opposition to the United States and European Union, which he—as a high-ranking intelligence officer of AISI—had sworn to defend. Like a word once spoken could never again be unspoken, he saw no way to undo what he had done. At the same time he saw the word TREASON in big red letters flash across the arc of his vision. His country's real powers took an extremely dim view of anything that distanced it from the USA and the EU. Now fifteen dead crows that he should have known about and the lab that was one of his projects put him in a bad light. Not only crows die, he thought, people too die. Still, he'd felt flattered when the Greek brought Stuart-Stuart to tell him about the birds. After which matters moved rapidly in multiple directions. He made the one day's trip to Ukraine anyway … good PR for himself and shows a Riccardi on the ball, alert to details. The lunch with Gianluigi and Stuart had set things in motion, unstoppable things, and quickly the three-man lunch transformed into the Group as he referred to it; first François-Marie. Why that Marie? he thought. Another of his dislikes: Maria or Marie as a second male name. Was he/it an hermaphrodite? Still, he'd loved the actor Gian Maria Volonté in the film *Investigation of a Citizen Above Suspicion.* Ermanno was cognizant that he showed too many eccentricities for an intelligence agent and tried to suppress or transform them into exceptional qualities inherent to the profession. Then François-Marie introduced his flame, Helen, the red-head who, contrary to Ermanno's experience with gorgeous women, turned out to be a totally different kettle of fish. Thus his excruciating doubt about himself for his misreading of everyone present. Himself included. Excruciating? he wondered. Can doubts be excruciating? Well, his were. His second wife left him for that very reason: his doubts, she had charged. Nonetheless, he was not used to doubting himself and his instincts. And as this red-headed fireball understood, she did not necessarily need him to organize her young chemists of the world. That lady had the makings of a revolutionary. A rebel who had found a cause. Just a word from him could easily get her fired, but the collateral damage would be worse: it would make her both a martyr and besides a full-time professional revolutionary. His famous instinct about people and their motivations was shaky indeed. It must have been her hair, he thought. And what about her French boyfriend? Bird-lover. Was he made of the same stuff as the red-head? Ermanno doubted it. He would speak with his pal Gianluigi about him. And as far as doubts were concerned, what about the self-proclaimed communist, Stuart-Stuart. Don't trust anyone with the same first and last name, he muttered under his breath … and felt better for it. Nothing that man would like better than finding something Communist to join. His to-do list: ask their man in Glasgow to send him back copies of the Scottish magazine Stuart wrote for. He suspected what he would find there: the usual left-wing armchair communist comments on international matters no one could challenge anyway. Even his old pal Gianluigi Logreco, who was he really? Who knows what he truly thinks about anything when sober? Like Freud and Jung must have felt of their failure in that they couldn't reach the utmost depths of the human psyche where man's most secret self was embedded. Gianluigi didn't leave AISI only for the Greeks, he thought. Was he already back then a secret drinker? Or did he already have other political-ideological obligations? Greek mythology after all was a unique cover. Ermanno thought he knew the details of all the important parts of his old friend's life. They had practically grown up together in Puglia, went to the university in Rome together, and had many of the same friends. BUT, not all, he remembered. After Ermanno married the first time, there was a secret woman in Gianluigi's life ... who suddenly disappeared. Who was she? Slavic, it seemed. What happened to her? There must be more to his story. Or was the Slav he loved a he? Thinking such thoughts, Ermanno told himself that he had a very suspicious mind.

After Helen read her manifesto, he cut the meeting short, again asking Gianluigi and Stuart to remain. He would reveal casually, very casually, some of his doubts. And he had doubts! If the others only knew! No, things could not go on like this; there were people and people. Some persons could and must be trusted. Yes, I will share what knowledge I have gathered. The three sat at the table: Ermanno uncertain, Stuart distracted by thoughts of Férnande, Gianluigi drunk and dreaming of bottles of gin.

"Here is the overall situation in a nutshell for both of you to mull over," he began:

"Russia presented evidence of the use of biological weapons by the United States and Ukraine.

"US pharmaceutical giants oversee military biological programs in Ukraine.

"The Pentagon is moving incomplete Ukrainian projects of biochemical research to Central Asia and other Eastern European countries.

"The transfer of bio-research to third countries allows the USA to deny its existence.

"The United States is blocking laboratory inspections through the Biological Weapons Convention (BWC).

"Work in US biological laboratories for the production of pathogenic bacteria is carried out without clear control."

21.

Stuart navigated the Elevated over the ex-roundabout and made his curvy way to the gate where the lone guard waved him through the Great Wall. At home, he fell into the huge bed and straight into Sophie's calling arms. Love without dialogue. Love without analysis or with Mashad carpets spread in his mind. Back in Sophie's arms where he knew he belonged forever and ever, amen. Back into an embrace he understood and loved. Enough running up that hill. Enough therapy at the top. Enough mystery and strange encounters on thick Persian carpets with a stranger who wants to be him. His shame. His guilt.

Now Stuart didn't consider himself a liar by nature. He didn't resort to little white lies about the silly situations that arise in everyday life: Did you telephone x, as you promised this morning? Yes, of course. He would call in the afternoon, so what difference did it make? He hated the falsehoods all around us like, from advertisers and nasty people trying to sell us something or to destroy the reputations of others. He didn't lie just to attract attention. But this, his strange and confusing relationship with Férnande was a brutal deception of Sophie which he had allowed to happen, chiefly because of his maniacal fascination with the world of dreams. Férnande was like an alien in his heretofore seamless ten-year relationship with his wife. He had thus discovered the significance of a deep lie and it sickened him: he hated being in the position of feeling he had to lie to the person he loved most in life, thus dichotomizing their relationship in such a way as to create a sort of inequality between them, as if he were to some degree superior to her: as if he could lie or not lie to her at will and *sans arrieres pensées,* or that Sophie was inferior because she accepted his lies used cowardly to get out of tight situations. And in any case, he felt he had degraded their relationship each time he ran up that hill. He also recognized the reality that Sophie was Férnande's friend; they worked almost vis-vis, Férnande on the hill and Sophie in the valley.

They often lunched together, two intelligent and open young women—natural that they would eventually confide in each other. But come what may, Stuart didn't want to know any more details. From this moment, any relationship at all with Férnande would be of a sincere therapeutic nature. And hopefully she would send that Mashad back to where it came from.

In the late morning, Gianluigi rang their doorbell, Stuart and Sophie later assumed because of the enormous hangover that had left him so nervous, as he said, he felt he would jump out of his skin. He'd missed his two classes and by the time he'd gathered the courage to call his faculty, it was too late. "As the Greeks say, fuck it all," he muttered without a sign of embarrassment since that was Sophie's lingo too. Ignoring his plea for at least a beer they got him to a comfortable divan and gave him a hot tea spiked with a few drops of a liquid tranquilizer and two aspirins during which procedure the professor insisted on relating to them his incubus, he believed, early this morning in which gigantic worm-like creatures threatened to eat him like the whale did Jonah. "The huge pinkish giant worm was at least ten meters long with a body the size of a lion. I kept walking toward it, it toward me. I kept searching for its mouth but never found it. Maybe it was in his tail."

Sophie laughed and said: "Fucking dreams, fucking worm-filled dreams!"

Stuart chuckled, not at the dream, but at Sophie's linguistic reaction. In reality, he wanted nothing to do with dreams and nightmares either so he broke down and went to the kitchen pantry and brought Logreco a beer … to Gianluigi's surprised delight.

"So what's the news from the front," Stuart asked, aware that hangovers alone never sufficed to keep the professor away from his lectures, the one place in the world he felt safe and secure, as he expressed it, "in this modern world of turmoil." In that same moment, the cat rubbed against his leg in greeting on which Professor Logreco sneezed loudly several times. The cat scampered away, and Stuart said, "Ciao, Paco, *non importa*, he's a friend despite his allergies."

"Not everyone thinks so," the professor said. "Like not everything we've ever done in our lives is fixed forever. Time passes. Things change. We change. We're not the same today as we once might have been … even if ever so briefly. My big mistake was joining AISI, too young to know what I was doing, to understand its purpose and my potential role in it. The ancient Greek political philosophers taught that man is by nature a political being. By this they meant that human beings are suited naturally–by nature—for life in a particular sort of community, a polis. My problem has always been to which polis I belong."

PART TWO

22.

It was Saturday, a week since they moved into the rear apartment at the Hotel Imperial. Over a late breakfast, Helen asked if he didn't feel the need for a normal social life, like friends for dinner, an evening in an intimate wine cellar, an art show, a film now and then—well, that kind of thing. "Not when I have you," he said, cognizant of the difference, if not a dichotomy between them, of which in the moment of their first passion he'd been unaware. He still felt like a loner; she was a social animal, an existential fact he could not ignore, as if their views on how life should be lived didn't matter. He'd already perceived in her signs of a growing sense of isolation. Now she'd made that clear. For her, a week in the Imperial was exciting and appealed to her sexual nature, but now that the newness of what some might imagine just another relationship between office colleagues was winding down, it was up to him to make some adjustments or their togetherness would soon prove to have been an illusion, no more than an ordinary short-term fling. "But I've been selfish in holding you in hiding in the Imperial Hotel. Actually, a social life—our coming out, so to speak—is fine with me. You're too beautiful to live holed up in this hotel and the Institute. In fact we two make a handsome couple—and moreover, two scientists, one major and one well-traveled minor."

He suggested they visit the hamlet—"a little like going abroad," he said." A strange, in some ways a futuristic abroad that he knew somewhat, he mused: the Elevateds, the ex-roundabout, the labyrinth, the Great Wall and the twin towers, the hillside where he once lived, the long Via San Nicola, the trapdoor to the underground laboratory. They could drop in on Stuart and Sophie and maybe Professor Logreco too—a start in a social life even though perhaps not exactly what she had in mind. But her eyes did light up when he mentioned the trapdoor; she was curious about the ultimate result of her work.

"I want to go down into the innards of the Research Center," she said. Those sixteen Russian soldiers are still on my conscience."

And so shortly before noon they drove slowly over the South Elevated at which Helen looked down on as from a plane from New York or Tehran on its final approach to Leonardo da Vinci Airport. "What's that mess down there?" she asked. "And where's the incinerator? I didn't know the city's major disposal center was so close."

"That mess down there was once a traffic roundabout marking the entrance and the exit from Casale di San Nicola. Now people dispute whether its aim is to keep strangers out of San Nicola or to keep residents in. Helen, hold your breath and crack your window a bit."

She did. "God in heaven, what the fuck is that?" she gagged and closed the window.

"That mess is everything. Trash and junk and garbage from God knows where, wild animals, some alive eating others. Everything rotting, undisturbed. This is one of the reasons there's so little traffic in and out of San Nicola. But wait till you see the rest," François-Marie said as they entered the twisting approach road to the Great Wall.

"For heaven's sake," Helen said, "who wants to travel this route."

"Nobody that lives here does ... well, actually some of the old people don't mind. They feel protected by all the obstacles." After a dozen or so sharp changes of direction, Helen began to giggle which ceased when the two German guards stepped into the gate under the twin towers. "Why, they're the guards or something at the Institute. So that means that whoever runs the Institute also runs San Nicola."

"Right. I know them pretty well, and I think I'm still on the San Nicola Control Commission. Nearly all of its members are Institute personnel," he said, lowering his window and handing the guard his pass. "We can go to the top of the tower on the left for a good view of the area … including the Radio Vatican transmitter masts and its walls too."

"Why don't we save that for the next time?"

"Ok. We're at the right time to visit Stuart and Sophie. Maybe they'll ask us to lunch—and you'll get to know Sophie," he added … deciding not to speak of Sophie's friendship with his wife. In this moment, he told himself, Férnande was a stranger, distant from his new life. But deep down in his inner self he was aware that was more desire than reality. Férnande still had a foot in the door to his heart and someday might push it open again. At times he had the sensation that he was living a hiatus, like on a sabbatical; a leave of absence from Férnande and that Helen was a metaphor for vacation time. Maybe temporariness was the reason he'd preferred the hotel residence rather than taking a more permanent apartment in La Storta or Olgiata. He'd momentarily taken leave of permanence. Not a sensation he desired, but from the depths of him an obsessive preference for temporariness kept resurfacing. Was change always like that? he asked himself. Though changes—changes of direction as well as internal changes—had occurred and continued to occur. Thus far in his lived life it seemed that something of the past always remains … or returns. He had undergone changes before; this time however he'd hoped for more: he'd hoped for a complete transformation of himself of before. He wanted what lay in the beyond as suggested by those yellow letters on his computer spelling out "beyond the limits. The changes he'd undergone thus far in life only affected the past, reforms of what had been. That past was dangerous, and sometimes, he knew, the distant past returns, victorious. He now yearned for the kind of transformation that would change his future life, in which he would be free of his guilt and his shame of his non-science, his old-fashionedness, his love for real things like the animal world. The changes he had faced were insufficient; they barely grazed his consciousness.

They were like the air through which he passed, untouched and unaltered. He wanted more. He wanted to wake up and feel that he was now a different François-Marie Dolon, metamorphosed into a new being. He looked sideways at Helen and wondered if she were the one to help him keep alive the spark of transformation.

Sophie welcomed them warmly and spoke so openly in her spontaneous language that her passing mention of Férnande rang natural to Helen who responded in the same manner and conversation moved on to Institute affairs and Helen's role in Ermanno's anti-chemical warfare group.

While lunching on the shaded terrace Helen said casually that they were headed to the underground lab … if they succeeded in getting in. It was the weekend and most likely no other visitors would show up. Besides, as employees they had a certain right to be there, François-Marie said, adding that he had snitched some keys at the Institute that would hopefully work.

"No problem," Stuart said. He went to the kitchen and returned with his two keys. When Helen insisted they come along, Stuart said that four persons entering through the trapdoor would be like tempting fate and that besides, he as a non-employee had no right to be there. To Sophie's disappointment, he declined, but he briefed them on the trapdoor mechanism, the ladder down into "Professor Logreco's Tartarus pit", the light switch, the tram and the tunnels each with its own tunnels and the cages that he'd found opened shortly after they discovered the fifteen dead crows.

So after coffee, François-Marie and Helen set out to explore the San Nicola depths. Leaving their car at Stuart's, they walked down the main road of San Nicola. François-Marie was surprised at the distance to the clearing where it all had started: from his house on the hill at the very edge of San Nicola, it had looked so close, as if the hamlet were a mere extension of Institute grounds. The afternoon was hot, scattered lambs' clouds lazed around northeastern skies, the Great Wall and the twin towers behind them seemed to attract like a magnet the haze created by the heat mixed with drifting vapors produced by the garbage mountain at the roundabout. When they reached the place from which Sophie had first spotted the glade and the dead crows, they put on surgical gloves and masks in case of botox vapors and made their way through the bushes and undergrowth to the trapdoor. Their keys from the Institute opened the lock so smoothly that François-Marie suspected that it could easily be picked with two pieces of wire. He trained his light down into the blackness. As Stuart had described it, the darkness appeared eyes like an impenetrable solid living substance, a thing, an object, truly the blackest darkness he could imagine. For anyone who doubts the existence of multiple shades of black, here was the counterproof: the darkness darker than dark of Logreco's Pit of Tartarus in the other world under our world. When they reached the bottom and their eyes began adapting to this new dimension of darkness, François-Marie found the light switch. The yellowish light quickly defeated the devilish otherworldly black and Helen exclaimed, "*E luce fu!*" And it was like some creator god creating the first light. They stared at each other, surprise on their faces, as if meeting another human being for the first time.

"There's the tram," François-Marie muttered. Something else new, at this depth. He had heard the word pronounced by Stuart but never having been in a coal mine he had hardly known what to expect of a tram underground with no entrance nor exit. He was conscious of the mystery they had created in their minds of what in reality was a simple descent into a cavern under the earth, a place with its own sense of normality, the kind of place in which civilizations have been born and developed. On such esoteric thoughts, he ordered himself to cease his endless bestowing extraordinary qualities on what in effect was actually just a cave like kids and old people love.

"Actually, Helen, now that we're here I realize there's little to see. The darkness, the tram, the caged birds that other chemists keep injecting with organic altering substances. But what can a tram down here transport besides people. There are those tunnels and sub-tunnels, Stuart mentioned but they have little to do with the botox project. God knows what else they have in mind!"

"Yes, but Botox offers defense ministries and the military in general countless possibilities and uses. That's why our petition addressed to chemists of the world is important. Which reminds me, I wonder how that guy Ermanno got involved in this. What do we know about him except that he's an old friend of Logreco? In reality we know very little about him … except that he's a high-ranking intelligence agent. I have a funny feeling about him. He's almost too smooth, too laid-back. Anyway, let's take a tram ride and get an idea of the layout of this place."

As they passed up the first tram car, François-Marie pointed at the lead car. "We'll get a better view up there. When he started to climb in he stopped dead. "Don't move, Helen, this car's occupied."

"What do you mean occupied? We're the only … Oh God, why that's, that's Professor Logreco."

François-Marie leaned into the car and got a look at the face. "It's Logreco all right. And Helen, this man is dead."

"Here, I'll check, I'm a doctor of sorts." Without hesitation, she climbed into the tram car, turned the man's body over and stretched him out flat on his back. "Dead all right. Not a sign of blood or anything broken and he hasn't been dead more than twelve hours. Rigor mortis has ended and his body is cold. He died in the early hours this morning."

"But of what?"

"And where?" Helen said. "Here, in the middle of the night?"

Helen stared at the corpse, looked up at him and said: "Well, considering all the circumstances—that is, the things we know which is not much—I would guess he died of botox inhalation … and not here. Walk into his bedroom at three a.m. where he's sleeping the first sleep of the dead drunk, a few drops of botox on a cloth over his nose or wide open mouth and it's *kalinichta*, Logreco old friend. Good night, forever."

François-Marie looked back at her and murmured: "Someone also wanted to put an end to unofficial visits like ours to the underground lab, so they moved him here as a warning. At the same time, they—whoever they are—intend putting an end to the revolt of the chemists."

"Meaning?"

"Meaning you and your friends and chemists-supporters. Meaning me too. And Helen, I keep returning to your doubts about Ermanno Riccardi. I would bet he'll show up soon. This whole charade of secret meetings of the so-called 'group'. Fico d'India is not very secret. It happens to be the most popular restaurant in La Storta. And switching meeting times and places, as if all that rigmarole guaranteed secrecy! It all seems childish and even clownish now. Yet we know it's deadly serious. Botox. Dead Russian soldiers. Stuart had no idea of the labyrinth he was entering from the moment he saw the dead crows. And Gianluigi Logreco was in mortal danger the moment he reported what he knew to the AISI chief himself … his lifetime friend—so he thought—Ermanno Riccardi. Stuart's in danger not only because he saw the dead birds but then found the underground lab where they came from, and you and I for the same reasons and because of your manifesto. Look, let's go back to Stuart and talk this thing out. But in any case, you and I have to go into hiding. Sounds weird, I know, maybe a little romantic too for me at this crucial time of my life but we must go underground … but not this one! My old life of many little things is over. I don't think Riccardi said lightly or off-the-cuff that we're safe in our jobs for another couple of years. Who wants to be safe in a job that includes botox and people dying from it? Of course, he wants us to stay in our jobs, where we're visible and easy to find and easy to silence. Now, let's put Logreco back the way we found him and get the fuck out of here."

They were pensive on the walk back to Stuart's: both felt overwhelmed by the events sweeping over them, each of them attempting to get a handle on the meaning and possible outcomes of the situation they faced. Now the uninvolved observer of the events of this story might underestimate what was at stake here for them and for several others. Just their visit to the underground lab was enough. They had become dangerous to the powers that be. The powers up the hierarchical ladder to NATO and CIA. François-Marie was convinced that Professor Logreco's botoxed dead body in the underground tram changed the whole game also for them. Should they feel not only fear but also guilt that things had reached that critical stage before they even wondered what was really happening at the Institute and spent their time wooing each other? There were more fundamental matters that counted than their own satisfactions, he thought, more than their own tranquility and those 'little things' of their lives. This was one of those times when he felt it necessary to be aware of what was happening in the real world, the world of things much greater than himself. Were they acting appropriately? Helen had the chemists rebellion to deal with, Stuart had his political writing and he had birdlife and world ambient stability on his agenda. Was that enough? Could that ever be enough now that they'd murdered Gianluigi Logreco and their botox had killed the Russian soldiers. On the one hand, there was no question of simply good and evil at play here for either Helen or himself. Their doubts concerned the right course of action to defend themselves against threats from *their* unlimited power centers: Aisi-Aise, CIA, NATO. This was not the society they had anticipated when they set out in life, she in Rome, he in Orléans. Was it true as realists claim that nothing can be done to change things?

That's what he had wondered when he was that shy boy in the Orléans Lycée: Why? he'd asked. Why can nothing be done? Yet now he was faced by new realities, grown-up, no longer fairytale realities, realities that seemed so evil and powerful that he had to go into hiding. Why? Because he has seen the evil. He and Helen were witnesses. And now he knew witnesses exist at various levels. Some witnesses were minor simply because they were only charmed by the symbolic manipulations of power and hypnotized by substitutes for unpleasant facts: while in reality they knew nothing, had seen nothing and suspected nothing. Public evil was merely a theory. Others, at a middle level, knew things, suspected things, and studied conspiracy theories, and thus reacted AS IF they had seen more. Hence, they were under observation. Then there were the menacing witnesses who had seen and experienced the evil, who sought the occasion to reveal what they had seen. They were a danger to society. Other-thinkers, rebels, who say no. They must be silenced. Not even all his years in hiding in Greek mythology saved Professor Logreco. He had seen the evil beast. He was a witness. But did he intend to testify? François-Marie didn't know. If anyone knew, it was the boss, Ermanno Riccardi. Moreover, his and Helen's backgrounds and their individual situations were diverse, even though the dangers confronting them were similar—though not the same either: she had released her manifesto and her rather dreamy intentions: she was first category of intolerable danger. François-Marie had only taken care of the birds and had been present in the Group's meetings. He could hide, then go back to Orléans and vanish from circulation; yet he too would remember Professor Logreco and for the rest of his life he would look over his shoulder and wonder about a visit from two courteous men.

Helen had in mind her marital situation from which she had escaped and was now cognizant of the error of her hasty acceptance of the job in the mysterious San Nicola-Research Institute complex simply because it was near home, rather than examining more closely the openings in a major hospital complex in Paris and a research center in Vienna. Though her meeting François-Marie had seemed to justify her precipitous decision. she thought herself much more realistic than the romantic Frenchman. She knew—even though chiefly from hearsay—the brutality of her Rome deep state neo-fascist power structure. So it had been since the assassination of Julius Caesar and so it was today, and so it would remain forever.

When Stuart, who, his friends believed, knew everything worth knowing heard the news about Gianluigo Logreco, he told them that in one form or the other Ermanno Riccardi's puny Internal Intelligence and Security Agency or AISI had existed in Rome for two millennia. "Duties have not changed much today," Stuart began. "Nor has the general atmosphere of intrigue surrounding it. AISI is responsible for safeguarding national security within Italy's borders and for protecting Italy's political, military, economic, scientific and industrial interests. Yet because of corruption and the clash of interests you never know who or what is on your side. When Gianluigi Logreco quit AISI years ago, he hadn't yet learned the full truth even though he must have suspected something was rotten in Denmark when he resigned. His old friend Ermanno knew what he was into but he did not resign. Ermanno could have killed Gianluigi for his foresight. Ironic too that to outsiders AISI seems all powerful, while in reality it is infiltrated, partially financed, and controlled by the agency of today's dwindling empire, the Central Intelligence Agency, the CIA. You see, my friends, we hear these things and many believe it's just rhetoric and legend. It is not. Listen, friends, newspapers print articles the agencies write for them. Rome radio stations recite news scripts most likely written in CIA offices on Via Veneto. Keep in mind that the CIA runs the intelligence show right here—in Italy, in Rome, in the hamlet of San Nicola. Keep in mind that behind Italian terrorism in the past stood many secret services. The same CIA and its many helpers are the semi-secret sponsors of biowarfare labs that abound around the world. So we can assume, they run also ours, just two kilometers down the road from us here.

"In the Roman Empire, the *Frumentarii* were originally a military organization used as an intelligence agency, police force and eventually an imperial spy agency. They also carried out assassinations on orders from the top. Botox? No! They had lead—a deadly poison too. By the second century—sorry for this leap back in history—the need for an empire-wide intelligence service was clear. But not even an emperor could easily create a new bureau with the express purpose of spying on the citizens of Rome's far-flung domains. So there was a lot of conflict about authority over such a powerful agency consisting of police, secret police, intelligence agency and spy network. Anyway, when they began to be seen as a tyrannical plague, the *Frumentarii* were replaced by the *agentes in rebus*—enigmatic!—secret police agents, undercover agents, and spies."

For François-Marie, everything was deranged, *scombussolato*—the word Helen had taught him recently—as if his life had never known calm, order and tranquility. Everything was in Camus's becoming stage, as it was in his Lycée years when he, the outsider, struggled for direction. Since his liaison with Férnande, order had at first gradually, then piece by piece fled from him and his quiet studies of birds. Maybe it began when she first branded him a minor scientist, the category into which she had always classified him. He himself had never thought of it as science at all: ornithology for him meant study and admiration and love and recognition of the importance of bird life for the world. Yet there had remained the official doubts about their respective fields. Most certainly ornithology was a science of birds. But psychology? It is said that psychological studies are designed very much like studies in other scientific fields. He found that doubtful. Its status as a science is grounded in its use of the scientific method, others claim. Really? He wondered. Férnande claimed that her professional practice was based on knowledge obtained through verifiable evidence of human behavior and mental processes. Bah!

Then, after a great leap ahead in time and as fate would have it, science or no science, he and Férnande visited Stuart that day and the great disruption began. And along separate lines, in a sort of crisscross fashion during which Férnande became friends with Sophie and he with Stuart who, in turn became Férnande's patient—and perhaps more.

Because of his fifteen dead birds, he let himself be sequestered by the "Group", ironically because of his "minor science", ornithology, that heretofore had seemed to degrade him. Crows, crows, crows. Birds suddenly assumed the importance they deserved—but in this case, for the wrong reasons. A Black Angel in the person of Ermanno Riccardi stepped into his life. A time to ask: better to have a black angel at your side or no angel at all? Black angel? A fallen angel? An angel fallen from paradise because he was evil? Did he fall because of his accumulated human sins? *Jamais de la vie* could that man be considered a spiritual being, an intermediary between good and evil. Was he the black angel of Logreco's death? Was Ermanno an angel of evil in disguise? Even as a kid he had never resolved the issue: was evil simply a permanent aspect of human nature? Was there no atonement in life? Forgiveness and pardon? How horrible if there was no absolution available. Were humans condemned to black angelhood from birth? Férnande never gave him answers. Kafka, he recalled, seemed to think it was the human condition ... and permanent. His characters showed no surprise that it was normal life. They didn't seem to expect life to be otherwise. You were born evil and evil you remained. You don't know why. You try to live as a good person. You try to help others. You think you love others. You don't even claim like Sartre your love for all of humanity in order to cover up misdeeds against individuals. You are more specific. Yet hopelessness is your inalterable destination. And absolution is withheld. You too are a black angel. You too had a bit of paradise, but like Erysichthon you ate the apple. And as a result, you faced the wrath of a system that eliminated the mavericks. François-Marie's disillusionment today was for him a landmark, a well-beaten path traversed by others like him. He could no longer accept that people were spineless, submissive, devoid of spiritual values, ignorant—that they pursue soulless activities and are the authors of their own downfall. He marveled that he too once believed the bad egg myth, that the other-thinkers were the bad guys. The contorted body of Gianluigi Logreco dumped like a piece of trash from the roundabout in an underground tram car appeared like the sign of an evil world.

23.

What to do? François-Marie was especially apprehensive about Helen because of her anti-botox manifesto which had found adherents among the other chemists at the Institute. It had stirred the enthusiasm of Logreco—for which he paid with his life. Even Ermanno Riccardi—now nicknamed 'fucking son-of-a-bitch'—had praised Helen's ideas: praise your victims' values before you kill them.

They were sitting on the shaded terrace with the picturesque views of the Abruzzi mountains to the east. The caps were still whitened with what remained of the great snowfall. The sky appeared broken into pieces, between the blue and the swiftly moving gray-white clouds. Patches of sun warmed the fields and turned the olive trees on the rolling hills to silver. The towers of La Storta's cathedral soared even higher than the twin towers at the entrance gate, together making the ugly township resemble from a distance Etruscan San Gimignano with its fourteen towers, already back in in the Middle Ages an attraction for fervid believers walking the Via Francigena—the pilgrim route from Canterbury to Rome. Today the old route has been renewed and passes through the eastern edges of La Storta. Again young people walk it. Not in search of Jesus but in the spirit of Goethe's *Wanderjahre*. Stuart mused that walking the old Via Francigena was again fashionable, and commercial too, generating thousands of bed and breakfast offers along its route.

Helen and François-Marie were sitting on a swing, she with one arm around his shoulders, the other possessively across his body. With her thick red hair she looked like a man-eater, but in reality, Stuart knew, Helen had the mind of genius and artfulness. Her warm embrace of François-Marie had a way of including everyone else in her embrace—she was not only admired but also loved by all. Sophie who retained her genuine love for other women was fascinated by her, a reaction even stronger than her attraction to Férnande. She didn't speak but her eyes fixed on Helen the entire afternoon spoke for her. Gradually, Helen became aware of her fixation and from time to time rose from the swing and stood at the terrace wall staring mute and expressionless at the mountains gleaming in the sunshine. And try as she might, she couldn't avoid casting glances in Sophie's direction only to meet her unwavering gaze: Stuart's wife was as if transfigured. Stuart was vaguely aware of the sensations passing between Sophie and Helen, and between himself and Sophie. Sophie had told him of her bisexual period—however, as if it were a mere curiosity of her past youth. He fidgeted around in his chair or he went to the kitchen for drinks. A tall drink in hand he walked nervously up and down the terrace, his hands locked behind his back as if in deep thought, but at the same time he followed Sophie from the corner of his eyes.

While Stuart observed Helen and Sophie, his thoughts wandered along other lines: how could he have once believed the stories that in every group of human beings there was inevitably the bad apple to take the blame for all evil. And the other-thinkers of all times? Were they really the bad guys ... those to be controlled? The image of the contorted body of Gianluigi Logreco dumped like a piece of junk in an underground tram car gnawed at him like a sign of a new and evil world. He felt his helplessness about violent death in general; yet he was incensed at the "murder-execution" of his friend Gianluigi Logreco and felt no qualms about labeling Riccardi "terrorist" and felt an inchoate longing for revenge.

'He's a criminal guilty of crimes against humanity,' he thought, 'not only because of Gianluigi, but also because of his role in the military use of botox and the spread of secret biolabs. He should be arrested by Interpol and incriminated by The Hague International Criminal Court. Enough bullshit! The ICC after all arrested Serbia's Milosevic, sent him before the Hague Court, and he died in his cell.

"Fuck'em," he said aloud. "Let's indict some real terrorists-criminals for a change. Ermanno Riccardi should also pay for those sixteen Russian soldiers dead of botox. Enough is enough."

"Meanwhile," François-Marie said, thinking like Stuart, "we're at their mercy now. Riccardi can toy with us at will, or he can botox us too."

"Not only botox. Too obvious. They could imitate the ancient Romans and use lead!" Stuart said.

"Lead?"

"Lead. I once researched lead poisoning for an article about its use by the ancient Romans. Lead is surprising and its effect is unpredictable and dangerous—and deadly. Yes, lead is useful. Contemporary generations have found it to be an essential part of civilized living: pipes, pewter, pottery, paints, and even potions were made with it. Toy soldiers I made as a boy were cast from it, port wine was protected by it, grey hair was disguised with it, church roofs covered with it; cosmetics contained it, and cans of food were sealed with it. Now historians theorize that lead caused the fall of the Roman Empire! A major role of the Praetorian Guards was to protect the Emperor from lead poisoning. But they too were corruptible. So lead sneaked into the palace and the Emperor's chambers through every hole or crevice, killing left and right. Institute chemists know the secret: Romans boiled down grape juice in their lead pots. Lead ions would leach into the juice and combine with the acetate from the grapes. The resulting chemical syrup was sweet and used in wines and a wide variety of foods. Pure poison is the result. Assassination for beginners. Wives poisoned their husbands. Husbands, their wives. Senators, emperors. And especially bosom friends, like Gianluigi. So don't drink anything at work, you two! Nothing at all, especially not sweet grape juice."

"Jesus Chistus! Ugh!"

"So no more playing games for us. No more mucking around

with phony conspiracies like Riccardi's third level rogue intelligence service which he allegedly directs. That lying son-of-a-bitch. In one way or another that bastard is going to pay for Gianluigi.

"Now listen, I've been thinking day and night of plans. First of all, we've got to protect ourselves, especially you and Helen. One idea, François-Marie, both of you might keep working as if nothing were amiss. You might consider returning temporarily to your home here in San Nicola—the house is assigned to you and Férnande can hardly object—you can even fill her in on the reasons. She'll get over that 'minor science fixation', as you did. And Helen," he began tentatively, sorry that he'd had the idea and looking at Sophie whose eyes were still fixed unwaveringly on her, "Helen you can stay here in the small apartment we have upstairs for guests. If they look for you after work hours, at night—which is possible—they'll search the whole big city from La Storta to Ostia. We've never had any guests so the place is virgin and officially non-existent. Then one day you can just disappear without any official break. At that point, it won't matter anyway. But at the same time we should take some action. We can't just sit back and accept things because 'that's just the way they are.' That's gutless surrender. Helen, you can put the brilliant manifesto idea on hold for a while, or we can look for someone in another country to launch it. Meanwhile I'm writing a major article—a kind of exposé—for my Glasgow magazine about the secret biolabs in the world and your institute's underground lab in San Nicola –and I will accuse intelligence services for crimes against humanity … but then I too will have to go underground."

"You'd better run fast and far far away," François-Marie said. "Actually, I think you are in more danger than me—I just study birds. You influence public opinion."

"Less than you think. Still, it's too bad we can't count on the western press to back us up," Stuart went on. "Our media won't say a fucking word. You'll see! But someone will. Somewhere someone will echo it. One result could be a parliamentary investigation of our intelligence services. There have been many. Nothing Rome parliamentarians like better than a good corruption scandal! Investigations of the secret services started back at the birth of the *Frumantarii* in the second century. They reached a high during Italian terrorism in the 1960,70s and 80s. Today, they have botox to deal with … but they should keep in mind ancient Roman history of lead."

"Time is the problem for us. Such things take time and we don't have it," François-Marie said. "Maybe I should go back to France—with Helen of course. And just fade away into anonymity. No need for Férnande to run ... she's not involved anyway."

Stuart however prevailed. They would do it his way.

24.

François-Marie's conundrum was: Should he or could he go to Férnande? Easier to go to some faraway land like New Zealand than to her in his own house on the hill. Yet Stuart and the others thought it the safe thing to do. So he went. That evening, when he proposed to Férnande the solution as almost inevitable, a *fait accompli,* she seemed surprisingly pleased: the prodigal son come home attitude. Rather taken aback by the turnabout and the lack of recriminations for simply not coming home one night and vanishing, he succinctly related the series of events: the birds, Stuart's discovery of the underground lab, the "Group", the involvement of the secret service, then the unexplained death of Professor Logreco, and the evident danger to him and the others. And that the unanimous decision was to maintain an apparent modicum of normality in all their lives, like his return home. He underlined the temporary nature of the arrangement and mentioned the other woman she'd likely heard of, Helen.

"Oh, yes. I understand she's quite striking … and very beautiful."

"Well, she attracts a lot of attention."

"Must be her red hair."

"Not only. She's also a scientist and very intelligent."

Férnande smiled.

"Like you," he added

"Intelligent people attract other intelligent people. That's how we got here from apes and dinosaurs. The story of life," she said.

"Strange then the many aberrations and … regressions."

"Progress is that way; two steps ahead, one backwards."

"We seem to be moving backwards everywhere today. Is that still part of progress? Shouldn't there always be some territories or at least pockets of progress—of people moving ahead? Now, here in our lives, a high-ranking Italian intelligence chief I met assassinated his best friend because he supported Helen's petition calling on chemists of the world to demand official investigations of the secret biolabs springing up all over the world—devising new ways to kill large numbers of people."

"Such efforts of human beings to kill each other help me understand better than I once did your interest in birds."

"My interest in ornithology was at first more academic … and admittedly also hobby. Then I learned of their importance for the entire ecosystem. Now that I've seen examples of humans killing other humans, I appreciate more the little things that help men. While men are killing other men, birds work to the benefit of public health—it's their nature. Besides, they're beautiful and sing better than most people."

"Yes, there's that too. You know, François-Marie, I believe I've come to understand you better than I did at any other time in our marriage. I've got my hang-ups too, don't forget, many of which you know … but not all."

Her eyes were darker than usual, and calm and searching. No sign of that crazy blue that sometimes appeared in critical moments. He perceived that she was feeling a certain anxiety about something besides his safety.

"But I'm learning to know myself," she said, "and it's hard work. Anyway, where is Helen now? "

"In hiding."

"In hiding, where? She could be here too. Nobody would ever think of looking for her here … of all places."

"No, that's true. But none of us thought of it. Seems rather bizarre, doesn't it?" he said, feeling a nervous trembling in his legs and staring at his wife strangely, as if he were seeing her the first time. On the one hand, she appeared her usual dark, and even inchoate self. On the other hand, she'd never been as sensually attractive as in this moment. What does it mean? he wondered.

"Férnande, something about you seems new … and different. Maybe we're getting to know each other too. And that's scary … and unexpected—after all this time. You and I know that humans are much more complex than birds."

"Certainly human nature is mysterious. Then sometimes we wake up and find that things are different from what we thought they were. François-Marie, bring Helen here. It will suit her better. But who knows?"

Much later, during the early morning hours, he was still awake when she slipped into his bed in the upstairs guest room now reserved for the eventual arrival of Helen. She lay on her side, one leg over his. He turned his head slightly away from her toward the window as if to reject her, but the twelfth chamber of his wildly beating heart said yes, yes, yes.

Meanwhile, in the mansion two kilometers down Via San Nicola, Helen, alone at last, began an unintentional review of her life … and waited. She knew very well for what. It was past midnight, she was in bed wearing only her T-shirt. The windows were open, a playful sea breeze was blowing in from the Mediterranean. She watched the fluttering of the beige window curtains caressing gently the nearby art deco floor lamp while she counted the number of beats per minute of her heart. Counting the force of the breeze and counting the amps of the lamp, she was waiting for the knocks on her door. She knew who it would be.

Later, toward morning, she was alone again and wondering how she had arrived at this exciting but totally unexpected return to the past. Oh, yes, she had told François-Marie her life story: her Italian mother, her Austrian father, studies in Vienna, but she had omitted a period that she termed reductively as "somewhere else"—like a place or a time where she'd lived before coming back to Rome and where in the end she married Romano. She never revealed details to her parents about that lost year spent "somewhere else". She never spoke about that period in Vienna-Grinzing, that back then had seemed so far away but that in fact you could get to on a tram. She had met Gudrun at her school. They became friends, intimate friends. Helen, in the early morning hours in the bed in Sophie and Stuart's guest apartment was thinking in German, as she sometimes did—always when she thought of Gudrun. The time that would never end, they'd seemed to think. Since Gudrun was very rich, they didn't think about work or chemistry or family or men … as both had before. In their togetherness they seemed to merge and become one thing. Time seemed endless. And yes, it would last forever. The first summer came and went while they lived their first passion in Grinzing. In the fall, they traveled. Down the Danube to the Black Sea. To New York and San Francisco. In the winter, to Bali and the Maldives. Life was exciting. They were close and both repeated that today was endless. And their union seemed permanent. Helen's beauty blossomed so that wherever they were, they were the center of attention; she attracted men like a magnet. From the very start, Gudrun always beamed in pride, never displaying signs of jealousy. Yet, as time passed and another summer was arriving, their frenetic travelling became boring. And again they spent more and more time at home in Grinzing: Helen returned to her books, reading days and weeks at a time, while Gudrun, more and more frequently, visited her parents in Munich. Helen seldom felt lonely; she came to actually enjoy the days when Gudrun was away. Yet as her absences became ever more frequent and ever longer, Helen felt increasingly uneasy, not because of her absences but of the possible significance. In that respect, she felt a tingling of guilt herself, because once the newness of their relation and the excitement of constant movement, of new people and new experiences abated, Helen came to realize that her own sentiments were changing—weakening and fading away. Or had they always been mendacious and spurious?

she asked herself. She had always considered herself an honest person, but was it true? Truth was her dilemma … about herself. Was her conviction about herself only illusion? Hoping that was not the case, she couldn't detach herself from that hope, the hope of truth. Inevitably she told herself that either she had misjudged and overvalued the role of love in their relationship—as often happens in life—or that neither Gudrun nor she had been misled from the start and in reality they had been aware of the fleeting nature of their togetherness. That not even a whisper of the permanent was at play in their togetherness made Helen feel like either a fool or a whore. Yet she consoled herself that she had known in the innermost depths of her heart that they couldn't continue to live at the heights they had in Vienna-Grinzing.

25.

In his sprawling third-floor apartment in Via Panisperna in the Rome's Monti District, Ermanno Riccardi had been ruminating over his lives with his ex-wives and their children now out in the world doing their own things. The secret agent imagined he looked as disheveled as he felt lying on a couch in the front room facing a small park. He had just put an eye drop in his right eye as he did twice a day in his twenty-year old bout with glaucoma and had the sickening thought that these hot days were the kind Gianluigi had hated, on which his face took on the tormented look of those moments when he removed his public mask and became the person he once was. He was wearing jockey shorts and a t-shirt that barely covered his protruding belly. Trying to find a comfortable position on the lumpy couch, he constantly shifted around from one side to the other while without moving his head his eyes remained fixed on a small crack in the ceiling plaster, convinced that was where the worms he saw around the house came from, which reminded him of Gianluigi's dream of the huge worm with no mouth. Crazy dream world anyway! He massaged gently his sensitive left side just below his rib cage where it seemed to him a big piece of his colon was causing his chronic constipation and subsequent diarrhea when he took laxatives. Gloomily he looked around the room, wincing from time to time when he saw an object that awakened sad memories, and again he asked Norbert what the fuck he should do with his life … now that he'd burned most of his bridges with AISI, alienating key people in his variegated projects as well as with the Agency overseers, the Italian ones and the others. Those fifteen fucking dead crows had led to the breakdown of AISI relations with the secret biolab operating out of the research institute in San Nicola, and as if that weren't enough to interrupt the flow of his life, that French kid François-Marie had run off with the one woman he had met in many years who challenged him in the way special women always had.

"Hang on and wait out the crisis; it too will pass," Norbert said softly and sticking to the far side of the room.

"Bullshit!" he muttered. "Nothing really passes. Didn't you know that?"

Ermanno Riccardi knew that he was a complex man. His entire life, once so perfect, was now upside down. Suddenly everything was inside out, reminding him of his former desire of being born old and becoming progressively younger until the day he could return to the safety and security of the womb and rejoin his first self, the core of the man who was once Ermanno. As a man, he'd had two wives and four children, two with each wife. Today he had no one. The two wives and the four children had gone their respective ways. His first wife was American; first the children, then she too moved to the USA and made new lives of which he'd never been a part.

"Norbert, I've suspected that the real reason you asked to live with me is that you're my son's spy on me; Edgar was always concerned about my erratic ways."

"Ed only told me you had a lot of free space here, but that you lead a dangerous life. He thought I might be able to help."

"Sometimes I suspect that my son Edgar—and maybe even you his best friend—is in cahoots with AISI. The big bosses, the secret ones in their comfortable ministries, must think the same: I'm too erratic, too independent, too politically untrustworthy. And in a way, they're right. I am."

"What do you mean? May I report this to Edgar," Norbert said facetiously, and snickered as was his way. "I'm just kidding. If I told him about the life you lead, I think he would be on first flight to Rome to pick up your pieces."

"Something you didn't know and that Edgar has forgotten, when I was a lot younger, I supported a far left party as well as some of my country's political enemies. I've even led AISE internal opposition to arming certain foreign countries. That's why I was transferred to our

FBI of AISI. But recently I unofficially backed a petition against the web of secret biological warfare labs in Europe. We've got a mass of them in our country, you should know that. But to read our press or listen to our TV you would think we're a bulwark of peace and prosperity in the world. I say publicly that our media are carbon copies of what our masters across the pond write. The last straw was when they learned that I supported the nucleus of a small civil opposition group against our own biolab on the outskirts of Rome."

"My God, a miracle they didn't suicide you."

"They will, some day. Meanwhile, somebody killed my best friend just for being in that Group. But it was a message to me. That's what it really was. Gianluigi died as a warning to me. A martyr. No wonder I feel like shit."

"So what is happening with your 'little Group?'?"

"Disintegrated. My cowardice. And that a sexy red-headed vamp turned me down."

"Is that the Helen you mentioned before?"

"Yes. Truly a stunning woman, and besides she's a brilliant research chemist. When I declared myself the one time I was alone with her, she just laughed and treated me like her father."

"Well, you are old enough!" Norbert said. "What a let-down though. But you seem to have trouble with the reality of age in general."

"True. And I don't like it, so I go on operating on several levels, one incompatible with the other. You know, Norbert, my very life seems at odds with life itself. Considering that wives and children have left me, that my employment is incompatible with me, and I work at a job where I'm both esteemed and mistrusted at the same time, I seem to be leading multiple lives in one. I think Edgar had a tough role in mind for you. Like keeping me alive and also doing the right thing—maybe those two things are incompatible too. I must be incompatible with myself. My psychiatrist says I'm like a man in search of my first soul. Of my core. She says that many people never find that first soul—that many don't even know they have one. And I don't want to be one of those."

Ermanno was eternally surprised at how many people he met were so different from him. He recognized that he had his dark side, and for him that side was vastly different from his first soul that he missed and needed. He'd learned to accept others as they really were; he didn't try to remake them no more than he'd tried to remake his wives and children. Maybe they'd wanted him to try, but that's the way he was, he reminded himself: generous. If asked what he considered his most meaningful quality, he consistently replied: generosity.

When Norbert left the room to get back to his studies, Ermanno perceived a light breeze waft across his face while he lay there on the couch, twisting and turning in search of a position in which both nostrils were free. Finally in desperation he said, "fuck it", and recklessly sprayed extra strength Narivent into both nostrils, said "ah", and lay back in wait of the magical effect. His uncomfortable position seemed like just penitence for his egocentrism: his uncontrolled aspirations to sensual enjoyment of life as it came to him. Yet his material success and accompanying enjoyments seemed just, a sign of his having mastered life; he believed that pleasure was the reality of a properly lived life. And when he sometimes heard warnings from his conscience, he shushed them … though with only partial success. So when success and the satisfactions and pleasures it brought began to evade him, his life of wives leaving him and suspicions about his political reliability circulating behind his back, his worries about his compatibility with life began. Ermanno Riccardi of today didn't consider himself still the same man of ten years earlier. Yet though he readily admitted that he aspired to success and the good life it provided, he tried to master his desires as he theoretically mastered life itself: he told himself that material rewards would never be the final goal in his life. Not even happiness was an acceptable goal. Still, there was something unsettling in his nature, something contained in his oscillation between self-control and abandonment to sensual pleasures. Mulling over the flow of his life, he divided it into three phases: the sensual enjoyment of life when he arrived in the capital and began ascending the hierarchy of the secret life; the second phase was the time of solidifying gains and family-building; and now the third phase was the rough, gloves-off treatment he faced when he began paying for his errors and presumptuousness of earlier times: though his ascendency had continued, the number of enemies he made to get there likewise grew. The more conscious he became that the world in which he moved had values he didn't share, the more he felt like an outsider, different from other people. He still performed his work efficiently—sort of—but the moral rewards remained truant. He thought: how can I work seriously in the secret world, when love and passion are the things that make life worth living? He'd seen the difference in these days with his biolab and botox Group. They all know what I mean That red-headed beauty knew and understood him and wanted nothing to do with him personally.

He looked across the room at the tall mirror in which he saw his reflection as if magnified. In the mirror he looked strong, still with the strength to overcome his present difficulties. Which reminded him of another quality that he believed redeemed his physical decline: resistance. His resistance to things as they really are had begun in doubt and had now reached the stage of confrontation. Still, Ermanno vaunted that he was capable of saying, no. No, to the temptations offered in the form of comfort and ease. Once, when he was young, he'd unerringly chosen the easy way, the comfortable way, the way his friend Gianluigi had rejected. But no more. Today he said NO to Power which continually tempted him, offering him more of the good life. "You have to resist," he repeated aloud, slapping one hand into the other. "Resist temptation." It must have been Foucault who said that where there is Power there will always be resistance. Yes, definitely, it was that French philosopher he used to read, Foucault. Also

Dostoevsky attacks Power, in every circumstance and in every time, and writes the bitter truth that most people just don't want complete freedom because of the responsibility it entails. The tragedy of the human condition, Ermanno thought. Most people are simply afraid of freedom. The constant drive "to be happy" limits real freedom. But happiness, he knew, is not a positive goal. Nothing to strive for. And anyway since happiness is forever ambivalent and elusive, the result is fear of not achieving it—which means failure. Meanwhile, we take those dainty steps along our life avenue, softly, quietly, just to avoid the stinking trash and the red dirt and the sticky mud of our reality. Fear. The symptom of our times. Fear of non-achievement. And today, we put on stalwart faces before all those artificially created fears, the fears of terrorism and school shootings, crossing imaginary red lines, false flags. Human fears, yes. But because of those fears, resistance requires companions so as not to face the threats alone. Otherwise, fear wins out. At that point, Ermanno silently told Norbert now in his room, 'once you are on the inside of resistance, once you are involved and committed, each step becomes easier.'

'I should do this more often,' Ermanno thought. 'A good long period of meditation gives a man the strength of a lion so that you can roar, 'fuck it all.' For now, I think I'll take a long walk and get that spy Norbert off my back. I'll buy some newspapers and sit on a bench in Villa Borghese and for just one day live the life of a gentleman … or if the mood strikes me I'll just get stinking drunk. Yes, yes, all of that for at least one day.'

26.

It was the first time Stuart had been in the city in years. Strange, he thought, that everything was about the same. That's the way Rome is: like the old saying, everything changes so that nothing changes. Or something like that. He'd never really understood that classic adage, taken from some film or the other. Stuart felt like a stranger anyway, despite memories of those wonderful, halcyon nights and days when he'd lived near here with his friend and their respective women and feeling it could go on forever right up to the day of disaster, when happened what happened. After Stefano's death, nothing would ever be the same again. But that was something he forbade himself to recall. It was like a pre-life, a life seen through a gossamer amnesia long since cut out of his life. Pain and regret had replaced his non-stop festivity. Another, a more serious and down-to-earthliness kind of life began.

He was about to enter the Piazza Barberini metro station and head for San Nicola when he stopped for a look at the unchanging surroundings: just across the piazza, the old Hotel Barberini where they used to go for the dancing on the roof garden; down at the end of Via del Tritone, the outline of Palazzo Chigi and the government complex; up the hill, the great curve of Via Veneto and the fortress that was the U.S. Embassy surrounded by walls and steel barriers and patrolled by Marine guards—and, he knew, backed up by sharpshooters posted on the roofs of adjacent hotels; the sirens of ministers' bulletproof armored cars racing down steep Via Barberini. A world no longer his, Stuart was thinking as he turned toward the newsstand and abruptly met the eyes of Ermanno Riccardi who was still holding a newspaper in one hand and the change from the seller in the other and a look of surprise on his face. A second passed before Riccardi turned on his charm, grinning at Stuart like at an old friend you meet after years of wandering around the world.

"What a coincidence," Stuart exclaimed. "I haven't been in the city in years and the first person I meet is you—our leader," he added with a certain irony.

"I'm a cop as you so pointedly call me," Ermanno said softly, moving away from the kiosk, "so our meeting in this God-forsaken place can't be a coincidence."

"I know, I know, I use the word a lot. But it's because I've always wondered why cops don't believe in the coincidences? My whole life seems like one huge coincidence. But still, if it's not a coincidence, then what can you call our meeting like this—of all places—at a kiosk in the huge Eternal City? An act of God?"

"Maybe it is," Ermanno said, taking Stuart's arm and starting down the dull street of Via del Tritone, "but all that stuff about police not believing in coincidence is just for detective stories and films."

The thing about the central Via del Tritone leading downhill toward Palazzo Chigi and the magnificent piazzas on all sides, Stuart recalled, was that despite its intriguing name, Tritone, the street had nothing of great artistic note. However, hidden behind a row of innocuous buildings just one short block away reigned Bernini's world-famous Fontana di Trevi, its waters and its art, and there amid tourists' coins jetted into the fountain's waters to assure their return to Rome were also the Greek gods, Poseidon and his son, Triton, at home among an imposing array of symbolic art and statues of other gods of the Ancients. Professor Gianluigi Logreco had told him that Triton lived with his parents in a golden palace on the bottom of the sea and is represented as a merman with the upper body of a human and the tailed lower body of a fish. In art and literature, Triton was a generic term for a merman.

"I was going to say it's chance, but then you would insist that chance and coincidence are the same thing anyway. More puzzling to me is that you see me as a cop ... when I'm really not. At least I've never thought of myself that way even though I'm a functionary in the Italian FBI—and by the way we don't do the same things the real FBI does. Not anymore. I mean, at least I don't go around arresting people. But then we do have our problems: our top brass takes orders from the USA. And as I told you we do have our rogue agencies and they are bad, bad, bad. But Stuart, that's not me."

"What? Then if you're not a cop, what are you? You command other cops, you run a biolab, you meet with other international cops, I assume. I suspect you go to secret meetings right up there around the curve in the U.S. Embassy. Maybe you just came from there! You get funds for your projects and great lunches for your contacts. What does it all mean then?"

Ermanno reddened for an instant. Then: "I consider myself a government official, an …"

"An agent. A secret agent. They're cops too. And you probably carry a pistol … or maybe two. Like they do in films, one belted around your ankle. That's what a cop does, no?"

"Well, I'm not a real cop in any case … whether I carry pistols or not."

"Ok, ok, I really don't care about your pistols even if they are symbolic of those who do the policing in the world. And Ermanno, I prefer anyway the side of those who are policed. But I still wonder why police say they don't believe in coincidences."

"Stuart, actually I really don't believe in them —but that doesn't make me a real cop. Coincidences just don't exist. Philosophers and religious people don't believe they exist either. There's an explanation for every event, for everything that occurs. The prevailing idea seems to be that everything happens for a reason."

"Oh, what crap! I read on Google that some people think the word *coincidence* should be removed from the dictionary! Anyway, boss, I have an almost unbelievable story contradicting the doubters— all likely in bad faith anyway."

"Let's hear it then."

"Ok, Ermanno, here goes. As a rule, I read in bed every night, novels or literary stuff. Last night I was reading random parts of a great book by Erich Auerbach, *Mimesis*, a 600-page tour de force, a history of the evolvement of reality in world literature starting with the Greeks. I've read the whole book straight through before but for the last week I've been opening random pages and if it attracts me—and it usually does—I read that part. At the same time, as every night, I had the Rome classical music radio station on. Now imagine this: it's about ten o'clock, the time for grand opera. I flip open the book, by pure chance on page 396. I read about a small novel of 1732 by Abbé Prévost, a love story of a young girl named Manon Lescaut. Simultaneously the radio speaker announces the second act of Giacomo Puccini's opera, *Manon Lescaut*. All by pure chance. So I have at my disposition from two simultaneous sources the tragic love story of the sixteen-year old Manon who meets in Amiens the seventeen-year old Chevalier des Grieux: great literature of the eighteenth century and grand opera of the nineteenth!. The two kids fall in love and elope to Paris but there their romantic life turns into tragedy. The story is about betrayal of love, virtue and eroticism, rivers of eighteenth century tears of high-flown bourgeois sentimentality. At the very same time I read in *Mimesis* the name Manon Lescaut, I hear Puccini's nineteenth century des Grieux exclaim in desperation at the loss of love: 'Manon! Manon!'

"Stuart, my friend, I agree that your experience is at the very limit of reality. You've convinced me—this time. Still it's the kind of exception that proves the conviction of most people that coincidences don't exist. Eighteenth and Nineteenth centuries, eh? Great image though: two centuries amalgamated in a sixteen-year old love-struck girl."

"You're quick, you know. I think I always knew it, and then Gianluigi always spoke so highly of you. But the quality I like most is your ambiguity. I mean that in a positive sense; you seem to have one foot in your secret services and one foot out. In life too, I imagine. An outsider in general."

"Are you a psychiatrist or something like that? You describe my life the way it really is, and the way I feel about it too. But I'm lucky. A few people would agree with you: Gianluigi did, a kid named Norbert who lives with me—my son's spy, sent to keep an eye on me, does—and a woman I once knew. Listen, I've got to go now, I've got a date with a bench in Villa Borghese. But come see me sometime, at home. We communicate well with each other. Uh, one more thing. I had the feeling that some of you of our littler group believe I had something to do with Gianluigi's death. I didn't. I swear to you, I did not. I'm still mourning his death these days."

"Ok, I can believe that. I do believe it. But Ermanno, mourning for his death does not mean innocence. Some killers and probably many executioners cry when they kill their victims." In the same moment, Stuart thought that he didn't mean that jibe at all, so why did he say it? 'I suspect the truth is that this man has a lot of guilt on his shoulders , he's alone, and he needs help.'

Looking out the suburban train windows and ruminating about the strange and maybe tragic man named Ermanno Riccardi—not the son-of-a-bitch Ermanno—Stuart waited for the magical moment when signs of the city abruptly end and the whole world returns to its original pastoral nature, the Arcadia he had come to love—a life and world that had been interrupted by the arrival of the Research Institute and its secret underground biological laboratory near his house. While mulling over the significance of the birds killed by botox and his descent into Tartarus' pit, the fortuitous meeting with François-Marie and Férnande, and now the unresolved and hushed-up death of Gianluigi, Stuart was conscious of the meaningless buzz of the chatter around him in the train car: the usual gossip about their neighbors between two women across the aisle, here and there comments on the weather and climate change, another stupid TV show. On the other hand, no one had the slightest complaint about the degeneration of public transportation, the ever less coverage offered by the national health service, no mention of the war in Ukraine, praise for the USA, no mention of sanctions to teach those Russkies a lesson once and for all, one hesitant mention of Putin responsible for the price of gas, no criticism of the European Union, and above all no mention of Italy's new Fascist government and the media specials on Benito Mussolini. When a man across the aisle dared mention the disgraceful roundabout and his indecision whether to sign a protest petition, no one even responded. Stuart listened, hoping for more—just any small signal that people cared about their world. Cared about real freedom. Nothing! Not one fucking word. The train was slowing toward the Giustiniana station when Stuart said in a loud voice to no one in particular: "I'm a communist and I support President Putin and Russia against NATO and the United States," on which in one synchronized movement every single passenger in the car got up and crowded the exits at each end of the car. Stuart eyed them grimly and thought: 'Revolution? Hardly. Docile people like this accept whatever you give them. They would freeze in the winter, pay triple for gas and electricity and even eat dirt rather than rise up against the system.'

Now alone in the last car of the suburban train, Stuart began piecing together how something similar happened in nineteenth century France. There it was before him. Fresh. Ten years after the Revolution of 1789, Napoleon established a dictatorship, lasting until his destitution and two exiles, to the island of Elba, then after his return and defeat at Waterloo, his final exile to the remote island of Saint Helena. He remembered that the Bourbons returned to power and a moderate constitutional monarchy lasted until 1820, followed by a period of reaction so severe that liberals and moderates revived, leading to the July Revolution which marked the end of the Bourbon Restoration. Stuart slapped his head, muttering '*dummkopf, dummkopf*' and realized that the abandoned and emptied train car, the silent people, the idiotic chattering about nothing, this period of k*now nothing, say nothing, do nothing* that was the Italy of today resembled the Restoration in France: its public silence, its historical amnesia, its acceptance of tyrannies and fascistization. What in France was the Restoration, in Italy was the *Three Tyrannies* period: the quiet tyranny of their own Fascist government; the blatant tyranny of the European Union, the no longer even dissembled tyranny of the United States of America over its European colonies. In France, the Restoration was the age of the new, fearful bourgeoisie, fearful of losing their newly acquired wealth, fearful of a new revolution when the new upper classes clamped down on the defeated classes, a time when everyone, the winners and the losers, preferred boredom to risk, while ambition and the thirst for more prodded the new classes ahead. In Stendhal's *Le Rouge et le Noir*, Julien Sorel observed these revolutionary events crushed and people eating dirt, then the return of the people, however this time in the form of the vicious beast, fascism. The triumph of the worst of the past. The culmination of that history was also Italy.

A sudden silence interrupted his meditation. The train motors fell silent and passengers from other cars moved along the platform. He too stepped down from the silent train and wondered how he would proceed on to Olgiata and San Nicola. Looking around for other options—buses or taxis—he noted groups of people pointing toward the roof of the station building.

"The bird's there again."

"Looks like a black crow."

"It's too big for a crow."

"I think they're called ravens."

"He comes every day and just sits there and looks.

"As if he were waiting for someone."

"What can it mean?"

Stuart looked up. A black bird was perched on the ledge of the roof of the station building: It seemed to be looking beyond the tracks and the parking and out toward the rolling green hills like those in San Nicola. It was a raven, exactly like the one in his freezer. An American raven, François-Marie said.

"Does that bird live up there on the roof?" he asked a bystander.

"They say it comes every morning and stays all day"

"I wonder why?" Stuart said and called François-Marie. He should come immediately. "An American raven is sitting on the station roof!"

The ornithologist was there like Jumpin Jack Flash. They passed through the station and out toward the tracks, turned and peered at the raven on the roof. François-Marie held up his phone with the picture of the raven in Stuart's freezer. "Your raven is male, and the station roof raven is female. Yours is bigger than her. And I would bet she is his companion and that she's waiting for him. That has bothered me from the moment I saw your raven. Where is his mate, I wondered? We can only guess how they got here in the first place. Either someone brought them and they then escaped or they flew the Newfoundland-Greenland northern route together and followed other birds migrating south. The trip would've taken them weeks of flight, rest, food and, since ravens have strong, long wings, sleeping in flight and dreaming raven dreams. Maybe they nested in the fields between here and San Nicola. Yours was foraging or exploring. Who knows? And he got the last of the botox in trees around your clearing. My God, why? Coincidence? Still, the fact is we'll never know the answers. Stuart, I wish we could capture her and take her to her mate. Ravens, you maybe didn't know, are monogamous and partners for life. And these two are not old yet, no more than four or five years."

"I think capturing that lady up there pretty unlikely. You told me how smart they are and they sure as hell don't trust us humans."

"Listen, I've got an idea. Ravens have a powerful sense of smell. We can bring that cloth you wrapped your male in—now permeated with his smell—and bring it here. If she's his mate, she'll react and we might be able to cage her and gradually become friends. She'll be sad when she sees him dead, but in the long run she might become attached to one of my remaining crows—if they don't kill each other first—and then crossbreed. Ravens and crows belong to the same family but they are two different genera and they hate each other … still, it sometimes happens. With our help they could nest in the wooded area in your gardens."

"Sounds like fantasy to me. But you decide. Birds are your babies. I've got to get to work now on my writing. Too many distractions lately."

"Distraction is a light word to describe the big things happening to me?"

"Helen, you mean?"

"Helen, yes. But it's more complicated than that."

"François-Marie, what's up What are you trying not to tell me."

"Stuart, you will think this crazy, but I've fallen in love again with my wife. And there's more. We're thinking of moving back to France. To Paris, this time. Orléans can remain as our 'back home' So if we do go, it's Paris."

"First of all, congratulations. It sounds right. Solid. Much of both your lives stand behind it. But still I'm curious about one aspect."

"Then, shoot, as you always say."

"I mean, how do you really *feel* about it? I mean Helen is still there and you were mad about her … only yesterday."

"I expected you to ask that, for it's certainly still on my mind, constantly: How do I really feel about it? I have to confess, Stuart, that in a sense I feel relieved, for deep in myself I knew I was far out on a limb … that that was not real life. But my passionate relationship with Helen concealed all other feelings. My feelings for her were like those of a person just released from prison. I could say or do what I'd always wanted. And I felt loved by her. It was freedom … a new kind of freedom, but still somehow limited. I felt free but I was tense and confused. I must have known I was out of place. But now, in this moment, I feel guilty for misleading Helen, but strangely I'm calm, maybe even serene—and for the first time in my life. I feel stronger. Free of my complex of inferiority to Férnande. I, François-Marie Dolon, am deciding my life—not Férnande Volkov. I don't worry about whether my life occupation is a real science or not. It seemed so important to her. Now my differing outlook is mine. Extraneous factors don't bother me either—like jealousy ... of you too, by the way—all your trips up to her studio. I no longer feel like a stranger in my own house. Stuart, for the first time in my life, I feel me. And I feel free. So that I want to shout it to the world. I am here, materially. And free. My life no longer seems like someone's else's bad dream. And I'm grateful to Helen for liberating me."

27.

François-Marie dropped him at the Olgiata station where he'd left his car. It was mid-afternoon and strange things were in the air. A general kind of excitement seemed to have infected departing passengers and station personnel. When Stuart approached the entrance to San Nicola on the northern Elevated, he saw why: a wrecker at the southeastern edge of the dump had lifted one end of the carcass of an abandoned bus and was pulling it slowly away. And two Rome AMA garbage trucks were loading dripping crane buckets of waste, garbage, and trash. Strange things indeed! He zigzagged through the approach road and abruptly stopped in confusion: the steel protective wall had been removed and the gate widened. The German guards had vanished. He drove through the space between the twin towers and stopped to look up the green hill toward François-Marie's house behind which a work crew was dismantling a section of the Great Wall. Stuart smiled to himself. He'd known change was in the air but not so soon, nor so profound. Ermanno had shown that he was still a force to be reckoned with, even though his life now was not worth two lira; his situation was much worse than Gianluigi's was. Along pine-lined Via San Nicola small groups of people were talking and pointing in all directions. Infectious excitement was written on the faces of people used to others deciding everything for them—good or bad, beneficial and propitious or disagreeable and harmful. People who didn't want to take such decisions themselves. Who just wanted to be taken care of. Stuart had understood that many people here had grown to like the Great Wall, the garbage dump, the Elevateds. They felt protected. They didn't need freedom. What would they do with that old-fashioned concept? After all, the Hamlet Commission, the City Council and the national government in Palazzo Chigi had the well-being of their people at heart.

Still, for most hamletians, Stuart thought, the atmosphere of change in San Nicola as a whole was generalized, like the changes in the world as a whole, just the random, superficial and unexplained end of a period. Actually the end times atmosphere they had perceived since finding the fifteen crows in the glade was on a completely different level. The rejoicing people of today were the same ones who were comforted by the Great Wall and had felt protected by the restricted entrance to the hamlet. Those *masses* were still unaware of the Tartarus underground biolab and the Research Institute on the opposite hill. They knew nothing of botox or the sixteen infected Russian soldiers— nor would they care much if they did know. Meanwhile, on the hidden level, revolutionary changes were underway: Gianluigi Logreco was eliminated; Ermanno the intelligence agent confessed his innermost self and it was he who had ordered the liberation of San Nicola; François-Marie had fallen back in love with his wife and wanted to return to France; red-headed Helen was stashed away in Stuart's house to tempt both him and Sophie.

Stuart found them together on the afternoon terrace: Sophie and a fiery Helen, and to his surprise across the table from the two women sat Ermanno.

"The uninvited guest arrived," Ermanno said.

"How'd you get here so fast? By helicopter? "

"Sort of. Someone dropped me off at the Institute. And I had my walk! Anyway, you will have noticed the latest improvements in the hamlet. It's all my doing, my friends and comrades if you will permit me the use of that binding title. Those corrective changes are in fact the reason I'm here, in hiding, so to speak. All this to do downtown about the hamlet will either blow over, or they will do to me what they did to Gianluigi."

"Well, you're welcome here, boss, we'll do our best to make your hideout comfortable and secure. Man, our house has become really popular in these days. For years the only people who even rang our doorbell were Gianluigi or Jehovah's Witnesses or census takers. Anyway Ermanno, I think you've done the right thing."

From time to time, Ermanno looked longingly at Helen, and each time he pulled in his stomach and pushed at his thinning hair, patting it down over spreading bald spots and talking nervously. And while talking—about himself or the accomplishments of the Group or the clean-up of San Nicola—his fear began to show. Fear of the unknown waiting in the dark around the corner. Fear of the punishment for what he had done so impulsively. Stuart watched Ermanno reach for his gin and tonic and how when he saw the unstoppable tremor in his hand, he withdrew it, sat back and looked at Stuart watching him, shrugged, and said: "What the fuck does it all matter?"

When in that moment the bell at the gate rang, long and loud, he literally sprang back to an erect position. "The front gate," Stuart said. "No problem. It's François-Marie to pick up something: I'll tell all of you the story later."

The total silence inside the freezer was disturbing down in the cellar. It was the silence of an abandoned graveyard. The silence of eternity. François-Marie peered at the bird uncertainly. "I had the thought," he said in a near whisper, "that the cloth inside which this raven has lain for weeks must be permeated with botox in some form or the other. Dangerous, I should think."

"We can ask Helen. Do you mind if I bring her down to take a look? Chemists make this toxin so she might have some ideas."

"No, I don't mind at all. Bring her down. She and I can ignore each other." His bravado like his words gave Stuart the impression that his friend still had doubts, doubts about his sudden decision to try again with Férnande and start their life over again, doubts about abandoning Helen. He may have intended his words to sound harsh and sarcastic; instead they rang weak and diluted by another set of feelings: since he couldn't surrender Helen easily, he might even try to live a double life.

When he spoke to Helen on the terrace, she grasped the situation quickly: the bird on the station roof and the bird in the cellar with François-Marie.

"He's in the freezer too?" she asked off-handedly as they went down the cellar stairs, and laughed sardonically. "With the top closed? My lover boy! Eternal love! Anyway, no matter now."

When she saw the cloth lying on top of the freezer, she picked it up like any old rag—fearlessly, the two men thought, for they'd treated it like the Holy Shroud of Turin with the imprint of a body on it and were careful about even touching it. Stuart, afraid of infection, had even thrown away the backpack he'd carried the dead raven in. As if a sop to them both, Helen did hold it at a distance to smell it. "Hmm. It has no smell at all. Maybe the freezer kills the toxin instead of conserving it. An interesting chemical development. So if that's the case, then the bird on the station roof is the only being on earth that might smell the dead bird in this cloth. Just put the cloth in a plastic bag and find a way to let his mate sniff it. If she voluntarily gets in the cage with it, we were right. Shows how genuinely powerful emotions exist in the animal kingdom.—of great interest to ornithologists like my father and François-Marie. We humans just talk about love, while she may have flown the Atlantic Ocean to find him. Now that my friends is real, total devotion. Anyway, if it turns out the cloth has no raven smell, then, well, we were wrong."

"Ok then, I'll be on my way back to Giustiniana with the cloth, a cage and a portable ladder. Thanks to you, Helen. And Stuart, give my regards to Ermanno. He did a brave thing—already this afternoon the Great Wall began disappearing near my house and you saw the gate. Maybe they could leave the towers, an unusual entrance into old San Nicola! "

"I'll tell Ermanno your suggestion … a good idea."

It felt like another meeting of the Group when Stuart and Helen rejoined Sophie and a now more relaxed Ermanno whose eyes—like

Sophie's—followed Helen's natural sensual movements like a hawk. She knew no other way. Her very walk contained both the invitation and its fulfillment. She nodded and smiled at the others and ambled sexily to the wall looking over the garden and the entrance gate as if to watch the departure of François-Marie from her life. Thinking that Helen had been more enamored of him than she realized, Stuart tried to sum up the confusion of the psychological situation between Helen and François-Marie: she has a good, intelligent and honest heart and she knows she is an ambulatory female minefield which, he had noted, she tries to play down so as not to scare away sensitive, fearful males. But she must perceive that disguising and minimizing the power of her beauty also increases her feelings of loneliness. So she has to be a strong and courageous woman to face the inevitable isolation that her sensual beauty creates. She has to be glad she's beautiful but doubtless feels it unjust that she has to pay such a high price for it: the men who step forward are always the arrogant, insensitive, egocentric persons for whom she is simply the beautiful object they deserve. François-Marie seemed different from the start. But now, after his betrayal, she must see him with different eyes. To her, his body that she'd seen as that of the long distance runner was now nothing more than a run-of-the-mill ornithologist. What she'd heard as a charming French accent now sounded silly and stupid. The reality was that they'd both been lonely and searching for love, but what François-Marie mistook for love for her must have been the usual passion for her beauty, more than it was budding love, more uncertain solace and revenge for his 'cared for' status with Férnande than it was love for Helen. The reality was that François-Marie was tied to his wife come hell or high water, as if she had some demoniacal hold on him, the bitter truth of which he must have been cognizant from the start of his adventure with irresistible Helen—but, he learned, the two kinds of attractions were not the same. And besides, he'd wanted to hurt Férnande, not Helen. Yet he couldn't even begin to explain that to her … not yet, at least. François-Marie's position differed in another way from all of them: his mind was filled with ravens; he even forgets himself; he didn't have the mental space to feel her emotions; he simply didn't feel her suffering over another failure at love.

Stuart contemplated himself and the others there on the summer terrace—the remaining four of them—the way their creator wanted them in this moment. Two were missing: the Frenchman was off on a mission to recover an American raven, and Gianluigi Logreco would never again return. While Stuart's thoughts roamed far and wide, he suddenly heard Ermanno's words … "so you see, that is just the way the way secret intelligence agencies and secret services work. Someone learns that botox is a terrifying poison that could wipe out the world and they construct the complex, extravagant cover for a bioweapons lab in Casale di San Nicola, they not only put it underground but they construct this elaborate secluded hamlet, the garbage dump interrupting a public roadway, the crazy Great Wall, the art deco towers, the German guards, and all that other shit and then the top dogs—the ones that run everything at the very top in the national government and the CIA—laugh and dance around together and drink crates of champagne and smoke cigars and take off their neck ties to celebrate sixteen dead Russian soldiers, their great victory. And then the same ones kill one of their defected agents, Gianluigi, just for spite."

28.

The more complex his dreams became, the longer the dreaming lasted; the more active his wake self's director's role became, the longer it was taking him to return to normal daily life. The morning after the first view of the raven on the station roof, he began waking at around seven and quickly jumped into the chaotic dream in which small colorfully dressed children played quietly while black birds and white birds flew around them, birds with big bodies and wide wing spans, so that he knew he had to do with ravens, all chattering in their language one to the other while diving and swooping around his head so fiercely that he threw his arms into the air to beat them off and it took him longer than usual to take control of the situation. He was cognizant that he got into his director's role just in time, actually just seconds before the dream would have bypassed the dreaming and set out on its own without his moderating management. But once he was again inside the dream action, he rather fearfully rejected the idea of playing an active participatory role, like sitting with the small children and pointing out to them the acrobatics of the birds. From time to time he thought he should get up and leave dreamtime but something magnetic held him and the dream part of him began to wonder if that which was happening in his dreamtime, was happening elsewhere too and that by staying in dreamtime and directing events he was creating new realities. Hence, he thought, if he stepped out of the dreamtime—as he could quite easily—the still unknown event would never happen and these two small children would never exist. For his dream created them and his direction and guidance brought them to life. But despite any decision he might make, he felt the dream's gradual magnetic power lessening. The dream began to fade and he knew it was ending; yet he was aware that he'd just experienced the real thing, not a scholarly-historical recounting of what the dreamings must have been for the Maya or the Aboriginals. He felt as if he were atop the crest of the great wave of time carrying him to unknown parts. That is the problem of us humans, he thought, we're uncomfortable with our doubts about transcendence and theories about how we got where we are and where we are going from here—even though the little we know or want to know is also falling in pieces. That we are merely part of someone else's dream is unbearable—if not ludicrous.

When he stood up and checked the time, it was only seven-thirty and though the dreamtime had lasted only those short fifteen minutes, his sensations in the aftermath filled him like a hangover from a late evening orgy. Quickly he made notes about what he saw and felt before his mind returned to its everyday state for which he had been trained by his education and science to accept as normal. Later, he would call Férnande and tell her the good news and that he felt destined to run up that hill again.

But the words 'first things first' churned through his confusion about where reality lay. He had promised Ermanno to take him down into Tartarus Pit this morning, and he too was curious to climb down that ladder again. Though perhaps he should not have been, Ermanno was pleased with the idea of seeing first-hand the result of one of his projects; even though he was in charge of the biolab project, he had never seen it. For that reason, Stuart believed that Ermanno and the others of his world had no idea of what they were really doing. He had asked Helen at one of their meetings what the fuck botox really was as if the fact it killed people didn't count. Only after his on-the-job training, after reports about the dead Russian soldiers, after his trip to Kiev, after gathering statistics about the secret biolabs worldwide did he grasp the essence of what he was doing: he realized that in effect he was producing lethal botox toxin that was killing people.

Stuart gathered his equipment, his 250000 Lumen Xhp90, the new backpack, shoes and jackets for both of them and they set out. It was surprising the number of people, walking or jogging along Via

San Nicola as far as the *manége*. Ignoring them, he and Ermanno continued on to the glade that time and nature had rendered almost unrecognizable. They pushed their way through the thickets to the trapdoor, which vines were already gradually covering. Stuart's Lumen illuminated the way down into the pit of darkness. During their descent, Ermanno breathed hard and fast, muttering, "good god, good god, good god." When they finally stood on the ground under the bottom of the world and Stuart turned on the lights, Ermanno blinked and said that only madmen could dream up something like this. "Though it seems unreal, it's also proof that humans simply don't know what the fuck they're doing. No wonder our world is crumbling around us. Look at this tunnel!" he said. "Where does it lead anyway and what the fuck were they doing here?"

Stuart watched him as he meandered down the lateral tunnel, sliding his hand along the smooth walls.

"Maybe this really is unreal," Stuart said when Ermanno came back, his mind still under the effect of the morning's dreaming: the black and white birds flying around the kids and a rabbit riding atop the little boy's head.

"Well, maybe as you say, it's only a bad dream. Now that I know you a bit and see the world you live in, I think you might mean that literally."

Stuart reddened. "But Boss, you shouldn't think I'm experimenting in the paranormal lightly, or playing games and indulging in magic. We all dream and our dreams do have meanings and sometimes they generate powers like clairvoyance. The ancients like the Maya and the Aboriginals had science too, but for them the dreamings were not only normal but essential to explain the origins and existence of human beings ... and sometimes to predict their people's future. Dreams were a power—closer to metaphysics than to the paranormal. But above all, I'm trying to harness a bit of my own hidden self."

"*Per l'amor di dio*, Stuart Stuart. I'm not sure I follow you, but meanwhile let's take a look at this place."

"Right! Now step over here to our own private metro—thanks to your concealed guidance! You get the place of honor in car number one. Now we'll take a little ride. The whole length of the Pit."

"Pretty good set up anyway, the underground labyrinth. Whoever planned it did his job well."

"Nothing much to see now that the birds are gone, although water is still running down there at the end of that tunnel."

They had ridden about five minutes, observing the side tunnels to the left and the right, when Ermanno said in an unnatural voice: "How much longer … all of a sudden I'm not feeling well. We'd better get back home. I need to lie down somewhere."

"Ok, hang on. We're at the end of the line."

They were under the right tower. He called Sophie to pick them up. Meanwhile, Ermanno managed the steps and immediately sank to the ground, slumped against the tower wall. His pale face was now chalk white.

Outside, waiting for Sophie, Stuart saw that no trace of the Great Wall remained in the vicinity of the former entrance. As far as he could see in all directions, it had simply vanished. It would have required a whole regiment to clear the wall so fast. Meanwhile, a fleet of garbage trucks was clearing the roundabout from which the junked autos, a second bus and furniture had already been removed. What garbage remained was now within the limits of the roundabout itself. At this rate it would be clear in another day or so. The road would be open and the Elevateds superfluous.

He went back into the tower and looked anxiously at Ermanno, sitting with his back against the wall, his chin on his chest, his legs drawn toward him in a cramped position. Was it slow working botox poisoning? Stuart wondered, thinking of Gianluigi and Ermanno's subsequent conviction that the same fate awaited him. He swore to himself that they would defy destiny and create a new one for Ermanno.

When they reached the house, Helen examined him still stretched out on the back seat of the car. Ermanno was only half conscious. He spoke little, his words slurred, "can't see, can't see right" he kept saying, breathing hard and trying to swallow.

"It's botulism," Helen said. "I'm not a doctor but I'm certain. We've got to get him to a hospital quick and he needs an antitoxin immediately."

"If he's admitted to a hospital in the city they'll find him in an hour or so … and finish the job. There's a small hospital, out near the town of Bracciano where we went for vaccinations. Let's go there. But even that's dangerous. After all it is Italy's corrupt secret service that wants to kill him."

Sophie drove. Helen tried to keep Ermanno comfortable and conscious. Stuart went through his pockets and removed every piece of identification or information about him. The emergency room at Bracciano Hospital was nearly empty and the doctors quickly got the picture. They gave him the antitoxin and wheeled him off for treatment. Later, they reported that he would likely survive, but with lasting damage. He had spoken a few incoherent words before the sedation knocked him out. Stuart could call at any time and see him the next day—if his pals don't find him first, Stuart thought.

"By the way," the head doctor said, "the infection was massive."

Stuart had spotted the youngest doctor, long hair, bearded, who looked like the typical outsider. He called him aside and explained frankly that their patient was in great danger, that the same people who'd infected him were looking for him in this moment—to finish him off. Could he do anything to protect him?

The young doctor grinned as if he relished the opportunity. He would remove Ermanno's admission file and post a nurse nearby for the night.

"Those white coats here are the big danger," he said. "They love following restrictive orders. A bunch of bureaucrats and cowards, aiming at becoming director of a hospital like this and imagining the happiness it would bring them. By the way, why'd you pick me to speak with?"

"I was attracted by your haircut."

The doctor grinned. Then his face clouded and Stuart saw that he was rethinking the whole situation.

"Look," he said, his perceptive mind assessing the situation and how to handle it, "the best way to help that guy is to get him out of here, quick. These guys here are a danger to the medical practice. More bureaucrats than men of medicine. One of them has probably already called the local police, who will contact Rome. Now I have a friend near here who will take him in; besides I know quite a bit— more than those other guys—about botulism. We had another patient here, a chemist who works in some laboratory. He believed that somewhere in this area there were people making the toxin for military purposes. Hey, where do you live anyway?"

"In the hamlet called Casale di San Nicola. You must know that roundabout on the road to Rome."

"Of course. Who doesn't? And I also know there's a secret biolab somewhere in the vicinity. Was your friend inside it today? That would explain it. I think he somehow got enough vapors to infect him."

"Yes, he did. And I was with him ... but not in the all the same places."

"I'll treat him myself but ... but you'll have to trust me on this. I mean, I'm not like the other so-called doctors here."

"Yes, though I don't know the real reasons why. Instinct, I guess. That sick man too was convinced of his instinct and look where it got him. Turns out though that he was partially right."

"Why partially?"

"He knew the people who want to kill him were evil, but he only half believed they would go so far as doing him in—even though they'd just botoxed his best friend, a former agent of the same organization."

"Agent! Organization! Wow! Then this is big time stuff."

"Does it scare you?"

"Some, but it excites me too."

"I'm Stuart Stuart. What's your name?"

"Doctor of Internal Medicine, Bruno D'Amato."

"So Bruno D'Amato, where'll we take him … if we get away with it."

"My girlfriend has a house in the town of Bracciano facing the lake. Teresa's a nurse, or soon will be, and she loves this kind of thing—working in the beyond, so to speak. And she has a guest room … just the place for him. I'll take care of medication and laboratory tests somehow. Look, Stuart—I like that double name … *fico!*— there's a back delivery door here. Drive around there and I'll bring your friend out somehow and we'll be off to Bracciano. Lucky Teresa's home today. I'll call her on the way. Then I'll come back here and discover the patient is missing. And you should leave the area as quickly as possible. We don't want neighbors to see anything."

Twenty minutes later, they left a near dead nan—who the doctors had said would never be the same again—in the back room of the house of Teresa Bersani hanging over the crater Lake Bracciano. Sophie and Helen couldn't believe such coincidences possible: only a couple of hours earlier Ermanno was dying in their car; now a doctor had concealed him in a nearly untraceable hideout and was treating a complete stranger and risking his own medical career. Stuart believed Bruno too wanted to defy fate and the rules of a sick society. There are such people in the world, he thought. But ever less.

29.

As soon as he was back home, Stuart called Férnande and pronounced the words only she would understand: "I've got to run up that hill again."

"Run then!" she said.

He headed for La Storta in the Panda. Near the former entrance gate to San Nicola he glanced up the rolling hills at François-Marie's house; it seemed to belong to another place and to another age. It was no longer part of the hamlet as it was when it lay inside the Great Wall. Only a few truckloads of garbage remained in the roundabout. Workers said the Elevateds would soon come down. Only the twin art deco towers stood like sentinels over San Nicola, symbols and reminders of what once was, like the raven, the carrion eater, the bad omen with death trailing in its wake. 'I'll take the peacock,' he thought. 'Beautiful and ostentatious because of its great fan of feathers, filled with grace and the colorful awakening of the senses.'

Férnande was waiting at the door, at the edge of the Mashad carpet, but not touching it. Mashad, Mashad, so distant its origins, so near its reality, a never, never land.

"Welcome, stranger," she said.

"It's good to be back from the changing world outside. A little stability won't hurt us, Still, I am rather nervous, but I have to update you on my dream life."

"Things are changing rapidly everywhere, Stuart. Like François-Marie and I."

"But not your studio. It stays the same. The color of the walls, each different one from the other. And the black wall is the same, the one you loved best. In fact various objects seem to speak of you, my analyst."

"Not really. I mean I'm not an analyst—just a psychologist, at best a therapist. As you once pointed out, I don't even have a couch for patients to lie on."

"But you're my analyst! And you know that many Jungians don't use the couch either. In any case, Férnande, for me this place speaks of you."

"So what happened that you had to run up my hill again? And afterwards, I hope you'll tell me about that secret novel you hinted you were writing."

Stuart told her about the complex dream that disturbed him. Though he recognized the objects, the birds and the people in the dream, the dreamscape seemed too simple to be meaningless. Black ravens, right, but why the bluish white ones? A child playing amidst the chaos, unconcerned about the blue-white ravens or the white rabbit on his head, a beautiful young girl sitting like princess on a kind of throne, mounted soldiers and mobs of people. What could it all mean?"

"Oh, Stuart, it's just the fantasist writer in you that makes a mountain out of a molehill. Besides, I think you're staying too long in dreamtime. That can play tricks on you. Besides, it's dangerous—like voodoo . You keep looking for hidden meanings—meanings that aren't there. Some things appear in dreams also to amuse us, you know. Frankly, I think this is another of the novelist's treasures that you often suspect of having some dramatic and menacing significance. You have to allow a little free space in your mind for Jung's shadow self—our dark side, yes, but which can also be your playful self. Just describing it is sufficient, if you like, play with it, but then let it go. Your dream is not like that terrifying scene in *Doctor Jekyll and Mr. Hyde* in which Jekyll wakes up and finds he still has the hairy forearm of Hyde! That's an example of why I think psychiatrists and psychologists have much to learn from novelists. In fact I don't know how we could get along without literature, which is much vaster—and maybe wiser—than psychology can ever be. You might read more of that Italian analyst, Mario Trevi's *Invasioni Controllate*. I like this in his book: 'Literature helps us understand the importance of the metaphor, and you must keep in mind that psychology is made up of metaphors.' So I think that sometimes you have to be able to just let them go."

"Another matter, Férnande: it's said that analysis is harmful to creativity. Did you ever read about Rilke and analysis? There's a story that still circulates that Rilke refused to be examined by Freud because he was afraid of losing something of himself. If he'd been analyzed, would he have written *The Unicorn?* You know, 'the creature that has never been but they loved it anyway and it behaved as if it were there and it raised its head with hardly a trace of not being there so that they fed it not with corn but only the Possibility of Being, enough that it could grow a horn. Only one.' So what do you think of that, beautiful lady?"

"Absurd that he refused treatment for a thing that never was! Your Mario Trevi said the same. He too found it ridiculous—in the short term at least. Though not a writer, he admitted that in the long run he came to feel himself invaded by his unconscious— though the invasion in him was *controlled.* Apparently, Rilke's was uncontrolled, the way a poet's unconscious must be, I suppose. Trevi said that the unconscious imagination was vastly superior to that of the conscious mind so that when you're short of ideas you can always put your hopes in your creative unconscious. When Trevi spoke of the mind, he said he meant both the conscious and the unconscious. And Fellini said that without analysis—he went to the best Rome offered in his time, the Jungian Ernst Bernhard—he wouldn't have been able to undertake many fundamental things in his work. So in other words, take that dream for what it is—a dream—and use it."

"You remind me. You know, I will always wonder what the analyst found so unique in Fellini's mind that inspired his mad fantasies in his Oscar-winning films that to me seemed taken straight out of his dreamworld. That's why straight people, I mean people who discount their dreams, or don't even believe that they dream, are seldom creative. I used to watch Fellini films; it was like walking along the narrow edge of an abyss during an earthquake. You grasp for meanings. And that's the way dreams work too. No?"

"Stuart, you and I can see that Fellini's films came from his dreamworld. Life as a dream must account for it. But I insist not all dreams must have some dramatic meaning. What happens in the dream itself is the meaning."

"I read that Fellini said a shadow or a memory was enough to work with. I understand that feeling. Sometimes, just one single word comes to me in life—or in a dream—and that ignites something in me. One day, apropos of nothing, I thought 'San Marino', that little republic in the middle of Italy and I wrote a novel set there—and I've never even been there."

"That's another reason psychology needs art, especially fantasists. Intellectuals can analyze and talk about what Fellini or certain writers create but they are shy about reaching the essence of … well, the essence of creation. And the individualism it requires. The Jungian concept that if a man goes his own way, his own individual way, it is the right way, I think—but it's always at a certain risk".

"Yes, there's a risk all right. Ideologically, I'm a collectivist, that's the communist way. But within my collectivism I reserve room for my own creative individualism. That's another reason to believe that literature dominates psychology. Why? Because art is free in one sense—or nearly. You can't tell a free writer what to write or a free painter what to paint. Still, I think that the rooms of my heart cannot be just for me, myself.

"And by the way, there's another curious thing about Fellini that I forgot to mention: the connection of dreams with death. I've read that the filmmaker was literally obsessed by the idea of death, especially death by mistake which must have been a burden throughout his life—maybe a burden of evanescence. And he was right: he died much too young in the operating room in an operation that he didn't need. So was his death on the operating table fate or destiny or chance?"

"Fate, this time, I think."
"Still, at least like Tiresias he had clairvoyance."

30.

A few days later Stuart's phone rang early in the morning, a time Italians call only in emergencies or for something urgent. Sensing bad news, he grabbed at his phone on the bedside table.

"He's gone," Doctor Bruno D'Amato said. "The antitoxins were working well and he was improving but when Teresa entered his room with the medicines at seven this morning our patient had vanished. We both drove around the town, just in case. *Niente*. Nothing. We asked everyone we met. No one had seen such a person wandering around. And everyone here knows everybody else in town. Only one rather anomalous matter—I mention this because you spoke of his connections with the secret world—when I went to check him yesterday and the day before, a black suv was parked up the street."

"The bad guys! Look, Bruno, you can't do anything more for him. I think he was afraid they would trace him and involve you and her. He'd become very observant of such things of late. His penitence, maybe. I'll head for the other towns on the lake where I think he had friends. Hang up now. No more phone calls. Ciao!"

Thirty minutes later, Stuart was in Trevignano on Lake Bracciano. It was already hot. Beach time. He realized it was Saturday when he saw the long water front crowded with people. There was a commotion several hundred meters down the lake front: a big crowd of sunbathers, police, medics dressed in red and white running back and forth between the beach and an ambulance parked on the street.

"What's happening down there?" he asked a woman hurrying past. "Some guy crossed the lake from the town of Bracciano in a speed boat carrying a dying man to the hospital. He thought it was here. The medics and two doctors came from the hospital in Anguillara across the lake. Too late. The man was already dead."

Stuart pushed his way through the crowd standing at the edge of the water as if waiting for something else to happen. The only sounds were that of small waves lapping at the sand. He saw Ermanno uncovered, flat on his back, his mouth open, eyes closed, his face watery cold and gray. He looked around for something to cover his face with. When someone handed him a cloth sheet, he looked up into the eyes of Bruno D'Amato and nodded imperceptibly. He covered Ermanno and walked away.

Stuart found the man with the boat. Police were questioning him. "No, I tell you, he didn't find me, I found him still in shallow water near the shore but trying to swim. He could barely lift his arms. When I tried to speak with him, he just mumbled Trevigano, Trevignano and kept trying to swim. When I told him I would take him in my boat, he stopped and just looked at me. So I got him to the beach and told him to wait there while I got my boat. When I got back with the boat, five, maybe ten minutes later, he was gone. Then I spotted him out in the deep, still trying to swim but going under, then reemerging. Lake Bracciano near Bracciano town gets very deep and very fast. He could've gone far down first. But he didn't. He managed to stay afloat. When I was a boy that famous deep sea explorer, Jacques Cousteau, was here with his crew to measure the depth. People say that his subs never found the bottom. But officially the lake reaches one hundred sixty meters deep, but Cousteau thought it was much deeper. That's the way these crater lakes are, you just never know ...."

The police walked away and Stuart kept the boat lover talking. "Ok, ok, I've read about the Cousteau thing, but what about this man?"

"Well, I raced out to him in my boat ... that's her over there, a real beauty and at full speed ..."

"You're in love with ... look you'll probably get your picture in the newspapers or on TV with your boat what with all the reporters hanging around. Ok, so what happened then? Did he say anything?"

"I pulled him in and he didn't look good at all. But I'll tell you what I forgot to tell police: he died in the boat! That man didn't die from drowning. We were about half way to Trevignano when he sort of gasped and I think he died in that moment. So, no, he didn't die from drowning, I don't believe. I thought that was strange. A man comes out of the water and dies but not from drowning. That was one very sick man and the only thing he ever said was 'Trevignano."

Stuart remembered that Ermanno had mentioned the summer days he used to take his kids to Trevignano and they always ate filetti di Tinca in a fish restaurant right on the waterfront. The kids loved it, he said, in one of his rare acknowledgements of his former family life, and that he missed those times. Memories, Stuart thought—not old friends—drew him back to Trevignano. He must have wanted to die there—and maybe he did. Ermanno had often mused about life and death and both the mystery of the act of dying the death—especially since Gianluigi died, as if his words that *they* might be planning the same botox death for him were more than mere premonition.

A stiff Eastern breeze had come up over Lago Bracciano. The ripples of less than an hour before were now small rapid waves, sunbathers here and there frowned at the sky and called to their children to stay close to the shore. The summer's end sun remained hot. Someone nearby turned up the volume of a radio: Kate Bush was singing the popular *Running Up That Hill*. The circle of people around Ermanno remained unbroken. All of a sudden, two rough looking men dressed in jeans and baseball caps and badges on their shirts arrived with a stretcher and pushed the crowd away. They lifted Ermanno onto the stretcher and without a word carried him to a black suv with CD plates waiting on the street, its motor still running. They slid Ermanno into the back and walked off into the town. Two other men wearing white shirts and ties got out of the suv and examined closely Ermanno's face until one of them nodded at the other as if to say, 'It's him.' They too were apparently agents of AISI, men of NATO and

CIA, Ermanno's colleagues, and more than likely the same ones who'd botoxed him. Now, all traces of their former boss would quickly vanish from the face of the earth: no autopsy, no inquest, no questions asked. Immediate cremation, and Ermanno Riccardi will have never existed.

31.

Pleasant late summer afternoon breezes from the Tyrrhenian Sea wafting over the hamlet conveyed a nearly forgotten normality back to the five hundred inhabitants trying to get used to the reality that they were again part of the whole corrupt world outside, as well as to their loss of the sense of protection and a certain exclusivity inside what they had called—many lovingly—the Great Wall.

Today, arriving from Rome, you circle the roundabout in a normal fashion and enter straightaway into the hamlet. The Elevateds and the garbage dump are gone. Older people lingering along the pine-lined Via San Nicola relate another story that is gradually becoming fable: the security they'd felt in earlier times when they proudly showed their permit to the guards and passed through the gates in the Great Wall into the hamlet. Many of them would stop and gaze in admiration and awe at the two art deco towers, the likes of which were unknown in these parts. Like an abandoned ideology or an abjured faith, they also perceived that many little things of the past still remained. And if they by chance ventured into the abandoned spaces of the open rural terrain unprotected by their Great Wall, they felt an inexplicable sense of unease about the intrusion of the unknown into their former "way of life" surrounded by their Great Wall.

Needless to say, those San Nicolians felt like survivors of a malicious tragedy that struck the fortress that had offered them the first real security of their lives—or as one elderly widower expressed it: 'since he was ejected from his mother's womb.'

The summer breezes also projected sensations of an aftermath, of that same pervasive end times atmosphere. Some such nostalgic people, especially of the villa crowd, loved the two remaining one-eighty turns of the road after you come off the roundabout into San Nicola, which actually serve no other purpose than remind them of how it once was behind the Great Wall. Such people, especially the nostalgic ones, were bewildered the day they found plastered on posts and fences an announcement—signed by members of the San Nicola Commission—of the Commission's unanimous decision to take down the two towers the following Saturday. Professional demolition experts had guaranteed not to damage the surroundings, especially not the tennis-swimming club and restaurant near the entrance that was reopening the next day after the two-year closure due to access problems. During the demolition procedures, San Nicola would be a closed area: no entry or exit via the roundabout from early morning until late afternoon.

Two days later, San Nicolians gathered at road blocks on Via San Nicola, or inside the confines of the tennis-swimming club or at the roundabout, each at least one hundred meters distance from the twin towers, to observe their official demolition, planned in the minutest detail. There was something festive about the occasion like once at public executions on Campo de' Fiori in the city; opinions were divided: older and more cultured people thought that the art deco towers—despite the nasty reference to the more famous Twin Towers—added a certain prestige to the hamlet and reflected a connectedness with the widespread art deco residential sections of their city.

One young guy there for the fireworks wisecracked that the demolition squad should furnish at least one helicopter to crash into the towers—one copter would suffice—to lend more authenticity to the felling of the twin towers.

"That was a terrible tragedy back then, Muslim terrorism's most heinous attack," replied an elderly man, another of the 'villa crowd' as young people referred to those who lived in the huge villas lining deep Via San Nicola where Stuart and Sophie lived.

"Pure magic, how they fell," the young guy added. "If two airplanes were enough in New York, one little helicopter will suffice here … for both towers. I doubt the Commission even thought of that—if that phantasmal commission even exists," the kid continued, despite shushing from all sides. "Who are they anyway? Where are they?"

While the populace stood by in suddenly hushed observation, a muted explosion sounded, the twin towers shook as during a 8.0 Richter scale earthquake and then slowly at first, almost calmly began to crumble, then louder and louder as layer after layer joined the lower parts of the dying falling walls gradually imploding and in a surprisingly short time collapsed cleanly, each tower separate, the left tower first, then the other—and without the fiction of a helicopter. No one jumped from the top. No sirens sounded. No cameras whirred. No journalists mingled among the people asking how they felt about the spectacle. Here or there, one person expressed strong feelings of support or condemnation, while only a few knew that a real San Nicola Commission actually did exist—a commission however appointed by the Research Institute, which in turn was run by Italian Intelligence, and it in turn run by NATO, the military arm of the European Union, both of which were controlled by the USA. The demolition was perfect. By the next afternoon, no traces of the twin art deco towers remained, just as no traces of the existence of Professor Gianluigi Logreco or of Ermanno Riccardi remained.

In this atmosphere of changing times, François-Marie and Férnande could not make the final decision to return to France. They too felt ties with San Nicola; each felt connections, similar, though of a different nature one from the other.

François-Marie felt a dreamy sort of loyalty to "his" birds, a solid connection with his dream images of peacocks with their trains of tail feathers spread in all their glory, and how they moved aside for his passage among them. In comparison, moving to France was a detail.

Férnande, was caught up in dreams too, now that she knew another François-Marie. Now that she had come to terms with roller coaster sensations, she desired more and more to be in her re-found euphoria in his arms—she thought, to make up for five years wasted on her "vapid and vainglorious egotism", as she depicted her former self.

The Dolons' house now lay at the very edge of San Nicola;

actually not even part of the hamlet. The other houses like theirs had vanished, dismantled piece by piece and carried away to an unknown elsewhere. It was as if the other houses had never existed either. For them, the vanished houses were metaphors of their former lives, mere figments like the so-called Great Wall was for a handful of skeptics.

In every room of their house, there were cardboard boxes, packed and ready for movers. They could leave any time they wanted. But they stayed.

The normalization of the hamlet—the destruction of the Great Wall, the clean-up of the roundabout, the straightening of the approach road, the dismantling of the Elevateds, the demolition of the twin towers, the removal of all the identical prefabricated modular houses on the green hill, except that of François-Marie and Férnande, and the grand reopening of the tennis and swim club and restaurant—was mirrored by the apparent return of quiet order to the manor house of Stuart and Sophie, except for the presence of their fugitive guest, Helen, stowed away in the secret upstairs apartment.

For several days, end of summer clouds had been gathering each afternoon and there was a marked crispness in the early morning air, which Stuart thought would have pleased Gianluigi no end. This morning, evidence of a light nocturnal rain dampened the flagstones in the garden and left behind big drops on the leaves of ferns and other plants on the open terrace. The meteorological changes bore sensations of nostalgia and a longing for return to something uncertain and indefinite, sensations that coincided with the physical-social-geographic changes underway in the hamlet of San Nicola.

Trying with all his force to remain apart from it all, Stuart was struggling with the opening of his long postponed novel on which he was working day and night or whenever an idea struck him: naming and describing his protagonist and other major characters, the physical setting, the time— the all-important question of time and its span— and zeroing in on his major and minor themes. Ostensibly searching for space and time, he was living, working and sleeping in a downstairs guest room in this trying period. Sophie occupied their common bedroom on the second level and Helen—who, after Ermanno's disappearance had resigned her job for personal security reasons—lived in the secluded third level paradise while she was trying to read every book in Stuart's library and received nocturnal visits from either Stuart or Sophie.

Ultimately, the rains came. The north winds blew. Summer was over. But nothing definite had yet replaced it. Stuart searched for a replacement. Maybe the seasonal change and the search for a replacement was the metaphor he needed. He laughed at himself and discarded the idea as banality.

Then there was the hamlet. What? he thought. You mean our hamlet where we live and work, suffer, dream and love? The hamlet, the breathing, living organism that was San Nicola was another matter. Its five hundred inhabitants, people of his times, penetrated his very being, breathed into his organism through his own nostrils and mouth. Though he thought differently from them and saw the world with other eyes, he was still part of them, from them had emerged the person he was today. Yes, he told himself: they are part of me, and I am part of them. It's there. There is the reality. But which San Nicola do you mean? old friend, he asked, admittedly meaning Europe, not just the hamlet in change. The old, old hamlet of pre-Great Wall times, or the Great Wall hamlet itself, or today's post-Great Wall hamlet. Which was real? The hamlet of the majority of mature, politically corrupt San Nicolians who rue the fall of the Great Wall, or the young who were already forgetting it and had cheered the crash of the twin towers? Or did he mean only himself and a handful of other-thinkers like him.

Yet, to write about the hamlet is like writing about the wind. It blows, but it is empty and vacuous and you walk straight through it. So was it real? After the experience of Great Wall hamlet, you might think the hamlet itself is unreal, only the shadow of a possible community of people. Yet the hamlet IS real. Often surreal. Stuart felt that with time and luck he would be able to embrace the hamlet per se, free of the element of time. But then, he thought, who or what is ever free of time? Time marches on freely, tramping and trammeling over anything in its path, unlike François-Marie's peacocks that with their trains of colorful tail feathers spread so courteously parted for his passage. San Nicolians had no worries about sinking into oblivion; it was oblivion itself. That is how they wanted things. San Nicolians were outliers by choice. The few kilometers distance to the city seemed insuperable. The hamlet. Its people didn't want to be at the center of things. They wanted to be outliers. They felt different from other people. Though the perfect place for artists, the hamlet had only Stuart—but no one even knew he was a writer. There is no intellectual life in the hamlet. No real culture or counterculture. San Nicolians read little. Only rare individuals even discuss the arts. People don't know what to do with the arts. What is bookreading worth? they would answer. The reading of books takes place in Milan or in out of the way places like Ferrara or Padua. Not in the hamlet. Nonetheless, the San Nicolians who had loved their Great Wall for the protection it offered had quickly come to prefer the lack of walls and garbage and the Elevateds. The supermarkets were more accessible, the tennis-swimming club and restaurant re-introduced the social to the hamlet. Rumors spread that soon small shops would be admitted in a new commercial area.

Each afternoon, the three of them met on the covered summer terrace for a drink and to speak of their individual activities. The most talkative, the one of the three who had the most ongoing pursuits out in the real world, was often Sophie: she told them that sales in her boutique in La Storta were booming, especially among San Nicolians who, like returned prisoners of war or rich plantation owners from the South Sea islands on a buying spree in Europe, were itching to spend money on things whose existence they had forgotten.

"An elderly lady came in the shop today", Sophie recounted,

"and while looking over every single necklace in the shop, said that during their two-year spell under the shadow of the Great Wall and the twin towers, people had stashed away money in secret places—some literally under the mattress."

"When I asked why that, she answered that it was because of widespread fears that bad times lay ahead. Just imagine, they feared times worse than those two fateful years of people and birds disappearing. But then the talkative lady left without buying one single item. I suppose she was saving her money too."

Then Sophie proudly showed them a check for three hundred euros and a warm letter from the editor of the Milan magazine that had published her first short story, *Life Without Love*.

For long moments Sophie's eyes remained fixed on Helen who had asked what the story was about.

"It's about a strange woman who'd never known how to love until she met again a man she'd liked and, I think, had slept with when she was very young."

"You *think* she slept with him, you say. But Sophie, you're writing the story and creating the people in it, don't you know everything about her?"

"Why Helen, dearest"—which Sophie pronounced lovingly and with the most innocent charm—"how can you know everything about another person? Impossible! I actually know little about you—though I should know more by now—and yet after ten years together, there is so much about Stuart that I don't know either."

"What don't you know about Stuart?" Helen asked, her eyes tentatively wandering in unexplored territories, as if in Sophie's lands of abandoned spaces.

"Like how he really feels about almost anything. He loves me? Well, yes. But I have no idea about how he loves me."

Sophie glanced at Stuart and then did a double take; he was

staring at his wife as if he'd never known this side of her. This was another Sophie. This Sophie was the writer she so wanted to be. Who liked to say she wrote stories and hoped someday to become a writer. A special kind of writer, he knew, with untold talents and the experience of lived life to sustain it. He was the opposite: he was a writer as he had told Férnande, but a writer who hardly wrote. That made no sense to Sophie. And he admitted that she was right again.

"Strange," Helen replied. "Here I am, living with two writers who don't seem to understand what they write, while I have so much to say but am unable to write it down coherently. So what actually should I do about it. *Nada de nada?*"

"Like most of us, Helen, Like nearly all of us," Sophie said. "We have so much inside us that wants out. We want to let it out. But …"

"But I sit up in my room and read. I read it all. And what do I learn? I learn that the writers I once admired dislike and criticize the writers I like most. The writers I thought were progressive turn out to be reactionaries who consider the ones I love the most totalitarian. Yet writers are loved and spoiled even if many of those that I'm reading fear the extremes which is precisely what I want to know about. And that's where I want to be—at the extremes. Some of the best writers consider their proper place the center. And they urge other writers to move to the center too, or—they preach—all is lost. Such writers, those who're afraid to risk out on the edge and under pressure, are not for me either. They simply don't exist. Better to let them be … and hope they vanish quickly. Surprisingly, there are many like that."

"Really?" Sophie said. "I've always thought that all writers have something interesting to say. That that's why they write. I'm surprised you think that way ... darling."

"I ran into an unexpected one, an American writer I once thought I liked very much: Saul Bellow, who died not long ago, was a Canadian-American, Nobel prize winner, the son of emigrants from Russia. He despised Russia like he despised progressives who dared touch the extremes, while he loved and bowed down to Washington's power and to capitalism. But then he had an excellent pen and handled words beautifully. It must have been easy for hm. His life flowed easily and he was very successful. He traveled around the world and commented on it but he wanted nothing to do with writing under pressure. Now if I were a writer, I would want to write ONLY under pressure. But he charged that D.H. Lawrence, Baudelaire, Nietzsche among others who worked under pressure represented intellectuals poorly. Poorly is the word he used. 'To the center!' Bellow said. 'To the center! Mankind's real struggle is at the center. At the center, humankind struggles with dehumanization for the possession of the world.' I think he meant Communism. Especially Russian Communism. At the center you can learn what human beings are and what our life is all about, he believed. But at the center, humankind is at war with collective powers for freedom! Get that! He equates the center with freedom! That is, it's a Cold War between capitalism and Socialism. And he chose the first and detested the latter. He equated extremism in literature with junk culture! He relates extremism ONLY with junk culture, with thrillers, shoot-outs and conflagration, with sadism and sexual deviations—certainly nothing normal."

"Good God, Helen, and to think you have been here among us all this time," Stuart finally exclaimed, stood up and walked up and down the terrace in an effort to release the emotions accumulated in his mind during Helen's unexpected exposition of her literary world. The twilight had passed in a moment and a light autumnal fog had descended on the hamlet preceding the gathering darkness. Yellowish lights from the street and garden lamps piercing the fog transmuted his confusing emotions into a sensation of romanticism that in turn somehow reminded him of that one special fraction of time spent with Férnande on the Mashad carpet back then.

"I'm absolutely shocked at your words about poor Bellow," he said from his position at the terrace wall. "I too thought I loved him—obviously for the wrong reasons, I see now. I was blinded by his ability with words as the Nobel Committee was by his super Americanism. My love just died together with him in his center. I too will always want to feel under pressure.

"Anyway ladies, to return to real time, I ordered pizzas and beer from the tennis club restaurant for dinner. But I think I will skip the pizza and retire to my desk—too many ideas churning in my head. I always write better when it's foggy outside and the yellow street lamps come on. You won't miss me."

32.

Stuart's idea was a scouting maneuver: a second return to the city to see what was really happening in the world outside. In the morning, he boarded the train headed for Piazza Barberini. There was no particular reason for going to that area again—except for the memory of the Hotel Bernini where they used to dance on the roof garden club-restaurant. The piazza was the place he met Ermanno that day and talked about the role of chance in life and whether Ermanno was a cop—it turned out he was not a cop but a top intelligence agent. The hotel on the piazza also brought to mind all the diverse people of those pre-Stefano times. Where do they go, he often wondered, the people we used to know? Looking around for a face he might recognize, he saw only aliens and at the same time, he felt running through his veins something refreshing about his total anonymity: his rootlessness and his freedom. He felt San Nicola a world away, from which, in this moment, he felt deliciously detached and alone in this city that was once his. He perceived his solitude as both an ache and a joy. Contemporary man's eternal conundrum, he thought. The crowd or solitude? And he thought of the Donne poem that François-Marie loved, some words of which seemed written for him too: *No man is an island*. And he was glad that he too was involved in mankind. Purposefully he passed through an alley and whispered to himself that no, he was not a monk looking for a vacancy in a monastery; his place was among the others. And suddenly he stood as if by magic in the back row of mobs of visitors on the small piazza admiring the city's most famous fountain, Fontana di Trevi. Everyone was laughing and joking at the antics of two half nude girls splashing in the waters of Gian Lorenzo Bernini's illustrious art treasure. Bernini who created much of Rome's Baroque would likely have approved of that tourist touch. Stuart laughed, shrugged and walked on. Their freedom however was not his. Like the Great Wall had not been his freedom, nor the garbage dump and the Elevateds and the twin towers. The unfettered display at the fountain had nothing to do with freedom. Detachment, anonymity, lostness in the crowd awaited him. Solitude was his lot. Unthinking and undecided he wandered over narrow cobblestoned streets, across small piazzas, through the ghetto, to Campo de' Fiori where he used to visit Giordano Bruno. As every morning, vendors at the open-air market shouted their wares, children raced among the stalls and dogs barked. Normality. He sat down at the foot of the tall bronze statue of the hooded heretic philosopher who dominated the Campo when the market was closed, but in this moment stood unobtrusive and lonely, though just as mysterious as he was in his day.

"Not many people do this," said an older man sitting close by.

"Do what?" Stuart asked, surprised.

"Dedicate time to the madman the Inquisition burned alive right here over five hundred years ago," said the dark man who introduced himself as Nullo. It turned out that conversation with Nullo was exciting and above all influenced by the philosopher Bruno. And he wanted to talk about him.

They sat at the base of the monument almost side by side listening to the din of barking dogs and the cacophony of the market hawkers' cries and smelling the smells of fresh fish wafting across the piazza and the smoke rising from ovens with chickens turning on the spit while all around them swarms of shoppers competed for space and service. As always the Campo emanated a concentrate of the smells of the city—fruits and fish, flowers and human sweat, and in the afternoon after the market closed down, a hint of sea air. Mornings, women push baby carriages among the stands and small children play among the vendors' stalls, their cries muted by revving motorcycles and honking delivery trucks. Market stands are loaded with the production of the Mediterranean world: vegetables, fruits, meat and fowl from all of Latium, from the south as far as Sicily, from the islands, from the regions of Umbria, Abruzzo, Tuscany, Le Marche, from across the seas and the mountains, all exploding into color here in city's heart.

"Old Bruno," Stuart ventures, trying to prompt the other to speak about the heretic, "seems to pale before life here on the Campo. He would've liked this place today—if not for the memory of his fiery end."

Smells drift across the Campo and ricochet off its ancient walls in an erotic dance before converging on them sitting under Bruno's shadow image. Nullo sniffs the air as if to test his olfactory nerves and notes only that smells come and go and you can never describe them.

"Listen to me: I've thought about Bruno most of my life, especially when I too was a … a, uh, a fighter for the revolution—like him, I could say, even though official history has not yet formed a stable appraisal of him."

The elderly man clears his throat and peers at Stuart, a glint of mischief in his cobalt eyes and on his face the hint of a smirk like a Renaissance smile in a classic painting: "Oh, yes, he was a revolutionary and would be the same also in our time when the idea of revolution is fading. Only a faint light in the fog remains—although as you say, his eventual end would be about the same as then."

He stands up and stares at the bronze figure hovering above them. "The difference between Bruno and Lenin can determine your life," Nullo pronounced enigmatically, finality in his tone.

Then: "At least it did mine."

Again, silence.

Then: "Oh, yes, like him, I was very involved in revolution too." His eyes sweep over the noisy piazza for a moment before he adds: "but as you know our movement ended years ago. I was one step from the grave, one step ahead of the others. That was before Premier Moro was killed by the CIA that couldn't digest Moro's desire to bring the Communist Party into the national government—his body stuffed in the trunk of an old car like a punctured tire. That was also before the secret services took over our infiltrated revolutionary movement. We had believed our chance to change the flow of history.

Get out of NATO, we shouted in those times. Get out of the European Union. Look eastwards. And now? Ironic that our demands of then are the demands of some of the Right today.

"All revolutionaries have grandiose plans … ambitions to transform the world. Our goals were never limited to changes that just somehow occurred—our goals were those that we ourselves could bring about. Like revolutionaries of late nineteenth century Russia, we imagined the coming revolution as a transformation, not just of Italy's political and socio--economic order, but of human existence itself. Like Leon Trotsky and like the poets Shelley and Keats who rest in the Testaccio cemetery, we too wanted to overturn the world."

"So what really happened with the revolution you fought for?"

"What happened? What happened to me—to us—usually happens to revolutionaries. Changes were out of our control. We thought we were doing the right things to accomplish aims that we believed the political party from which we came shared. We were wrong. It did not. So we tried to make a revolution. And we were loyal to our aims. But often as time passes, the objects, persons, faiths, ideas, nations in which you believe and to which you belong can betray your trust. That happened to us. When the time came, our party no longer shared our goals. The objects of our loyalty became disloyal to us. We were outcasts. Like Giordano Bruno. The priests of back then labeled him mad. And banished him from their ranks. From their perspective they were of course right. For he was convinced that religion—the established order of the day—was a mass of superstitions. Bruno's unstinting rebellion on all fronts led him to the stake."

In a moment of silence, they watched a seagull circle slowly and light on Bruno's head. Stuart waited, so as not to interrupt the stream of the old revolutionary's remembrances.

"The priests who today promote the crying Madonnas were the same ones who burned him back then ... here on this piazza where we're sitting. But his hate for the establishment and his nonconformity would make him both hero and heretic today. He didn't wear masks. Nor did he have to *act* different. He *was* different. He would have rebelled against any system. Oh yes, he would have opposed capitalism like the Black Plague. He would have fallen on the barricades of Paris in 1968 and he would have fallen with us in the Italy of the 1970s. His extravagances were part of his method, as revolution was ours. Bruno thought in universal terms. He would have labeled barbaric the dumbing-down of Westerners who like the priests of five hundred years ago reject knowledge. The priests who burned him would rejoice in the people's ignorance as they do today. Incapable of even understanding their false faiths and beliefs, they were ignorant people who would have gleefully torched the whole Renaissance."

He looked at Stuart speculatively before asking: "Do you feel close to Bruno?" Then without waiting for his answer, he added: "I feel very close. Today, closer to him than to my Lenin."

"Just shows that revolutionaries are revolutionary."

"But there's a world of difference. At the moment they make the revolution, revolutionaries believe they are breaking through the continuum of history. We believed we were exploding history. Remember that French revolutionaries even introduced a new calendar. Though Lenin lived the revolutionary life, he was a realist. *Liberté Egalité Fraternité* interested him chiefly as a slogan. His revolution did not aim at restoring the lost Garden of Eden. No thoughts about Utopia or a Golden Age. Lenin's struggle was for the creation of a society with less inequalities than in capitalism while also allowing man a minimum of little evils—evils controlled by the hand of the state. But I don't think he ever believed justice even imaginable. Lenin the realist understood that would require blindness to man's nature. He limited sociopolitical systems to two: communism and anticommunism. His communist state aimed at more equality and applied more limits on man's evils; anticommunist states aimed at less of both. Some Russian

Communists believed that Lenin's great accomplishment was to take over failed capitalist Russia and create an anti-capitalist state in its place. Eventually his new state would again change, but it would remain Russia. Lenin was in a hurry. He had little time for fluff and frills. Marx understood revolution in a similar way to Lenin. The leap ahead in time is a dialectical one. History is not homogeneous. Time is always now—though different than before.

"Think about this: America announced the age of the individual and the American dream; yet the state has never had more powers of suppression. Extraordinary, no?

"Now Bruno was a revolutionary but it was his morality that was revolutionary. And it was never abstract: he called his morality a *heroic furor*. That's the metaphor of his thought. For Bruno was not only a philosopher, he was a hero. He grasped the unity and infinity of everything. All is all, he said. Like beauty and ugliness, like truth and lie, like good and evil. In the plurality of the world he lived in, sins seemed so petty. He opposed the sense of differences and nuances in things. He doubted a difference between good and evil, both of which he believed are present in everything. Thus the notion of evil tends to disappear and all is one. Every soul and spirit has a certain continuity with the spirit of the universe; everything has divinity latent in it. Everything that makes up the differences, he believed, is pure accident. So everything is in perfect unity. Good and evil are united. No wonder he opposed the tyranny of his day. The archaic beliefs. The primitive superstitions. The paranoid obsessions. The ridiculous lies of the powerful. The false morality and the corruption of the clerics. Mankind's long line of misery. And no wonder they burned him. The price tag on morality has always been high."

Stuart was incapable of a response. When he was a boy he'd been embarrassed when his father said such things, but spoken by Nullo those words were intoxicating. Spoken to him a stranger, an outlier. He felt he was entering into the *Sanctum Sanctorum* of revolutionary lore.

Clouds were gathering in the Rome skies. In the late afternoon it would rain. The crowd at the market was thinning and the pressing around Bruno was easing. The beady eyes of the bird sitting on Bruno's head were fixed on them. It was a Mediterranean crow. Nullo stood up and gazed at it for a long moment as if trying to emerge from the web of a distant past, and then turned and continued his discourse as if uninterrupted: "The importance of Bruno was that his thought was immeasurably rich. We have to accept that a priori. You see, what for him was the good, for Church power was evil. What was evil for Bruno, was the evil nature of 'the good' that he said existed in that Church … and in most people. In the same way, he said that the earth was not flat and that prayer was useless … and good and evil are relative. None of that was acceptable is to the Church."

His own words exciting him, Nullo's voice rose: "Bruno has been called the 'forgotten philosopher' who predicted infinite life and that the sun was only one star among many thousands which like our sun have many planets around them most probably inhabited by living beings. His ideas about infinity earned him the stake. Right here. Five centuries ago. Now he is nearly forgotten even though he was the intellectual peer of the greatest thinkers. A creature-thinker whose universe foreshadowed ours today. That's Giordano Bruno. His thinking was so consistent that he seemed inconsistent to his critics incapable of even following his thought. For reactionaries of then as of today morality is revolutionary. Real heroes are never part of the crowd. They soar high above. In the clouds. In the beyond. Alone.

"Romans love their heroes at first. But not for long. This is a city of clowns and crowds, of priests and kings, whose heroes quickly become outcasts. From the beginning condemned to the stake. That's why Rome is so little literary; they burn their heroes. Or they throw them out of windows onto our Sanpietrini stones. Defenestration is an old Rome story. Largely untold. But that story is not the stuff of literary heroes. Little meaningful literature is written about Rome. Contradictorily, unhappiness is less celebrated in Rome's culture than are rites of life. Too intent on their individual well-being for self-contemplation, Romans don't even reflect on unhappiness. As a rule they're too egocentric, cynical, grasping, and cunning for poetry. Poets come from somewhere else. What is Rome? Rome is a city of silent and empty churches with frescoes and Madonnas and images of popes and cardinals on its facades … but with few heroes. Real Romans are plebs who fall for charismatic leaders. But like children, only briefly. The era of charisma is ending—again. Also the era of individualism. You will ask what Bruno and heroes and charisma have to do with contemporary Romans. You know that Romans are too busy with Sunday drives in unbearable traffic and following new fashions to worship anyone for long … even the gods. Or they're packed shoulder to shoulder on the black sands of Ostia beaches among their I-phones and I-pads and lotions and sun glasses and unpacked lunches."

Stuart shuddered, afraid that he lacked the backbone to keep out of the city's centrifugal draw sucking him into Nullo's damning tragic vision. A madman at the very least.

"Romans are neither loyal nor literary. Overnight they create and worship their heroes but just as quickly they rip them down and trample them like disgruntled children. And they sometimes build monuments to them … but later they tear them down too."

Stuart rushed across the Campo feeling like a man charged with a heroic mission. A man with a goal in mind. Ignoring the misty rain, he concentrated on thinking before concluding that real thinking is hard to do on command. My new life is not just another film like one in the old cinema theater across the Campo from old Bruno. He had met none of his old friends but as coincidence would have it, he had made another, with a raving madman who spoke much truth: Nullo-Bruno; they seemed like one. Still feeling Bruno's spirit roaming around the piazza, he headed for the train, humming under his breath *running up that hill, make a deal with God, you be me, I'll be you*, but he thought of Helen. That fateful day of the burning the priests had chanted their mournful litanies, facetiously sorrowful, secretly elated: burning him was their duty … and their deliverance. Was he not mad, convinced as he was that their religion was superstition? Ignorant market people and well-indoctrinated spectators—men, women and children—looked on horrified in their fascination while the philosopher's body melted and Stuart thought of Ermanno, dead on the beach at Trevignano.

33.

He found Sophie and Helen on the summer terrace drinking gin and tonic. Feeling like an intruder, he greeted them and made the same for himself. He thought he would like to get drunk again like the time in the bar in Olgiata: four gins and tonic while waiting for Stephen Dedalus who never came. But he didn't. The ghost of Stephen reminded him of a story he once read about a plantation owner in Santiago de Cuba during the Castro revolution. The corrupt Battista government had confiscated all his sugarcane fields but he had all his money so he sat around and ate only plantain bananas and drank gin; the green bananas caused the chronic constipation that was killing him, but the gin kept him so drunk he didn't realize it. Self-restraint, Stuart thought. He told Sophie and Helen about Nullo and Giordano Bruno and that he felt he too should do something revolutionary. They both shook their heads as if perplexed, their eyes gleaming quixotically.

"Delightful idea," Helen said as if speaking of trying out a new restaurant or a Mediterranean cruise in the spring.

"Why don't you do it?" asked Sophie just to say something. "It's up to you. Only you can decide what you can and want to do."

Since their responses were malapropos to his story about Nullo and Giordano Bruno and Lenin, he looked closely at both and found that their starry eyes got in the way. On which he made himself another gin and tonic and decided to think things over, major decisive matters like those that fill Nullo's mad brain.

He thought of the random writers on social media, the city's random intellectuals, journalists, thinkers and commentators, who suddenly step from their random personal circumstances and are confronted by the great and all-important issues facing humanity, such as God and the origins of the human species, pandemic and the survival of mankind, concerning which individual reactions are the most serious and as a rule the most tragic matters—and of serious concern to all other individuals. Stuart pondered his place in the confrontation and concluded that although he felt he was consistently on the side of the just, he, like everyone, all too often misjudged which side was the just. Hence, his sense of futility and indecision. His experience with the birds and botox and his awareness of the sixteen young Russian soldiers dying of botulinum toxin in Zaporozhe had left its mark on him. He too was an individual emerging from a retreat in the hamlet, suddenly snapping awake to the realization that he must do something about the state of things in his world. He would perform an act of love. Not an act of valor as an expression of collective love for all mankind as that claimed by the Church of Dostoevsky's Grand Inquisitor, but an act of love for suffering individuals like each of the sixteen Russians in the Zaporozhe hospital. After the deaths and disappearance of Gianluigi and Ermanno's bodies, he had begun feeling that he had no function in life, no goal, as if his usefulness as a human being was dwindling and dwindling toward zero. Only concrete action could halt the sinking sensations of which Nullo and Giordano Bruno had made him conscious. Then and there, on the summer terrace, gin in his gut, two beautiful women waiting for his decision, the idea came to him: he would go to Zaporozhe.

34.

When Stuart stepped off the bus from Simferopol into the hectic world of Donetsk, a world of ice and fog and cold, snow-packed streets and crashing Ukrainian missiles as evidenced by damaged buildings here and there and the non-stop Promethean reconstruction of yesterday's devastation, he felt like Don Quixote out to prove himself. Prove himself amidst Russian military forces in the Donbas, it too once Russian, now again Russian. Prove himself? He too was a victim among victims, a shameful and guilty victim of the life people like him lived in Rome—as if extravagant public life showings were an obligation—faced with horrific dilemmas like which discotheque to spend his nights in. Yet, victim he was. And guilty. And ashamed of his guilt. Sitting those long hours on the super first-class bus, loud music and a lovely Asian woman occasionally serving drinks and *zakuski,* he had dwelled on his dark side. Observing the new Crimean bridge, the new people, the new way to live so different from his, he again felt his old life was dwindling and withering, and running out. The shame and the guilt he felt for his non-descript social class with no role, no mission, no raison d'etre. In comparison to what he saw here, he felt no real challenges, no significant visions of the reality of the war raging around this whole people. What did he know first-hand? He had experienced the Great Wall, dead birds, an underground biolab and yes, the death of two friends; yet he was aware that most of what he had seen and done thus far was also just the random happenings of a degrading life in a declining society—a society that lived as if war were not raging less than two flight hours from Rome. He had come to perceive his guilt for the death of the sixteen soldiers, kids dead of botox like his two dead friends. Guilt for the botox and the howitzers and the armored cars furnished by his own people cheering the death of the Russians.

He put down his bag on the ice-packed street, looked around in a daze and said spontaneously to himself: "Dreamscape". Observing the activities of people trying to live normal lives in the most abnormal of times, he tried to chase away memories of his own former times, of pre-Great Wall times, one said the good old times. But he saw here in the reality of Donetsk that those old times were not good times. The unreliability of his powers of recollection caused no end to the matters that bedeviled him. Matters that blocked his fluent passage through life, obstructing the development of his real self. From the beginning, untrustworthy memory plays lurid tricks on you, diabolic and sometimes melodramatic, but as a rule, true memories—be what they may—are underrated or ignored. Remembrance is anyway problematic. You think you remember, but you don't. Or you remember events in ways diametrically opposed to what really happened … or did not happen at all. It was all a dream. Even when you want to believe in some redemptive sweetness of things past, you might simultaneously recall them like dark invaders conveying inexplicable mysteries. Those times and the frustrations and the pain are the insuperable obstacles of our dreams. They are the shadows of ourselves. After Gianluigi and Ermanno, everything, life itself, had from one day to the next accelerated and time began passing at an astonishing speed, then ever faster and faster, while perceptions of the past warped and changed and false memories of what really happened formed. For some unfathomable reason, there on the Donetsk *maidan*, he was suddenly tormented by his incapacity to remember his own voice as a child. What and how had he thought then. And he felt powerless to do anything about the barriers between him and his own past; by the impediments to full recall or the doubt that he really wanted to break through. It was what it was. Or the past had become so malleable that he could mold it as he liked. He could alter it and give it meaning and intelligibility. He had the power to make the past dovetail with his present needs: here on this square in mysterious Donetsk, one side of the buildings looked brand new— rebuilt yesterday as they were. On the other side of a wall a series of damaged or partially destroyed buildings, some hit on the top floors, some on street level. You still puzzle over your life and what happened or what you believe happened. But instead of becoming clearer, the past, distant or recent, appears ever more incomprehensible and blurry, thus creating in one's recall those vast, almost limitless spaces for dreams or for fiction and make-believe, or for outright lies because one realistic particle of your memory tells you that things could not possibly have happened as you once imagined … or preferred. When at a later stage you examine yourself, you see so much absurdity and deceit that you have to wonder if it was worth the candle. Still, that does not mean that you do not get uglier, he thought, stupider and even more corrupt with age. There was a writer he had liked, Céline, who wrote in his *Journey* that "in the end your features are marked with that hideous grimace that took a whole lifetime to compose." In his own psyche, he thought, reality and fiction, pretense and sham, roam around inexplicably free. He compensated by filling his amnesia with a brazen and unabashed tendency to fictionalize reality. Sometimes, he stopped and wondered which is the most active, powerful and influential in his psyche, the present or the past. For there are times when each single event seems absolute. Yet from one moment to the next, things change dramatically and fundamentally so that you come to believe less and less in absolutes. You have to mistrust absolutists who demand specific answers, who put you on the witness stand: 'yes or no?' Absolutists who most definitely prefer white to black, this to that, and use expressions like 'in the final analysis'. Now he knew that he had seldom understood what was happening to him while it was happening. Still, he had long been aware of the helplessness you feel when you are unable to see what it is you yourself are doing. 'Am I alone in that?' he asked himself. And here in Donetsk, he was nervous and unclear about what exactly was going on. If you open your eyes and really see, he thought, you understand everything is ambiguous, ambivalent, two-edged and paradoxical. And one says that is life. He needed a hotel. The choice! The absolutist dilemma in another guise. A top floor or a bottom floor? Russian roulette! Wherever he was, whatever he was doing, he had hated to choose; as if he knew the correct answers, the right choices. There is so much he knows he can't understand, that he can only guess. He might have had some minimal influence on events in his life—maybe as much as one grain of sand influences the level of the sea. And even if he could exert any influence, it would most likely only cause damage as our political and military leaders prove day by day. So perhaps quiet and stillness is the best strategy, trying not to disturb things but trying not to be untouchable either. Yet despite your trepidation, you do come to feel you know something. That something lying beyond words or thought. Even though disturbing and confusing, the moment of intuition is wonderful and mysterious. If you could only speak its name you would know. For words pack great power. But the obscure musings he has in mind are beyond words; they are those that cannot be transformed into words … not even into sensations of thought images. It is the sense of the beyond—the *mas allá* he'd begun calling it in Mexico. It is the spirit in you that is greater than your body of skin and bones and water and without which you would not be a human being. You know such things without being able to transform them into syntactical thought. You want to know more. Helplessly you feel the idea dangling near you, you nearly have it in your grasp, but then it slithers away just out of your reach—unnamable, unpronounceable, intangible. Hence, one thing follows the other, so that later it seems you were just acting a part.

His tourist trip to Moscow now years back and his few lessons of Russian language enabled him to say hello and read signs. But the sensation of this all-Russian reality surrounded by everything and everyone Russian intensified his entrenched outsider self to the degree that only the thought of that phantasmal hospital where an obscure journalist reported that the sixteen Russian soldiers died of Ukrainian sprayed botox buoyed him up in his "quixotic"—as his women, Sophie and Helen, depicted his search. His women, he chuckled, like having two wives, he the Scotch-Italian bigamist. Precisely in that unguarded moment, he saw what he needed in the moment: a two-story, new-looking building with a big sign on top, HOTEL, and as fate would have it, parked in front a green taxi and inside a bearded driver, his Sancho Panza. And so it came to pass that in the bomb-scarred Russian city of Donetsk toward nightfall at a small HOTEL that in no way resembled a castle, Stuart's new companion and his worthy steed appeared as if from nowhere to transport him to a certain hospital on the road to old Zaporozhe/Alexandrovsk on the banks of the Dnieper River.

"Da, da, gospodin Zhurnalist, you sleep here first and at the crack of dawn tomorrow morning we'll set out in the direction of the big industrial city and river port of Zaporizhzhia in Ukrainan or Zaporozhe for us Russians which I'm sorry to say we won't see. But I'll put the *Journalist* sign on top of the car anyway. Makes road control blocks easier.' Misha had been a taxi driver in Chicago and was a man of the world. He said: "And, uh, yes, take a ground floor room. You never know in war. You see, Kiev is really, really pissed that we Russians control the whole region of Zaporozhe."

Feeling the familiar sense of exile and aloneness mixed with uncertainty about what he was doing, Stuart stepped into the penumbra of a narrow entrance way, stopped, and turned back toward Misha-Panza now standing on the street and watching him doubtfully, and said:

"You will be here tomorrow morning, right, Misha."

"At the crack of dawn, at around eight this time of year."

"And we'll find that hospital near the village Martinovka, right?"

"We'll find it. I know it well. And I think I know what you're looking for. The soldiers, right? I thought so. Everybody here knows about them, how they were poisoned by some strange spray in a forest, Sixteen soldiers, *you* think. *We* think many, many more, maybe two hundred, three hundred were poisoned. The Nazi legions of that Kiev regime are mean, very mean. They kill and lie, kill and lie. You know about the fifty people they locked in the Trade Unions building in Odessa and burned them alive? That's Kiev. That's this no-country Ukraine. A mean people. They once killed all the Jews and the gypsies and now they want to kill all us Russians. They've been bombing and killing us for eight years. Eight long and cold years. You should know that people around here think some of those soldiers survived. If they're still in the Donbas, we'll find them. And; Zhurnalist, tomorrow we'll have a fine day. *Tak, do zavtra!*"

Stuart sat in his sprawling, unexpectedly large room in the rear of the ground floor and made notes of everything he remembered about his arrival, his sensation when he descended from the bus into the ice and snow of Donetsk, the vision of the HOTEL sign, Sancho at the wheel of the green cab, the ex-Chicago cab driver, Misha, over fifty years old, tough, shrewd, informed—should've been a journalist instead of a taxi driver, the lobby-less hotel, just a desk under the dark wooden staircase, brand new, new like the walls, the window and door fixtures, the bed, the mirror and an ancient hand-woven carpet that reminded him of running up the hill to Férnande.

While writing down his notes, the feeling came over him that this mad trip of a certain purpose and hope—though uncertain outcome—was transforming into a major turning point in his life, albeit like all authentic turning points they too filled with conundrums, surprises and joys and the awareness of the threat of again losing control of events—and the subsequent disillusionment. Later, he thought, this might seem nothing special—as if his travel and Misha and the taxi trip through the steppes, the dying soldiers—that it just came about, willy-nilly, or as if Fate had willed it. Though wary of the unknown that such turning points conceal, he accepted the unknown factors as part of the bargain of the exchange of a former familiar life for the discovery of a new kind of life. In his experience, turning points may seem like maledictions—the malevolence of the gods—which produce not only new connections but also fearsome separations. And you don't know if you should curse Providence or cry for yourself at the ignorance of the equivocal wisdom of Destiny.

Stuart in fact denied the reality that he had chosen to step into the unknown as he did the day he descended from the trapdoor in the bushes near the glade into Tartarus pit under the bottom of the world. In retrospect his climb down into darkness seemed something more than choice, something inexplicable. Maybe it really was destiny, which left him hesitant and unsure about what he had so arrogantly considered choice. Keeping in mind what happened to Gianluigi and Ermanno, he thought that sometimes it seems the spirit Destiny even decides when and where to place those ambivalent turning points. He recalled Baudrillard's story about the workings of destiny in "Death in Samarkand". *On a street of the town, Death makes a sign to a soldier, terrifying him. He goes to the king and tells him that Death made a sign to him. And therefore he was escaping immediately to Samarkand. The king summons Death and asks why he scared his captain. Death answers that he didn't intend to frighten the soldier, he just wanted to remind him that they had an appointment that evening in Samarkand.* Such rules are truly confusing to consider! He realized that he had interjected Destiny's role into his life because this trip to New Russia could eventually turn out to be the prime container of other incredible turning points to come—negative and positive—of the rest of his life.

Dawn was just breaking when the next morning he stepped warily out the door into the icy cold onto the snow-packed Yuzhno-Donetskaya ulitza. Working people rushed past and barely glanced at his tall figure. Nearly all were wearing Valenki boots. They had told him that time in Moscow, see a pair of Valenki passing by and you know you're seeing a Russian. He grinned when he saw Misha park across the heavily trafficked street and step out of the car holding two big steaming plastic cups and a bag of breakfast breads.

Balancing his cup between his legs, Misha u-turned, headed west and said: "We're lucky, a wonderful day. Just wait till you see our shiny sun."

Stuart, riding shotgun, drinking the strong coffee and munching black bread, asked how long to the border.

"Border?"

"With Zaporozhe Region."

"You never know on Russian roads. I know a guy who was driving all the way to the city of Zaporozhe. He came back in a few hours and said two wrecks had blocked all traffic for the day. Crazy drivers, these Russians. I keep a distance from other cars, but you know, that's dangerous too. If you're in their way. they don't even slow down; they crash right into you from behind. Anyway, that's not on our program today. I feel luck is on our side. We'll be in Martinovka in two to three hours. *Da, da, dva chasa.*"

"If there're no wrecks and crashes, eh?"

"Not today! Today is a good day ..."

'A positive man, my Sancho Panza,' Stuart thought, chuckling to himself. 'Sees the worse for others, the best for us.' They drove over the highway cutting through the eternal steppes and plateaus of snow-covered fertile black earth, once the "bread basket" of the Soviet Union. It looked surprisingly like the lands of Sophie's *abandoned spaces* in San Nicola. They drank coffee. They ate *pirozhki.* Time passed quickly. They passed a check point. Soon after, Misha pointed at a small sign and turned into a side road. Two kilometers on a narrow road, snow banks on either side, and there was the village of Martinovka and a sign with an arrow: *Gospital.*

Misha explained their visit first to the head nurse, then to the director, Russians both. 'Major international journalist from Scotland to speak with the Russian soldiers ... survivors of the botox attack.

Important support for Russia's petition to the OPCW. Major international issue. He doesn't speak Russian. I'm his interpreter.' Personnel was overjoyed. International attention: the Martinovka hospital on the world map.

The small room on the sunny side of the two story structure had two beds and two medical chairs, a big window displaying a view of the same snow-covered steppes through which they had driven, the same steppe-like landscape as San Nicola during the anomalous snowfall. Two persons were sitting in the chairs facing the open fields, one near the other. The beds were made. One look at the men and Stuart and Misha became reverent and soft spoken: the two men were dying. Twenty-two years old and mere shells of themselves, they looked forty-two, sixty-two. Ageless … gray. Botox. Their gray-white shriveled faces reminded him of Ermanno's face when he lay dead on the beach at Trevignano on Lake Bracciano. These two were living death. Their dead eyes shifted from Stuart to Misha and back to Stuart, as if his height designated him as the one. Stuart paled. Words failed him. These two boys, Mikhail and Leonid, from the eastern steppes of Kazakhstan, from a village much like Martinovka, were dying as in a dream, dying slowly in an alien place that only looked like home. They seemed to sense that they were being done in by an unfathomable combination of circumstances of insanity in all of creation in which justice was alien, as if they knew they were at the mercy of a vast and mysterious control committee that itself was completely out of control and had no idea of the existence of two ordinary boys from a distant Kazakh village that they themselves were forgetting in their dying. In their simplicity, they conveyed their ignorance of their real condition or of the reasons for it. They only knew, the two now old men at age twenty-two, that the only thing they still had to do was to die. They didn't want to die, but they accepted. Dying was the only thing left for them. Striking was their look of persons who have never been a part of the action in the world; they were apart and completely devoid of hope for themselves. Mikhail and Leonid could just as well be named Alexey and Vladimir. The conditions of life had alienated them from mankind. They were not part of the continent as the poet wrote, they were apart from the main, and always had been. Their memory was fading. It was if they'd never experienced the emotion of thrill or curiosity—not even of the thought of death. No color in their lives. No hue. No warmth. No cold. They didn't count. Neither for God nor for mankind. Their life was truly a dream. They answered his questions in a low desultory monotone that struck Stuart more than their few words. He wondered about the tone. Did they speak to each other in that same tone sitting there in the medical chairs looking out over the fertile fields of snow and ice ? Did they speak about their unfinished lives in their village in Kazakhstan in the same tone? Maybe not. For the tone was death. He asked if when they were well again would they return home, to their own village? Misha translated. They didn't answer. Why did they join the Russian army and leave their homes? Ever so slowly they turned their heads toward each other. They didn't know the answer.

"See the world," Mikhail finally answered anyway.

"Da, to see the world," Leonid echoed.

Then silence. Stuart wanted to ask about their comrades and how they died. He did not. He wouldn't invade their inner spaces. The word death was unmentionable. Stuart felt he had to leave. He was overcome. He wanted to fall to the ground. In a sudden flash of comprehension, he grasped the simplicity, the honesty, of their answer: THEY WANTED TO SEE THE WORLD. He perceived what he felt was a supernatural revelation of a simple truth: it was the beauty, the simple deathly beauty in the two dying boys who had only wanted to see the world. It was like a revelation of his own existence. And there was something similar to that which Férnande had wanted to say about her feelings on the Orléans roller coaster. No one else had ever revealed to him their awareness of the occurrence of the same sensations in their lives. Maybe it was an epiphany—a divine intervention communicating to him its message of truth. Milosz believed that it is out of the commonplaces of life that occur the wonder of transcendence. And such was the basis of Joyce's conception of the epiphany, the 'showing forth' of the spirit of Leopold Bloom from the trivialities of that one Dublin day. Only the fortunate would know what they mean. The creative life of Joyce the writer varies over different levels reflecting his varying sensibilities. The lower level, the more ordinary creative plane, runs through the work of all creators, until occasionally, like a bolt from the blue, it is overshadowed by a higher plane. At epiphany level, the creator surpasses ordinary considerations of elegance which on that high plane are necessarily coupled with an absence of restraint and control—even dignity and self-awareness. The transcendence in such a moment is infected with an ideological spirit; it is here that the deepest pits of the artist's consciousness can be revealed. In that light, Dostoevsky's *Memoirs from Underground* is defined as one long epiphany. It reveals at once the writer's essential self. It transcends art and stands among the greatest mystical revelations of man. Thus, for writer, reader and the character experiencing it, the epiphany lies on the highest level of human emotion. The conviction crept over Stuart that in the presence of the two dying soldiers who just wanted to see the world he too had discovered some tiny part of the essence of himself.

On their return drive, Stuart asked Misha if he believed the story that when Saul the persecutor of Christians was struck blind on the road to Damascus, he arose as Paul their defender?

Misha had never heard the story: Damascus was the city Russia saved and epiphany the holiday when Russians take a swim in the cold water of January.

"Never mind," Stuart said, "When you come to Rome I'll take you to a church that has the great painting about another kind of epiphany by one of Europe's greatest artists, a madman named Caravaggio.

Stuart imagines the artist painting his Saul-become-Paul on canvas and wonders if it is honest. Then he tries to see himself watching his imaginary Caravaggio painting his epiphany scene, watching his hand painting the painting. He imagines he has become a shadow of his other self, watching the hand painting the same scene he was looking at. His other self looking at the painting seems like a stranger, cut off from his real self, cut off from real life, unable to experience the epiphany. He held onto the moment for a while, then forces himself to return to authentic time where one person after another in his life had passed away botoxed like the Russian soldiers, maybe three hundred soldiers according to Misha. Gianluigi and Ermanno passed before him, through him, holding him fast in front of Caravaggio's epiphany.

Though truth had not been mentioned or thought in that little hospital in the Donbas village of Martinovka, that must have been what he had in mind that day in Férnande's studio when they spoke about human nature. Truth!

Stuart looked at Misha. What were his reactions? There was a sad look on Misha's face and in his manners, but that was not the same thing he felt in himself. He shied away from the word epiphany. He knew it was dangerous and he, unworthy. But still, something of that nature had happened. In his mind, an epiphany points toward answers to questions like, 'What am I as an individual?' 'What is my life all about?' 'Do I count?'

Sophie had understood that when she said: "Do it."

The answers to such questions are misty and cloudy. He was just barely aware of that something that hovered in the beyond which some rare times and for brief moments seems within reach. It is like the longing for the impossible, the conviction that we are not neutral in life. He had often referred to that fleeting sensation, that hoped for glimpse of understanding, as the *It*.

Seldom do people speak of the essence of their real condition, which is shown to us only in fugitive glimpses that manifest themselves briefly and then vanish, glimpses that Tolstoy called the essence. After it has departed as quickly as it came, you stop and wonder if it was really there. Yet there is a residue. A shadow of its essence. And it is sad that it vanishes so quickly. And you long for its return. You feel nostalgia for that unnamable thing that you know lies within yourself, your essential nature. You hope it will return and stay longer and reveal to you once and for all the ultimate secret of who you are, and offer you a light and redemption and an exit from the darkness of your unknowing. Stuart thought Tolstoy might have had in mind a spirit. Or *the* spirit. The soul of which people hesitate to speak, the soul that is an embarrassing subject.

At the same time, Stuart felt deeply the dichotomy between what he did every day and that to which he aspired. That insuperable gap drove him crazy. He knew it was there, but it was out of reach, only rarely attainable. And it lies in that moment of revelation which is sometimes called an epiphany.

People in Donetsk were wary about Kiev's missiles but after eight years of the bombardment—eight years of bombs and missiles— they acted as if it were just part of everyday life. The few persons he asked just shrugged and many said that things never get better, ever. They get worse. Life is like that. Still, stores and offices were open, utilities worked most of the time, restaurants and night clubs were open all night and the Donetsk football team played important matches. There were policemen and courts and magistrates; crime occurred and criminals were arrested. Life went on. But people were still pissed that their armies and their militias—there were several of them—didn't push the Ukrainian artillery out of shooting distance. And couldn't they block ALL the missiles? Were there reasons they did not? It was a puzzle. Despite the falling bombs, Misha wanted to drive him northeast, to see the whole new country. But Stuart had had enough and his funds were running out.

He took the fast route home. In the early morning, Misha drove him to the airport for his flight to Simferopol. Faintly flickered scattered signs of urban illumination: people here feel no need to tempt fate, Stuart thought. Here and there, gas stations were open. Bakeries were already busy. A light snow was falling, sticking immediately to the snow-packed streets and gradually adding another white layer there where snowplows didn't pass. Traffic was scarce in the outskirts. Stuart started when an explosion sounded from somewhere nearby or maybe it was far away. Misha didn't blink. "The usual wake-up call in the northern suburbs," he explained. At the airport Misha hugged him and said he would never forget those boys in Martinovka and swore lifetime friendship with Stuart.

"Study your Russian," he said, "you Westerners are going to need it. And come back."

From Simferopol, Stuart flew to Varnas where he caught the afternoon return flight to Rome. Sophie and Helen would pick him up at the airport. After Martinovka, he was itching for San Nicola and above all for his two lovers.

They were there to meet him at Leonardo da Vinci International Airport. From inside the customs area, he smiled and waved at the two of them outside. They were holding hands like the lovers they were. He stepped out of customs and kissed them, each individually, then all three hugged together.

"The two women of my life," Stuart murmured lovingly.

"Everybody is watching us!" Helen said, her eyes beaming. "We do make a handsome threesome."

"It's envy and admiration," Stuart said.

"Maybe there is hope for us after all," Sophie said, "if we can only remain as we are today."

"Thus far it has all been quite an experience," Stuart added. "From the Great Wall, to an underground biolab, to fifteen dead crows and the death of two friends and a contingent of Russian soldiers and … and now the birth of our new hamlet."

"There's no going back now," Helen said optimistically, her hair brilliantly red under the artificial lights of Sector B of Europe's best airport. "Everything's in the best of order."

Stuart tightened his arms around Sophie and Helen and, though still uncertain about Misha's optimism, said: "As my Russian taxi driver in Donetsk believes, life is truly good."

The End